Lust fc

By Sean-Paul Thomas

Cover design by Gregor Muir - designbygm@hotmail.com - www.gregormuir.com

For Mum, Dad, Stewart, Michelle and Bianca.

Prologue

As I closed my eyes for just one overly long, tantalising second, I could see us driving that damn fine-looking convertible again on a stupendously hot and gorgeous summers day. Not even the faintest hint of white cloud could be seen anywhere above our heads, in the ocean of rich, blue sky. We had the roof down. We were laughing. We were horsing and fooling around like two reunited childhood sweethearts, without a single care in the world. As the lusciously warm wind rippled through our hair, we sang along, loud, proud, and with an infectious heart to any goddamn tune that dared play out at us from the car radio. My God, we looked so happy and in love.

As we continued to drive, I could see the beginning of some mountains emerging on the distant horizon to our left, while a delicious velvet carpet of deep blue sea stretched out into the smooth horizon on our right. For one heartfelt moment, I could both smell and taste that raw and exciting salty sea air, right in the roof of my nostrils and in the back of my throat, while my ever-more-tanning skin soaked in those radiant rays of sunshine with their delicious, affectionate kisses of warmth.

When I blinked again, we were suddenly naked on a magnificent, secluded, golden beach, our stripped clothes strewn here, there, and everywhere. We were playing around like kids again, spinning and jumping on the sand, then on each other, before wrestling ourselves onto the silky-smooth sand beneath our bare feet. Soon we were running and chasing one another into the cool, calm sea before diving freely into the deliciously inviting and invigorating waves of the crystal-clear water.

We swam, we played, we talked, we laughed, we whispered sweet nothings. We kissed and hugged with great tenderness, then made love with an even greater fiery and furious passion. We continued our romp on the shallow sandy shores of the stunning beach as the ocean waves lapped invitingly against our entangled naked bodies, enticing us to come back in for more.

We looked so happy. We looked so in love.

Real or imagined, it was the most perfect moment I'd ever felt in my life. I'd never experienced such pure and utter joy, so much good, raw, and positive emotion, until those short-lived but heavenly gifted last moments with her. I wished it could have lasted forever. I wished beyond all shadow of doubt, hope, and fear that it could have been real. That it should have been real...Was it real?

If I just kept my eyes tightly shut, surely the moment would never end. It would last, always and forever, in my mind, just so long as I didn't...open...my...eyes...

Present Day

I jumped into the police car. A sexy yet firm and official female voice on the car radio called out for the real owner of the vehicle to answer, but he was currently indisposed and wouldn't be replying any time soon. I switched off the radio. The keys were still in the ignition. I turned on the engine and accelerated away, not even looking back for a second. All I could think about was getting back to her and our new life together. Packing up our shit and getting the hell out of this goddamn country once and for all. Just take off to France, like Celine had suggested, and make a go of life on the continent together. Of course, I felt bad about Mum. I thought about driving back down to the borders to see her, if only for ten minutes, to apologise for what a horrible, inconsiderate bastard of a son I'd been to her all those years. How I'd never kept in touch. How I'd never looked after her and cared for her like any decent son should have watched over his only parent. I'd never even told her how much I loved her. Not once. And I did love her. With all my heart.

I shook those thoughts from my head. Realistically, there was no time. I would phone her, either on the road south or whenever we reached just wherever the hell it was we were gonna end up. If I owed anything to the woman who gave me life and did the best job she possibly could of raising me, I owed her that much.

Everything was going swell driving along the A1 from Dunbar to Edinburgh until I hit the Musselburgh turnoff and a police transit van exploded onto the dual carriageway directly behind me from the Haddington roundabout. The lights on the van were flashing wildly and the horrendous noise from the sirens echoed throughout the countryside.

This didn't look good.

The van was right up my arse as I accelerated. I sped up to well over one hundred miles per hour, continuing to weave in and out of the thin afternoon traffic. If I could just make it to the Newcraighall turn-off, I might have a flickering chance to lose the bastard. I spied another two police cars screeching down the opposite motorway lanes ahead. They must be coming for me, yet thankfully they had a fair trek to go to find a turning point along the steel barrier frame that split the two sides of the carriageway in half.

The slip road down to the retail park was fast approaching. The police van hounding me remained hard on my tail. There was no sign of any other police cars blocking my route ahead, so I took the turn off, gently applied the brakes and swerved around another four cars as they slowed for the red light. Not me, though, no danger of that. I bumped up onto a narrow curb and blitzed through the intersection like a bat out of hell, mounting the next pavement to avoid smashing into oncoming traffic from the crossroads. When I peeked into my rear-view mirror, I was shocked to see the large framed police van doing the same thing while clipping cars and taking out all road signs in its path. I returned my concentration to my own driving and rattled through another two roundabouts, passing through another retail park and hitting the approach road to the Niddrie estate. This would be as good a place as any to lose these persistent policemen fuckers. Niddrie! Sending a patrol unit into the heart of that schemey, war-torn shithole was every Edinburgh policeman's worst nightmare.

I drove along a boarded-up housing street, then another before taking a sharp turn down a narrow side street. The whole scheme was strewn with garbage, more stray dogs than you could swing a cat at, the occasional random fire burning in a garden or two, and smoke coming from the roof of another random building. Cars with smashed windows, cars without tyres, tyres without cars—all of this decorated the housing estate passing me by.

Then there were the dozens of tracksuit-wearing teens and neds (Non-Educated Delinquents) wearing their clan hoodies and baseball caps. All lounging around, sitting and standing, smoking and drinking, sniffing and staring. The police van remained glued to my rear and sped recklessly with me around the next street corner. I caught another glimpse of the groups of lounging teens in my mirror as they jumped to attention, fully alert and falsely believing for a few anxious seconds that the screeching police van raging behind me was coming for them. Then they relaxed, laughing amongst themselves while playfully pushing one another as the van whizzed on by, still close behind me in the police car out in front.

I made a sharp turn just before a row of shops and sped into a large park and grassland area. I swerved around a frail old man walking his dog as he entered the park. Perhaps he was deaf because he didn't hear me roaring up behind him until it was too late. When I swerved around him, he crouched to the ground in sheer fright, looking like he'd literally shat his pants. I zoomed on by, inches from his bum cheeks.

The police van followed, hot on my heels, into the park after me. It was like something from a car chase movie. The van was racing alongside me. I could see a crazy-looking policeman behind the wheel. Just by the glint in his eyes I could see that he meant business. No doubt about it. He pulled back and away for a second, then barged at my back end before pulling up beside me on the passenger side. I almost lost control during his sneaky manoeuvre, yet somehow managed to keep the vehicle from spinning away from me. I couldn't help but give an innocent little wave to the raging policeman. It must have pissed him off big time because he swerved into me again with even more ferocity, forcing me towards a group of trees in the swiftly approaching distance.

'Shite! Shite! Shite!'

I should've braked. That was the right and obvious thing to do. That was what the police driver had expected me to do. So, I accelerated harder instead. Fuck it. The police van sped with me, both of us dragging and scrapping the other along. As we reached the trees, I saw my split-second opportunity. There was a blind summit approaching. It was a deceiving little dip in the grass which led towards the small forest of trees ahead. I didn't think, I just swerved right, edging the van along with me. Quick as a flash, I swerved left, swinging the full front bonnet of my vehicle hard into the side of the police van. I slammed on the brakes, including the hand-break. The van was rocked off balance with the manoeuvre. The dip in the grass didn't help with its balance. The driver tried to turn his van away from the dip in a desperate bid to regain control...until the most amazing thing happened. The van hit a hidden log and flipped up and over onto its side, skidding and rolling down the grassy slope towards the trees. Watching it happen before my eyes was spectacular. Like a work of art I had randomly created.

'WOO WHOO!' I couldn't help but roar in a moment of pure exhilaration. I did hope the driver was okay, though. Hopefully he'd been wearing his seat belt like I had. If not, then hard lines, he wasn't very good at his job. I didn't stop to find out and continued towards the far end of the park. Eventually, I found another main road and realised that I wasn't too far from Edinburgh city centre. Maybe a mile or two at the most. It was time to ditch the police car.

I sped through another set of red lights, almost ready to pull over and chance my luck on foot when I spotted a speed camera dead ahead. No better parking place, I supposed, than on top of my second pet hate of all time. Second, that is, to traffic wardens. I headed straight for the steel contraption, ramming into its grey metal exterior, completely uprooting it from the ground while slamming the main body of the camera down hard onto the concrete road in front of me. A couple of passing cars beeped their horns. Some even cheered and waved from their rolled-down car windows with sheer and utter joy as they drove by. Some young neds waiting at a bus stop across the road started applauding and cheering me on too. One even toasted an already half-consumed can of lager into the air like he was accepting me as one of his own. A smashed-up police car on this estate was worth more than any million-pound winning lottery ticket, that's for sure.

I exited the car and waved back at the neds and all the passing drivers still beeping their horns. I smiled and took a bow before getting the hell out of there. I legged it over a nearby stone wall and made my way towards the southeastern foot of the volcanic hill, Arthur's Seat.

Chapter 1

A few weeks earlier.

I couldn't help but wonder if she gave good head as I sat opposite the middle-aged doctor inside her private office at the Royal Infirmary. She'd just told me I had some form of terminal brain cancer, but it hadn't registered properly because I wasn't paying attention to her words any longer. She was overweight, apple-figured, yet with a cute round face that could still turn heads when she walked past a building site... although couldn't anything in a skirt these days? I imagined she'd been one of the popular, pretty girls back in high school. Back in the days when she'd at least had her figure under some control.

I couldn't take my eyes away from a tiny bubble of spit on her lower lip. It aroused me as I watched it linger there all seductively, taunting me. I felt an irresistible urge to lean over and lick it gently from her face. But I controlled it and refocused. My mind snapped back to reality. Fear and sadness once again overwhelmed my thoughts. Something in the air felt wrong. Very, very wrong. I lowered my head and raised my hands at the same time. Halfway into the motion, the two met and I found myself buried face deep inside my cupped hands.

'I just, I just can't take this in.'

Even though I was Scottish and had lived in the country on and off since birth, the Scottish accent I'd acquired over the years never dominated my tongue like it did in most born-and-raised locals. The doc was proper south-of-the-border English, though.

'I'm so, so sorry, Liam.'

I tore my face away from my hands, gently shaking my head before smirking sarcastically.

'So how long, huh? How long have I got?'

The doctor sighed. 'Please, Liam. Don't do this.'

'Come on, eh? What's my sentence? Best guess. Give it to me.'

'Liam, I really couldn't say.'

'How about the last person you diagnosed. How long did they get, huh?'

The doc remained silent, curiously observing me with both sorrow and pity. She really wanted to give me a good, positive answer, I could tell. A wee bit of good news for the long road ahead. But, of course, that wouldn't be very honest of her now, would it? So all she could do was stare.

Briefly I wondered if she found me attractive. I imagined making my move on her. Would she welcome it? Would she let me stick my tongue deep inside her mouth and move it around, entangling it with her own, before letting me run my hands all over her soft, plump body in the process? Would she enjoy it? Would she make the move for my zipper and then...my wandering mind snapped back to reality and rage consumed me.

'Well, let's hear it then Doc, Jesus!' I exploded, unable to contain my mix of frustration and sexual desire. 'It's like waiting for the bloody *X Factor* results, for Christ sake.'

She shifted in her seat, shaken abruptly from her staring trance by my aggressive manner.

'With treatment, chemo, I don't know, Liam. Maybe a year, maybe less. That's my best guess.'

I refocused upon that tiny spit bubble. It calmed me. Soothed me immensely. It made me feel good. Fuck the chemo. All that shite just to cling to a few extra months of life. To hope for a year at best. My uncle had passed away a few years earlier with leukaemia. It made my stomach churn just thinking about all the crap he had to put up with when he could have been doing something else with his life. Something more memorable and productive with the remainder of his time. Screw that shite. I was out of there.

I nodded kindly at the doc. Thanked her for all the information she'd passed on and left. She stood abruptly, calling out about making an appointment with some other specialist next week. More tests. More horseshit clairvoyance. More wasted time and taxpayers' money. I wasn't listening anymore.

I walked past the cancer ward's waiting room, which was filled with more sad cases and zombified victims waiting to be told about their afflictions and survival rates. I kept walking. She fell out of earshot. I followed one of the ridiculously coloured lines on the hospital floor leading to some other part of the building. I chose the yellow path and prayed it would lead me to the exit. I felt like the fucking Scarecrow from *The Wizard of Oz*. 'Oh, we're off to see the Wizard....' But there would be no magical wizard with a new brain or magic cure lying in wait for me at the end of this brick road.

I made my way outside. Grey skies towered and rumbled above, urinating upon me with their wet drizzle. A storm was coming. A big fucking storm. When I reached the car park, a cool breeze hit my face like a soft fan on a humid summer's day. It felt good to be outside. To be at one and at peace with nature's earthly fresh air. It felt good to be alive. They say that some people, some lucky few on this earth, really appreciate life and its real meaning only when they're given their own personal expiry date. But oh, how I've pondered the meaning of it all these past few weeks since having the possibility of a near terminal end thrown in my face. The things we do to live a so-called long, healthy, and normal life. The empty, meaningless, monotonous, and mundane tasks, hobbies, activities, careers, love, sex, friends, family, people—and all the other trivial shite—we fill our empty lives with. All of them doing their very best to fill some hollow void in our conscious minds and distract us from the day-to-day process of growing older and nudging another step, another minute, another hour, towards our inevitable doom. Our species, Mother Earth's own terminal cancer, has never been more spiritually or intellectually minded in all our existence than we are today. Yet still, are minds are so narrow and rammed full of such pretentious and superficial self-importance, convinced that our own individual lives have more worth and meaning than those of any of our neighbours while still harbouring some hope and belief that there will be a simple, perfect meaning and explanation to it all in our final conscious hour. Our minds have evolved so far beyond our basic animal caveman way of thinking, yet we still harbour the possibility that there will be some kind of redemption. Some sort of beautiful ray of light or magical white-bearded wizard welcoming us at the end. Oh, what images and illusions of grandeur our minds conjure up in our most desperate times of need. Let me tell you about the meaning of life. We are all acts of a random nature, and none of us should even be here in the first place.

***

Before anyone starts feeling sorry for me, let me just say that I am not a nice guy. I want to get that out there into the polluted airwaves from the beginning. I mean, I'm not an utterly insane, mind-fuck, George Bush/Tony Blair mass murderer of millions and a shit pit of festering evil. Nor am I anywhere near the peak of Mother Teresa's rich, heavenly, Mount Everest of eternal goodness. I'd like to think of myself on the just-below-sea-level-mark on that particular scale. If I'd been born a country, I'd like to have been Serbia. Stuffed with a few deeply rooted rugged charms and not a complete and total fuck-up loss to humanity by any means, just 'not a nice guy' when it came to people. Especially relations and feelings with people of the feminine kind. Although, recently I had been trying. I really had. I battled constantly with this conflict more and more as the days rolled by. Like, the more I aged, the worse of an arsehole I moulded myself into. In all fairness, it was just too damn easy to be an arsehole... but an arsehole who, deep down inside, wanted nothing better in life than to settle with his own demons. To be completely devoted and faithful to one woman and one woman only. A woman whom I loved wholeheartedly and who loved me, without all the other mind-trap relationship bullshit games getting in the way.

I thought a lot about living in a house that filled me with pride, in a suburb and city I wasn't ashamed to call home. A home I'd be able to speak fondly and openly of some day while chatting with like-minded strangers on a family holiday abroad. Yes, this was what I dreamed about sometimes in the darkest hours of the night. A good life and a good home, surrounded by gardens, flowers, and freshly cut green fields. Surrounded by friends, family, and children I adored with all my heart, who adored me in equal measures. But for some people, life doesn't quite pan out like that. And the longer you resist putting off this comfort and happiness and fantasy bullshit of a good life, the harder it becomes with each passing day to find it again. To accept it and finally come to peace with it before letting go of all your insecurities and grasping it with all your heart, passion, soul, and desire.

Lately, I'd been coming to terms with the fact that I would most certainly die alone someday. And way before I'd been diagnosed with this untreatable brain cancer inconvenience. Yes, dying alone. Like some sad, old, lonely, sex-crazed fool with no friends, wife, children, or family to call my own. All I seemed to care about was where my next shag was coming from. This insatiable lust, which had infected my body and soul ever since my very first sexual awakening in my teenage years. A guilty lust which felt far worse than any incurable physical decease. Some days I woke up in the morning and felt, deep within my bones, that I could be truly happy with just one special someone in my life. Someone to love, protect, and come home to at night, cuddling up on the couch and spending free time together. A reason to get up in the morning. A reason to live and fight onwards and upwards.

On some rare occasions, I even longed to find that perfect someone who could make me want to be a better man. But alas, I knew it was useless and just prolonging the inevitable. What if I finally found that perfect someone and spilt my seed deep inside her soul and everything felt good and perfect for that short, singular, orgasmic heartbeat, trapped inside that perfectly wrapped, bubbled moment of harmony for one priceless and meaningful second, only for me to realise there was no such thing as a perfect compatible soul mate and that dark, sinking loneliness would eventually consume me and my feelings for her, just like everyone else who'd come and gone before her. Ultimately it would all disappear, fading like dusk from dawn. Evaporating into thin air, faster than a steam of hot piss in a frozen winter field, like those feelings always did. Always. And I, once more, would begin to long for something different, someone new. The never-ending monotonous circle of my daily life. That addictive chase for a new day. A new dawn. The grass is always greener...

I knew at the heart of this mental affliction I was what some might call a 'Selfish Narcissistic Prick.' Sex had always been a weakness and a downfall. I knew I needed sex a lot, and with as many partners who'd give themselves willingly to my cause as possible. It had always been quantity over quality over the years, that's for damn sure. And maybe that's the problem. Who knew? Certainly not me. I didn't really believe it mattered any longer whether someone was that perfect one for me. I really didn't. I knew I had this other horrible terminal lustful cancer embedded deep within my soul, and it was only spreading further and deeper through my veins with every new notch I claimed. This need, want, urge, curse... this longing. This goddamn disease which would absolutely be the end of me even before the real cancer had its wicked way. I needed to fuck. I wanted to fuck all the time and with as many different women as I possibly could. Christ, didn't all heterosexual red-blooded males want the same when you got down to the bare-knuckled nitty-gritty of it? I just didn't act upon it anymore as much as I'd like to, that's all. Maybe settling into a comfortable suburban lifestyle and approaching middle age had finally grasped a hold of my balls and slowly squeezed the final droplets of lust and zest for life right out of me.

But at the other end of that scale, I'd considered cutting off my own damn balls just to spite the suffering and finally live that so-called normal life. To end this cursed pleasurable and insatiable torment. But I was too weak... too goddamn weak to do it. Or then again, in hindsight, maybe I wasn't weak after all! Maybe I was just a man.

Chapter 2

I woke up around 10.30 in the morning. The fuckers next door, or one particular teenage fucker for sure, were playing their music at full volume yet again. Boom, boom, boom, BOOM. I felt almost immune to it. Feeling those vibrations had become part of my morning routine. Outside it looked grey and miserable, but on the plus side, the streets were clear of most traffic. For today, at least, I would put the brain cancer thing right to the back of my mind and become a self-employed plumber once more. I'd even convinced myself that yesterday was all just a bad dream. Shite! Was it a dream? Was it really?

The best thing about being self-employed and your own boss was definitely the fact that you got to dictate your own wake-up calls and working hours. Me, I loved to get up late. Beating the morning rush-hour traffic with all the nine-to-fivers, eight-to-fourers and ten-to-sixers out there who only ended up queuing in traffic for half their goddamn miserable lives anyhow. Trapped inside their steel four-wheeled coffins as punishment for getting up at such ridiculous hours of the day.

So, I worked as a plumber and I guess I did okay. I wasn't the best or fairest tradesman out there by any means but I certainly wasn't at the bottom end of that scale either. My only uncle, on my mother's side, the one who rotted away with the cancer too, prolonged his life by a few extra pointless months by taking every medication under the burning sun. Living out his final days in a deeply drug-induced, mind-warped state. By the end, he couldn't even tell what planet he was living on. Well, he told me once, back in the days when he was his real self and had full control over his mind, body, heart, and soul, that to be great at something you had to enjoy it immensely. You had to be utterly passionate about it. One hundred percent. It had to make you feel super excited to get up in the morning. Leaping and bounding out of bed with a big, fat, cheesy-arse grin on your face that said, 'Sweet Goddamn Mother of God, I love my work. I love my life.'

Sadly, with my job that was not the case, and never had been as far as I could remember. To me, plumbing had always been just a job, a trade, a career to get by. Something to fall back on in case I never made it as a rock star, movie star, racing driver, Scottish International Rugby player, male model, spy, fire—fighter, policeman...poet. The poetry thing had always been one of my more achievable goals in life. Dare I say, my dream. But, alas, it had died an ugly death many sweet moons ago, along with most of my soul. In fact, it was right after I'd joined the rest of the working-class arsehole elite and had to pay my very first utility bill, followed shortly afterward by taxes and more taxes, then an endless, spiralling combination of the two ever after.

I still dabbled in rhyming slang from time to time. More or less when I became super stressed or bored out of my tits. The women enjoyed it for shits and giggles when I brought it up in conversation at bars and clubs or while out gallivanting on first dates. In fact, most of them ate it up for reasons I can never fully explain. Drunk women and their 'struggling artist' fantasies, I suppose, when you put it against the backdrop of a handsome face. So, of course, I abused my mild talent and trust and ended up getting so dependent on using my poetry as an extension of my sexuality and pulling more girls into the sack that I never really pursued it on a more professional level. Is there such a thing as a professional poet in this day and age? Are there really people out there who still make money from this and nothing else? Or is it just a rolling fantasy, set up to the backdrop of one particular eighteenth-century Scottish bard? Right now, my own toilet wasn't even flushing properly. It needed a new internal flush cone, which I kept forgetting to purchase every time I headed out for work. Even though I'd bought countless numbers of them in the past for my customers. So, to hell with it. I guess my brain had been programmed to bypass any work for which I wasn't actually getting paid. I had to be content with pissing in the shower or kitchen sink whenever nature called. For the kitchen sink, I had to stand on my tiptoes, so it could get a wee bit stressful on the old calves. And remembering to take the dishes out beforehand became a constant nightmare. Especially in the middle of the night, when I didn't want to burden my sleepy eyes with bright lights. But it was the distant bathroom basin that worked best of all. Situated at a good height, much lower than the kitchen sink, to comfortably support my balls and slip the wee man over the edge without straining my lower legs. Of course, urinating in the bathroom sink turned out to be a real stroke of genius in the long run. It cut my bathroom time in half most mornings since I could do it while I brushed my teeth, waxed my hair and sprayed my armpits. And they say men can't multi-task.

***

Once out of the shower, I pulled on my dirty silicone-stained trousers, which I hadn't washed in months, followed by an old, thick but tight t-shirt to show off my fading muscular chest. In the kitchen, I swallowed a couple extra prescription tablets for my on/off headaches. Headaches that had previously awakened me to the fact that something was seriously wrong inside, and that I needed to seek medical help.

After boiling the kettle, I leaned against the worktop counter and slowly drained my black, sugary coffee. I took a moment to stare obliviously out the kitchen window at nothing in particular. My empty thoughts were soon interrupted by the faint sound of head-banging music that crept into my ear space from next door. I'd done a good job of blocking it out thus far. But it was back with a vengeance this morning. Especially when I clocked last night's unwashed dishes gently vibrating against the stainless-steel kitchen sink to the beats. Jesus, who the hell listened to such head-banging nonsense at 10.40 on a Tuesday morning, anyhow?

Due to the constant vibrations, one of my black-and-white pictures hanging on the neighbour-side wall and showing a gorgeous view of Edinburgh from the magical Calton Hill fell hard to the laminate floor. It landed with a thud, cracking the frame and shattering the glass. I stared at the fallen picture, then refocused my attention upon the vibrating dishes. I glanced up at the kitchen clock. I felt the rage brewing inside. It was growing and rising like bile from the pits of my gut. I wanted to hurt someone. In that moment, I wanted to inflict violence and pain upon another human being. I imagined storming next door and kicking in that noisy little bastard's front door. Finding the wee jakey cunt sitting with his back to me in his ridiculously untidy living room. Empty bottles of wine, beer, and take-out cartoons strewn all over the place. He'd be puffing away on a skinny joint while sitting on his comfy sofa, in his comfy little world. He'd be laughing to himself with his arms spread wide, resting them elegantly upon the top of his couch. Until I took my steel baseball bat and embedded it deep inside the hard centre of his jakey goddamn skull.

I refocused. I shook my head, trying to clear the angry, violent images from my mind. I closed my eyes and saw the doctor's little bubble of spit on her lips again. I saw myself licking it off with the tip of my tongue. The image of the action calmed me immensely while also giving me a ferocious semi. I refocused my attention on the present and opened my eyes. I finished my coffee, grabbed my keys, and left the house.

Outside it was eerily sunny. What the hell? Still cold as shit but the sun was shining brilliantly. That's Scotland for you. Sunny yet cold as hell. But even the sunshine couldn't brighten up the dreary-looking housing estate I'd found myself dwelling and rotting away in these past few years.

This was Burdiehouse.

How the hell had I ended up living in this spawn of Satan's shite? Take note. This is what happens when you don't pay attention in life and try to settle down with a nice bird, moving out of your pokey-yet-intimate party flat-share in the city centre to a bigger, more spacious pad in the suburbs. After a few months, your nice and faithful bird finds your not-so-faithful dumb arse in bed with her easy and over-flirtatious hairdresser sister. So, she dumps your dumb skinflint arse on the spot. Leaving you with a nice little twelve-month contracted house to pay for.

I took a deep breath and scanned the area. The major stand-out scenic attraction in these wonderful slumlands was always graffiti. It covered most of the surrounding walls, parks, and houses for miles around. Even my own home was not spared. Some houses in the street were completely boarded up, while black smoky stains lined the window edges. Looking like some daft ned had decided to have a barbeque indoors during a rainstorm.

I climbed into my work van and started the engine, half hoping the fucker wouldn't start. It did. First time. I drove down my street, heading out of the estate. A gang of half a dozen youths, all around the thirteen-years-of-age mark, loitered at the opposite end of the nearby park. They were watching other teenagers redecorate a bus shelter on the adjourning road. The baseball-capped, tracksuit-wearing vandals were stamping and smashing the glass windows from the inside while spraying red graffiti all over the metal framing.

I wanted to stop. I wanted to pull over and say something. Better still, I wanted to drive my car right up that curb, through that play park and ram it, full speed ahead, directly into that bus shelter. Taking out as many of those little bastards as humanly possible and making the world a better place. But would it, though? Would it really make the world a better place? I had strong opinions that it just might in the long run. I could feel the rage burning, building up inside me. I could envision myself driving into that bus shelter again and again. Right into the heart of those soulless, delinquent vandals, knocking them into their next shitty life. I could hear my cancer egging me on. Whispering from the darkest, foulest, deepest regions of my mind. I could see the headlines from the terrorist-obsessed media now: **Terrorist attack in Burdiehouse.** A *Muslim **looking** man* (I go to sunbeds a lot) *drives his van full of explosives* (plumbing tools) *into a bus stop, killing half-a-dozen* **innocent** *young* **children** (non-educated delinquents).

But in the end I didn't do anything. I just kept on driving and the teens kept on destroying.

***

I had to go to Mrs Patterson's house, which was way over on the other side of Edinburgh. She was a regular old customer of mine, Mrs Patterson. An OAP with a heart of gold. She usually called me up twice a month with plumbing problems which were either a false alarm or a blockage/leak that had been caused, I always suspected, by her own purposed meddling. I guessed she just enjoyed my company or talking to someone, anyone, about her life and memories. Plus, she lived all by herself inside that big old house of hers over in Comiston. So, if she felt obliged to pay me forty pounds an hour to just sit and have tea and biscuits while listening to more of her rambling war stories for the twentieth time in six months, then so be it. I actually enjoyed kicking back and listening to someone else's woes for a change, with neither one of us having any ulterior motives or agendas.

I drove through the city centre and up through Morningside in the direction of Mrs Patterson's place. Halfway along Morningside Road, I stopped at a set of traffic lights with the usual overly long waiting period when, quite by chance, I noticed a uniquely beautiful woman standing at a bus stop. She was that rare type of girl who made both time and your heart stand still. There were other people waiting around at the bus shelter but she clearly wasn't with any of them. She had long, flowing, dirty blonde hair, milky pale skin, and a curvaceous body to die for. What an arse. Even greater boobs. Most noticeable and striking of all her features were those deep brooding eyes. She looked so hauntingly beautiful and sexy that she took my breath away.

But those eyes. Those goddamn delicious, piercing, deep, hypnotic eyes. There seemed to be a deep, old, lingering sadness to those eyes which exuded a wise intellect well beyond her years. She wore a simple pair of tight jeans and a snug blue jumper which complemented the curvaceous body hidden underneath. A physique and facial features which reminded me of a dressed-down actress from the early 1990s, Emmanuelle Seigner. Just simply angelic and stunning. But the way she stood against that bus top, so casual and uncaring... I'd never seen such an aura of aloof sex appeal in my life. Even if she'd been wearing only a filthy bin bag, she'd still have gotten a rise from me. I mean, Jesus Christ! What the hell was she going to look like dressed up to the nines for a night out on George Street wearing a cute mini skirt, skimpy top, and high heels? I could only imagine.

I thought about pulling over and making haste on foot back down the street to boldly talk to her at the bus stop—but about what? I didn't have a Scooby. I chuckled at the ridiculousness of it. All those people around! Waiting, watching, listening. What the hell was I going to say to her? She would run a mile in embarrassment for sure, if indeed she didn't first blast me in the face with a can of pepper spray while sounding her rape alarm at maximum volume. I would forever be pathetically shamed for my foolish actions. No, the circumstances weren't right. Fate wasn't with me at that moment. So, I kept driving even though the cancer in the back of my mind was screaming at me to get the hell back there. Go and speak to her if she made such an impact and impression on you. You only live once. You won't even exist on the planet this time next year. Get off your lazy plumber arse and make something happen. Once again, I ignored its pleas.

***

I pulled up at Mrs Patterson's shortly after. When I turned onto her street, the first thing that caught my eye was another sexy gal dressed in a tightly fitted business suit. She looked to be in her late twenties, with one of those bodies you just knew had done some stripping to pay for that university degree a few years back. And no. She didn't make my heart beat fast or my body ache like the previous bus stop beauty. But still, she looked sexy and physically my type.

She walked along Mrs Patterson's street at a good pace. I deliberately slowed down as I drove past her to get a better look. I liked what I saw. This time, the cancer screamed at the top of its lungs to stop, get the hell out of the van and go speak to her. What's the bloody worst that's gonna happen? She'll tell you to 'Get tae fuck.' What's the best that could happen? You'll be ball deep in ex-stripper fanny by the end of the week. Now do it. You'll be dead soon. Man the hell up. Give in to your lustful urges and desires. You only live once, bro. Tick-tock. Tick-fucking-tock. The pleasures of the outcome far outweighed the pain of making the first bold move.

This time I listened to the cancer and pulled into the next available parking spot halfway along the street. Still a few houses shy of Mrs Patterson's, but I knew if I hesitated, hemmed and hawed about while looking for a closer space farther along there was a good chance I'd bottle it and lose the fox for sure. Usually, I went after women with only half her physical quality, along with the aid of loud music and alcohol to hide my insecurities.

The cancer had given me a boost. It made me braver, more confident, more determined, cockier, and carefree. If only I'd had it helping me during my high school days; the sick thought crept through my mind like a plagued rat, I'd have been an absolute legend with the ladies back then. Quickly I stamped that rodent thought down. Without further hesitation, I got out of my van and walked around to the rear boot, where I kept my tools. The fox strolled closer. I opened the back door and pretended to get some tools while pondering just what the hell I was going to say to get her to stop and talk to me. I could always play the old, safe, tried-and-tested 'ask-for-fake-directions' card and feel her out a little. Screw it. I'd start walking towards her, giving her that deep and lingering, bold-eye-contact stare. If she kept looking straight ahead, she wasn't interested. No harm done. But if she glanced at me once, just one time, even a fleeting look, I'd stop her in her tracks and ask for her number.

I closed the back of my van, turned, and made my way towards her. Wow, she looked even better from face on. Curvy, tight, and delicious. She walked with a real sexy wiggle in those high heels and tight skirt. With her head held high, she seemed to have an aura of great bitchy confidence about her, reminding me of some ancient Roman domina screaming, 'Only dare speak to me if you believe yourself to be worthy enough, mortal.'

Ha, I was going to enjoy trying to get into this one's panties. We approached each other. The black blouse she wore underneath her office jacket was unbuttoned by two, leaving the top half of her cleavage squeezing and almost popping out with every stride she took. I felt myself getting hard already. But unlike those lesser perverted males who just ogled from afar and never acted upon their instincts or desires, I kept my eyes firmly rooted upon hers at all times. Staring her down with a warm and friendly eye, but also a slight cheeky look etched across my face.

She was close. Those squeezed, voluptuous breasts and wiggling hips were almost within touching and smelling distance. She still wasn't looking at me, though. Her eyes remained focused on nothing but the end of the street and the direction she was walking. She was either in a happy budding relationship or hadn't seen me getting out of the van. If she never saw me getting out of the van, by the way I had dressed for my plumbing duties and without the support of my tape measure as the mark of a tradesman hanging off my belt, I could've been Brad Pitt walking down that street and still looked like a bloody jakey homeless rogue.

Just when I thought it was too late, she looked. The little fox looked. And not just any quick glance, but a long, lingering gaze, with a mischievous grin of her own. Wow, this was better than I'd expected. She'd totally checked me out and liked what she'd seen. I held her eye and felt the small fiery flame within. The sexual tension glowed between us with a lightning pulse. I felt the stiff yet stifled beast stirring inside my ripped, silicone-stained trousers, throbbing against the material inside. 'Let me out, let me out, let me out,' he groaned.

I waited until she'd walked by a few steps before turning around to face her. She half-turned too, glancing back while walking. She definitely seemed interested. But most women, being the shy and fragile creatures they are during the first encounter –especially without the lubrication of alcohol—weren't going to make any oral notions in the slightest to state their interest in a mate, bar the warm, lingering smile and glazing, obvious eye contact. No, that would be far too easy. It was up to me, the male, to go out there and make the first move, and I had to do it now. Quick and fast, with words and confident body language, before she slipped out of my reach for good. To delay a fraction of a second with futile hesitation would leave her questioning my manhood and kill all hopes of any future adventurous liaisons.

'Hey!' I called in a warm, friendly manner.

She stopped in her tracks and turned fully around. Of course she had to stop. It was the only polite thing to do when a handsome stranger called to you on the street and looked reasonably warm, friendly, and completely unlike a serial killer. Even worse was to come across as the stereotypical, loud–mouth, cocky, jerk of a builder who hides behind the towering shelter of his scaffolds and fences and other dickless, insecure workmates as he shouts down his sexual innuendos from the safety of a new-build high-rise to the attractive young females walking below. Oh, how manly they must feel at such confident and romantic tactics.

'How's it going?' I continued, saying the first thing that came to me. Still smiling warmly and looking as friendly as ever, I didn't wish to appear too confident and give off the impression that I chatted up attractive women on the street all the time. Which I didn't. Or even worse, to appear recklessly nervous like I didn't have an ounce of social awareness and confidence. No, a nice, soothing-yet-charming somewhere in between would be just fine.

'Hey thir yersel,' she replied with a flirtatious grin and a thicker Scottish accent than I'd anticipated.

'What you up to?' It was the next uncontrollable sentence from my mouth. I was instinctively acting like I knew her.

To my delight, she instantly followed my lead. 'Am just finished work and headin tae catch ma bus hame.' She was chatty and friendly off the bat. A good sign. 'Why did ye stoap me? Dae ye ken me or sutton? Are ye lost?'

I moved a little closer. She remained where she stood, still smiling, still maintaining eye contact—another good sign. Her breasts still squeezing up and out from underneath her tight top with each shallow breath. There was a baited pause. She waited for me to speak. I decided to come clean right away.

'Well, this is gonna sound really cheeky but...I saw you there, when you walked past ...'

'Aye, and ah saw you in all,' she interrupted, sharp as a tack. Wearing a big, wide grin across her puss.

'Well, I just wanted to take a risk and say hi, you know, that was it.'

'Okay. Well hi, then,' she replied with confidence, like she'd done this a thousand times before with countless other men in bars and clubs and perhaps even streets, all of whom were brave enough to approach. I moved closer towards her and stopped a few inches shy from her heaving bosoms. She smelt delicious. Cute, thin face, aging on the right side of thirty. But the breasts. Oh, my Lord, they were such magnificent creatures. A little too big and round for her body frame, so I was thinking boob job or else a really terrific Wonderbra, but magnificent specimens nonetheless. I imagined watching them bounce and jiggle away through a mirror as I took her slowly from behind, spread out on her hands and knees over the side of my bed. I bet they could jiggle away for Scotland, those things. I offered her my hand to shake and she took it.

'I'm Liam.'

'Nikki.'

I continued to hold her hand just a few seconds longer than I needed to.

'Look, Liam. Ah really need tae catch ma bus, ken, so...'

'That's cool. I'll let you go...' I deliberately paused, letting it linger until she was just about to turn away. 'But maybe we could grab a drink some time. Get to know each other a wee bit better when we're both not, you know...so rushed.'

'That soonds nice, Liam. Ah think ah might be up for that.' She bit her lower lip. This girl knew how to tease.

'Okay.' I pulled out my wallet and handed her one of my plumbing cards. She took it, glanced over it for a second, then put it into her purse.

'Yur a plumber, aye?'

'Aye, among other things.'

'You could come in handy.'

'I hope I do.'

'Ah might be in touch.'

'I hope you are.'

Our eyes lingered upon each other for another few seconds. Nikki turned away first.

'See ye then, plumber boy.' And just like that she wiggled off on her way again, down the street and out of my presence. I felt good. Christ, I couldn't believe that patter actually worked. Right out in broad daylight, too. I secretly thanked my cancer for giving me new balls. I felt like writing a poem. I hadn't written a poem in months and now I felt a burning sensation and the fire inside to do so. It was those breasts, you see. Those gorgeous, beautiful melons. They had inspired me to creative genius. I hurried back to my van, got inside, and hunted furiously for a piece of paper, anything would do. All I could find was my plumbing job receipt booklet. I wrote on the back of an empty page but all I could think to write about was her wonderful, delicious bosoms.

There's just something so wonderful about your breasts, you see,
So beautiful, hypnotic, bouncy, soft, and loose,
I cannot take my eyes away from them, please don't think me rude,
They're fucking gorgeous. What is it with your breasts I shall never know,
I want to suck them and bite them and taste them all day long,
Kiss them, caress them, love them as I would my own child,
Take them for a romantic walk underneath the beautiful, inflamed setting sun.
Tell them the story of my life and introduce them to my mum.
I prod the nipples gently with my tongue, then draw a swirling circle around the rim.
I wake up in the morning and all I can think about is them.

I let out a deep sigh and chuckled at the ridiculous words. I ripped up the paper immediately and crumpled it into a little ball in my hand, discarding it promptly out the window.

'Utter pish.'

***

When I drove home later that evening, it was dark with clear skies. Up above, the stars shone brightly. There wasn't much traffic on the roads, which was the way I liked it. Not far from home, I reached a set of red traffic lights at a crossroads in the middle of Gilmerton. At first, I didn't mind the wait. I felt calm and stress free, just sitting there and sitting there and sitting there...with nothing much happening in the slightest. Just minding my own business while thinking about all the trivial shite of the day. Then I became aware that I'd been sitting at those bloody traffic lights for a good five minutes and nothing was happening.

I checked left and right. Still no other traffic in sight. No pedestrians, no cyclists, not even ones without lights and helmets who cycled around the roads like they owned them. Nothing. Yet the lights remained red. I could feel the rage building up inside me again. I wanted to drive right on through those damn red lights. What would be the harm? What was stopping me? I imagined the police sitting in a hidden lay-by just farther ahead. Watching me. Egging me on to go through the red lights. The bastards were setting me up. A deliberate snatch for frustrated, retarded, and impatient drivers just like me. I imagined some secret underground traffic light control room in the centre of Edinburgh. A place where one sad, sadistic, egotistic, lonely, bitter old tosser controlled every single traffic light in the city. I imagined him sitting there in his wee secluded orifice, bored out of his bloody shit-faced skull because of the lack of traffic on the roads this fine evening. And when it did become quiet like this, he enjoyed nothing better than playing and taunting what few drivers were out on the streets with his silly little waiting games that were fucking amusing only to him. Making us wait and wait and wait for a goddamn eternity. He could easily have pressed one little button to make all the lights go green, sending every single one of us on our merry little way. But he was too busy laughing. Having too much fun with all his godly power to do a simple, good little turn like that.

I felt ready to explode. The lights remained red. I had visions of the traffic light controller's laughter getting louder and harder as he continued watching his CCTV footage of me just sitting there, going nowhere. Going bloody nowhere! I could see the police around the next corner, still rubbing their grubby little paws faster and harder.

'Do it, do it, do it,' I could hear them say. 'Jump the light, jump the light, jump the light!'

It would make their bloody week to have me run this red light. I was about to do it. I began revving the engine. Without even thinking, I started crawling forward over the point of white striped line of no return. I was gonna do it. The cancer burst my eardrums, screaming at me to do it.

'Live, you bastard. Live. Drive, you bastard, drive.'

Then the lights turned green. I breathed a sigh of relief and slipped into second gear, continuing on my way.

Chapter 3

The previous night I hadn't been able to sleep. I just laid there wide awake, twisting and turning all night long. The cancer kept talking to me. Whispering that I should be doing better things with the short time I had left here rather than fixing people's shitty toilets and leaky pipes. It told me to get a grip. Wake up to reality. Come alive. Feel alive. I told it I was scared. That I needed some kind of sign. I couldn't die. I just couldn't. I was fucking immortal, for Christ's sake. Everyone was immortal, weren't they? I didn't really have brain cancer. It was all just a sad little misunderstood dream. A horrible, bad, fucking nightmare. Or a dirty trick from some wido customer whose shitty bathroom I'd flooded accidentally when I first got into this plumbing lark. It wasn't real. I was too young for this terminal illness bollocks. This happened only to other people. I hadn't done anything with my life just yet. I hadn't made a name or something of myself. Who would remember me if I died right now? No cunt! That's who. Nobody knew me. I mean, really *knew* me. So I sure as hell wasn't going to be missed a year or so from now. By Christ I needed to change that, but how, where, and with whom?

I had to be in Leith by ten am to re-fit a tap that I'd installed a few weeks back which was leaking. If only it had waited a full month to start pishing water then I could've easily enforced my one month guarantee policy and charged the annoying customer a call out fee to come and fix my own mistake. So I was up and out of the house earlier that week day morning, and for my efforts, catapulted right into the thick end of morning rush hour traffic.

To be honest, I didn't expect it to be so bad since I'd avoided being out and about at this time of day for such a long time. But it was fucking horrendous. It was so, so bad. It looked as if every car in the United States of Europe had decided to pay Edinburgh a visit that very morning. Too many cars and not enough roads. It was just after 9.00 am, so where the hell was everyone going? What happened to the good old days of the nine to five rota? Was everyone late for work this morning? Or worse still, maybe they were all lazy self-employed fuckers like me.

I continued to sit in gridlocked city centre traffic just outside the parliament in Holyrood park, just off Queens drive. I thought I'd been smart. Avoiding the Royal Mile, the Pleasance and the North Bridge. But there was some fucking road works after the roundabout on Horse Wynd heading towards Abbeyhill, just after the palace that was now bringing the whole of Edinburgh to a stand still. Always road works in Edinburgh. The roads in this town have had more work done than Jordan's face, tits and arsehole combined. And don't even get me started on the bloody trams. Everything traffic related was fucked here in the city because of that fiasco. Everything!.

On a plus note the sun shone brightly from the heavens above. Two days on the trot which was a rare record for Edinburgh, so of course I'd take that while I could. I wound down my window and stuck my arm out into the fresh air just to amuse myself and calm myself down more than anything. With my other hand I turned on the radio. Radio Forth to be exact. It had just gone past ten am and Grant Stott's overly jolly voice, which reeked of far too many happy larry pills for a Scotsman on a week day morning, rang through my ears drums. 'Oh Lordy this and Lordy that. Auch aye and Auch noooo.'

My eyes drifted towards one of the many vehicles edging towards me in the opposite direction, also on the road to nowhere. This one caught my eye more than most. Inside, a lone middle aged driver with a dead hamster for a moustache, munched away on a wrapped bacon, sausage and egg roll, while sipping something hot. I watched him eat then sip, sip then eat, while crumbs and runny egg yolk got stuck in his moustache.

'Stashed away for a rainy day aeh pal?' I mumbled, amusing myself.

The man finished his rolls. Drank the last of his coffee and wiped his greasy fat mouth with the back of his paws completely missing the runny egg goo on his tash which had dried and looked more like a dirty big snotter. Our vehicles still hadn't moved an inch. I continued to watch the fuckwit cram the roll wrappings into his empty coffee cup, and then, without even the slightest care in the world or a flicker of remorse, he dumped the rubbish filled cup out of his window and onto the road below. Just like that. So bloody easy. What a fucking cunt. I could feel the rage building inside me again. I wanted to kill the prick. I wanted to commit blue murder all for the sake of an empty coffee cup.

I stared at the arsehole with a look of daggers. Giving him a glare of pure and utter loathing hatred like he'd sexually abused a squadron of brownies right in front of me. The man caught my glare and turned his full face in my direction, giving me his full attention. I kept staring. I wanted to say something. I wanted to educate this fucking parasite in the ways of taking care of the environment and our one and only home planet, mother Earth. In the blink of an eye I imagined stepping out of my van, scooping up his plastic cup filled with his rubbish shite. Grabbing the ignorant prick by the roots of his hair and forcing the cup right down the length and breadth of his scrawny wee fucking throat.

'Can ah help ye wi sutton thir pal?' said the man. 'Ye wanae tak a fuckin picture thir likes, aye?'

After a second I shook my head and turned away. The traffic started budging along by a rare few metres.

'Aye! That's whit a thought pal.' He spat, driving past me at a snails pace. 'Noo jog oan ye fanny.'

I drove forward. Getting this wank-stain the hell out of my peripheral vision. What was wrong with these people? What was wrong with the world when cunt's like that could just piss all over it with their shite and get away with it? Or was there just something wrong with me? Maybe I'm the wank-stain for getting so rallied up over a tiny wee bit of harmless rubbish. After all I was the one thinking about killing a man over a wee bit of littering.

After another forty minutes or so of more jerky wee nudges along in my van, I finally made it onto Easter road. Almost there. Why was it so busy up here too at eleven in the bloody morning? Why was no cunt working today in this city I wanted to roar. Cars everywhere. More cars than bloody people.

To my left I spied a dirty wee traffic warden. The bane of my existence. The bastards are like a plague of locus when you hit the city centre. More of these leaches than tourists and shoppers combined, I swear. But this was Easter road. I didn't think they ventured out this far, but kike a stray dog out of his territory, the fucker had.

I watched as he eagerly wrote out a ticket for an old red Astra. There were even two unattended young kids in the back seat greeting their wee eyes out, which you'd assume would have been the wardens first priority rather than the illegally parked fucking car, unattended brats. I noticed the hazard lights had been left on like it was a magical license to park where-ever the hell you pleased and also an indication that the owner would be back within the next hour or so. That was usually my trick. But the spunk-bag warden was having none of it. Commission, then Promotion to a better patch in Edinburgh first and foremost, then unattended brats later. The car was only parked on a single yellow for Christ sake, yet the warden's still writing away furiously like he's working on the next Harry Potter book.

Then he took a picture with his fancy wee camera. I glanced at all the other drivers around, sitting in traffic, waiting for the next set of never ending lights to change. They were all watching too, but said nothing. With a secret pleasure, watching someone else's misery unfold before your eyes was always more fascinating than anything going on in your own life.

Finally a man in his early thirties came clambering out of the tenement flats nearby carrying a baby in one arm and a pram in the other. His face turned to panic and dread when he saw the warden parasite up ahead. He rushed to the car, nearly loosing his grip of both buggy and baby. The parasite clocked him. There was a slight moment of hesitation in the warden's eyes when he saw the baby. The heartless parasite might have a pulse and soul after all. Until the young Dad started pleading and begging with him all pathetic like. That's what turned those sad bastards on more than anything. When folk treated them like executioners, pleading for their lives.

'Please ma man. Av jist been a few minutes like, ken, bringin the bairn doon ken.'

The warden's bout of hesitation lasted a mere second. His eyes sparkled with commission pound signs as he took out the fatal yellow and black plastic envelope, sealing the ticket inside with a wicked grin. He slammed it on the front window pane for even the Gods to see.

'Ah wiz anly goan a few minutes man. Please. Thir wiz naewhere else tae park man.' He continued to plead while the baby began letting out its own wailing sobs. The other two kids cried louder in the back seat too. The warden shook his head, turned away, and continued on up the footpath. He looked mightily impressed with himself.

In the early afternoon I had another job to attend to in the south west of the city

I hadn't officially met the customer yet but we'd exchanged some e-mails regarding the plumbing work to be carried out, so it seemed straightforward enough: a tap in the rear garden, up against the rear brick wall of the house. The kitchen mains were situated directly on the opposite side of that wall, so it shouldn't take more than a few hours to complete.

I hadn't officially met the customer yet but we'd exchanged some e-mails regarding the plumbing work to be carried out, so it seemed straightforward enough: a tap in the rear garden, up against the rear brick wall of the house. The kitchen mains were situated directly on the opposite side of that wall, so it shouldn't take more than a few hours to complete.

I knocked upon the front door of the old Victorian house and waited, a bag of tools in one hand, a drill box in the other. From how she signed her e-mails, I knew the customer's name was Barbara. I had visions of a little old lady or a middle-aged divorcee opening the door in a baggy sweater and loose, dull trousers, wearing a little bit of facial hair. I was pleasantly surprised when the door opened to reveal a relatively fit, curvy, smiling woman in her early thirties. Fair enough, she was taller than me, with love handles (must have had a kid or two hiding around somewhere). But she made up for those tiny little inadequacies with her sexy curves and more than two handfuls apiece of beautiful, bouncing bosoms.

'How's it going? I'm the plumber.'

I could see her eyes lighting up immediately as she gave me the once over, up and down like she hadn't seen a reasonably fit and ruggedly handsome bloke up close and personal in a good long while. She gave me a rather tenacious and flirty smile.

'Hi there, Mr Plumber,' she replied. Her eyes glazed, looking like she'd been expecting some beer-bellied, chain-smoking, middle-aged hog. Her Edinburgh accent wasn't too strong, either. She showed signs of living south of the border at some point in her past. Down south you had to lose the accent and adapt quick smart or else become a laughingstock tease fest for jock-strap, scotty and auch aye the noo jokes.

I put down my bag of tools and offered my hand with a flirty smile of my own. She shook it with a lingering gaze and held it. I couldn't see a wedding ring for love nor money. Not that I gave a damn about such petty things when it came to acts concerning my overactive libido.

'Thanks for fitting me in so soon. I'm Barbara. But everyone usually just calls me Babs.'

I watched Babs turn and seductively wiggle her way back through the house from the hallway to the kitchen, towards the back garden. I picked up my tools and followed her. I couldn't stop staring at her hips and plump, juicy arse as it wiggled away in front of me beneath a tight-fitting pair of jeans. That peachy round backside could've led me anywhere, even out into heavy afternoon traffic, and I still would have followed willingly to my road-kill doom.

As we entered the kitchen, a wee Jack Russell devil dog came yapping up to me from a hidden side cupboard by the fridge. Instantly, he started biting at my heels.

'Don't mind Rags. He's no even mine. Am just looking after him for my wee sister while she's on holiday. He's a well-behaved dog, most of the time.'

I had visions of booting this overgrown rat right out the nearest window. It was another pet hate of mine, when people referred to these oversized rodents as dogs. A Labrador, German shepherd, Collie, Great Dane. Now those were dogs.

'Unlike me, he's no a biter,' continued Babs with a teasing tone. I was liking her more and more.

She carefully opened the back door, shooing Rags away when he tried to make a run for it outside. She clearly didn't want the mutt anywhere near the garden.

'Little bugger's no aloud in the back garden the now either. He keeps attacking my wee boy's rabbits and guinea pigs and digging holes all over the place.'

I followed Babs outside and around to the kitchen wall. I set my tools down and made a mark on the brick where the tap would best be placed. I could instantly sense her vixen-like presence standing over me, arms folded. I was positive she was returning the favour of checking me out just like I'd done to her.

'You have a really nice tan on you, by the way.'

'Thanks,' I replied, trying to concentrate on my measurements. Just knowing she was standing there, eying me over, had given me a semi.

'Have you been on holiday somewhere hot?'

'Not for a long time, no.'

'Really! So, what's your secret then? Fake tan?' she smirked.

'I lived in Australia for a few years. Plus, I do work outside a lot.' I shot her a sly grin. 'And I guess there is that cheeky wee trip to the sunbeds every now and again too.'

'I knew it. Wow! Dinnae really hear too many men admitting to that these days, huh? So, you like to look after yourself then, I take it, aye? Wish I had time for sunbeds.'

I finished my measurements and glanced up at Babs. Her nipples were getting hard and showing through her tight beige sweater. I couldn't tell if it was because of the cool air or maybe...something else? I imagined what they tasted like. How they'd feel in my mouth as I bit down upon their erect firmness on the good side of hard. The mixed look of pleasure and pain on her face that the sensation would create as I bit down a little harder still before gently releasing.

'Is here good for you?' I asked, pointing to where the tap would stick out from the wall.

'Aye,' she replied with a sly wink and smile. 'Looks very good from here, Mr Plumber.'

I couldn't help but smile at her intentionally cliché comment. God bless forward and flirty thirty-something single women.

'So, I'll leave you to it then. If you need me I'm just gonna pop round the garage and pick my car up from its MOT. I'll be back in about half an hour. Then I'll just be upstairs working on ma laptop.'

She went to turn away, then suddenly turned back as something else came to mind. 'Can you do me a wee favour, though, and keep the back door closed while you're working out here, aye?'

'Aye, I can do that, sure, no worries!'

'I just dinnae want Rags getting into the garden with all the rabbits and guinea pigs about, you see. If he gets into those cages he'll eat the poor buggers alive.'

Christ on a bike, I wanted to eat something alive. For a second I found myself caught in a lustful daydream. I imagined what that wet patch between Babs' legs would taste like. What it looked like. Was it shaven, bushy and overgrown, or kept nice and trim like a little disciplined Navy airstrip? I wondered what she looked like when she had an orgasm. Was she a screamer? Would she like the dirty talk in her ear while I ravaged her from behind like the lustful savage beast I could be when the mood took me? Clutching her hair like the reins of a horse, fingers gagging her mouth, then spanking her plump, curvy arse. Scratching my fingernails down her back. I bet it was a beautiful sight when she came, perhaps like thunder.

I always felt amazed how peoples' minds held the power to create these perfect, pleasurable worlds, where everything inside your imagination was always the best it would ever get. But when you tried to make your fantasy a reality, it usually turned out to be, well, just...okay.

My wave of lustful daydreams continued. I imagined throwing Babs up against the cool, hard back garden wall in full view of the surrounding flats, houses, and neighbours. They'd cheer us on from above like we were two feisty gladiators in the arena as I pinned her hands to the wall with one hand while ripping off her shirt and bra with the other, revealing those beautifully curvaceous bosoms. Biting, teasing, sucking at those nipples, then turning her around and pushing her face-first against the wall to her shocked gasps and moans. 'No out here,' she'd moan. Trying to protest. But I wouldn't give a damn as I hiked that skirt right up around her waist and ripped those tight panties to one side with my bare teeth. Let her neighbours see that raw, lusting animal raging inside her. Spanking her backside hard as punishment every time she moved her hands away from the wall. I'd bury my mouth and face into those plump cheeks. Biting, licking, spanking. Running my fingernails down the entire length of her bare back again and again, all the way down to her curvaceous, peachy, plump buttocks. Leaving my trail of faint red claw marks upon her. Teasing her beautiful, juicy, peachy crack with the tip of my tongue until she begged for me to put my hardness deep inside her...but I wouldn't give her that satisfaction. Not just yet. Like the teasing bastard I could be, she'd have to beg even more for that.

I refocused on the present. What were we talking about again? Oh aye, the dog. Don't let him run about wild outdoors.

'Don't worry. I'll make sure he behaves himself,' I finally replied.

***

The job went smoothly. In just over two hours I had Babs' new outside tap drilled through the wall and hooked up to the water main underneath the kitchen sink. Job was a good'n. It was a nice feeling when a job went according to plan. Being a tradesman, I always prepared myself for the worst-case scenario and expected it on most occasions.

Five minutes later I found myself sat comfortably down upon the long, black, L-shaped leather couch in Babs' living room, waiting to get paid. She'd made me another cup of tea while she headed to the nearest cash machine just around the corner. When a glum-looking Babs re-entered the living room, she closed the door firmly shut behind her and came directly towards me. The couch I sat upon seemed big enough to seat at least six other people, just so long as they weren't too porky. There were also another two armchairs scattered around the scandalously huge living room. But with all the spacious seating area at her disposal, Babs chose to sit right next to me. Lightly but intentionally brushing against my thighs with her own legs as she parked her perky round behind beside me. I took another sip from my over-sugared tea.

'So, how much did you say I owed you for the job today again, then?'

'Eighty-five if that's cool. Sixty for the labour and another twenty-five for materials.'

Suddenly Babs slapped her hand upon my upper thigh and kept it there. She let out a deep, dramatic sigh and glanced away for a fleeting moment, biting her bottom lip. Her hand on my thigh, legs pressed firmly against mine, and that seductive biting of her lower lip—whether she was aware of it or not—were awakening my inner sexual urges like a newly budding rose. She turned back to face me and seemed a little worried as she released the tooth grip of her lower lip. I felt like I was in some kind of festival fringe show. I was about to chuckle at the bizarre display when Babs spoke first.

'Actually, you know what, Liam? My M.O.T. was a wee bit higher than I expected today. I even exceeded ma withdrawal limit on the cash machine to pay for it all.'

I let out a slight grimace. It was hard to tell if she really was into me or just using her womanly charms to defer payment until she had the money.

'Well, I don't do cheques, I'm afraid. It really has to be cash.'

'Aye, sure. That's fair enough...,' she pondered. Then her hand, which still rested upon my lower thigh, moved higher—within an inch of my loins, to be exact.

'Would you perhaps accept an act of human kindness, instead, for payment?'

She'd caught me off guard.

'Like what?' I said with a sly, fruitful smile. I didn't know whether to pounce on her there and then or stand up in protest. 'Another cup of tea and a chocolate biscuit?'

Babs grinned. 'No exactly...no.'

She slid her hand right up and over my groin, cupping the pouch as if finally revealing her sordid intent. In case I hadn't realised the subconscious hint the first time round. I did, but I was enjoying her little sideshow and wanted to see how far she would take this charade before I moved it on to the main event.

'I was gonna say, more along the lines of a cup of cock in mouth.'

So there it was, spelled right out in front of me like some kind of kiddie's alphabet soup. Couldn't get more blatantly clear than that, I suppose.

'Oh, I see!' I said, pretending I'd just cottoned on to her sexual innuendos that very second. But a second was all I needed. Usually in this situation, which had happened to me a few times before, believe it or not, I'd always take the money first before making my advances. It was the smart thing to do. But my cancer didn't give a shit about the money. It just wanted me to be happy and get my end away. Live in the moment.

'Well, aye, I suppose that might work.'

'Lovely!' Babs clapped her hands, delighted. 'Well, pop your trousers down, then. We huvnae got all afternoon. The wee one might come home from school at any minute.'

My loins were fully awake as I excitedly stood up. I pulled my trouser overalls down to my ankles in no time, followed by my boxer shorts. I sat back upon the couch and waited for the 'fasten-your-seatbelt' sign. God, I loved a woman of action who went straight for the meaty, gritty jugular.

Babs slid off the couch and down onto her knees, right between my thighs. My purple-headed warrior quickly stood to meet her gaze in a throbbing growth of girth and glory, giving her his full, meaty attention. Babs gazed at me with seductive glee. She unfastened a few buttons on her shirt, revealing half her hidden cleavage. Slowly and teasingly she guided her face, mouth, and tongue inches from my wee stood-to-attention general.

'Just dinnae cum in my mouth, though, okay?'

'Ummm...sure, Babs, aye. I'll try my best not to do that,' I said unconvincingly, still stuck in a throbbing glee of excitement regarding the pleasures to come.

'I mean it. Unless!' she paused. 'How good are you with boilers and central heating systems and such?'

Her mouth was centimetres away from the wee man's shiny purple head. I could almost feel those luscious red lips of hers wrapping themselves around my shaft. It was utterly tantalizing. She edged closer still, but not quite touching. I could feel her warm breath right upon the tip. The very thought of the sinful act to come created shockwaves of pleasure which surged throughout my entire body like it were an ocean filled with lustful electricity, and those ocean waves were getting bigger, wider, stronger, and faster. An incredible storm was coming and I was lost at sea.

'Well?' she grinned teasingly. Bringing me back up to the surface, but only temporarily.

'Ummm…pretty good, I guess.'

I knew fuck all about boilers. Just bathrooms, kitchens, and general domestic plumbing. Babs let out another mischievous grin.

'Well in that case, babes, just cum wherever ye like.'

And I intended to do just that. I closed my eyes as her mouth, lips, and tongue finally set anchor on my shores.

***

When I left Babs' place an hour later, I drove back down Morningside Road towards Lothian Road. My thoughts were on other matters (like my recent pleasurable indulgences, my next job, my up-and-coming due rent, renewing my gym membership, brain cancer) when, lo and behold, I saw her again standing at the bus stop. The hauntingly beautiful, sexy and curvaceous woman with the deep and tragically sad eyes, pale skin, and long, flowing, dirty blonde hair. She didn't look like she was from around these parts. Even with her pale skin, there was something foreign, exotic, and unique about her. I took this second viewing as a sign that I should at least attempt to do something.

She stood at the same bus stop, but this time by herself. I didn't need the cancer to tell me that I had to pull over immediately, even if just for a few seconds to run back to the bus stop and speak to her...but where? At the very least, take a chance and slip her my card. Hey, in my book, if you never ask, you never receive.

Of course, every available parking space ahead was taken. Did no one work anymore in this god-forsaken town? Double yellow lines followed me on either side of the road like a bad smell. Then, up ahead I glimpsed a narrow side street. Quickly I turned and parked halfway over a pedestrian walkway and an already-taken parking space. There was nothing else I could do. I flicked on my hazards like it would do any good when those heartless devil bastard wardens appeared. At least it gave me the desired comforting effect of having a temporary impenetrable shield against parking tickets. I jumped out of my van, left it unlocked, and hurried back up the street towards the awaiting beauty. The bus stop was in my sights. So was the girl. Then I saw a bus approaching.

Shite!

My heart sank. I was only halfway there. I wasn't going to make it in time. The bus stopped. I stopped. The girl stepped on board and made her way to the top deck.

Shite!

The bus pulled out into the main road and passed me like an untouchable summer breeze. I managed to catch a quick glimpse of the beauty on the top deck, but she didn't see me as she put a pair of headphones into her ears.

Shite.

I felt torn between two minds about chasing the bus in my van. Yes, what a good idea. I would've done the act, too, if it weren't for two giddy little traffic warden bitches who came creeping out of nowhere. Like two spineless, shapeless demon minions rising from the smoky shadows of the foul, bowel depths of the city sewers. Two stray dogs looking to shit anywhere. They turned into the side street where I'd recklessly abandoned my vehicle. They rubbed their bony, greedy little paws with more glee as they circled it. Hyenas, in for the kill at finding the stray wildebeest automobile lying mercifully before them.

Fuck them, I thought. Fuck them all. Let them write their goddamn tickets. I wouldn't give them the satisfaction of rushing back to rescue my van. What good would it do, anyhow? I knew it was already a done deal. Instead, I sat upon a nearby bench. I pulled out my job receipt book and pencil and scribbled a new poem with words that had recently infested my carefree mind. Even the thought of having my only source of income towed away couldn't stop the spilling of words onto the grubby, grimy paper in my hand.

Girl I've never met.
You haunt me, possess my soul and mind.
Girl I've never met.
The first time I saw you, you passed me by at the bus stop one day and all I could do was sit there and let you pass me by.
Girl I've never met.

I would lay down my life for you, fight to my dying breath for you,
just to see you smile a tearful smile as I fell defeated to my knees.
Girl I've never met,
You passed me by at the bus stop again today. The funny thing
was, I wasn't even waiting for a bus. I was waiting for you, like I
wait for you there every day in hopes that you might one day pass
me by.
Girl I've never met
Even when you do pass, I always swear the next time, the next
time, the next time, I will stop you in your tracks and say
something, anything.
For surely anything is better than nothing.
But saying something will only shatter my illusion and fantasy of
you. For if I say nothing, there is always a hope, a chance, that
you will always be mine.
Yet, girl I've never met, if I say something, anything, there is
always the chance that I will say the wrong thing, speak with the
wrong tone, pause at the wrong moment, look like a fool and lose
you forever...shattering my dreams, my soul, my humanity.
Girl I've never met -

I let out a deep, roaring sigh of frustration which made a passing elderly couple jump with frowning fright. I didn't even apologise, my mood was so foul. I glanced down at my written words again. More shite that quickly found its way into the nearest bucket.

Eventually the wardens finished slaying my four-wheeled beast, taking more pictures of the crime scene than a Japanese tourist outside Edinburgh Castle with a camera super-glued to their arse cheeks. Thankfully they soon left, but not before leaving behind their sixty-quid fine and seal of approval upon the windscreen, which I felt duly obliged to discard onto the neighbouring window of the next car.

My phoned beeped for a received text message.

'Guess who, plumber boy? x,' said the cheerful text.

It must be the lovely, sexy office girl, Nikki, from Mrs Patterson's street. Lucky for me I hadn't given out my plumbing card to any other attractive ladies for well over a month, so I think I managed to guess right.

Chapter 4

Later that afternoon, I had a job at a small barbershop on the Grass Market. It was a bastard of a place to get to. The closest parking happened to be on King Stables Road, streets away. I had to fit a new toilet, so it would require a few tools. I parked on the pavement outside the shop for a few minutes, flicking on those magical 'I'll park wherever the hell I like' hazard lights so that any passing traffic warden knob jockey would give me at least half a decent chance to unload.

I dumped my tools in the shop. The owner was a very nice Syrian guy called Ali. He offered me a coffee and a half-eaten kebab he'd been munching on for lunch and couldn't finish. I left the shop and parked on King's Stable Road before hastily walking back towards the shop to begin work. The entire job took an hour and a half and I charged the guy fifty pounds (not including parking), which he seemed delighted with, as the last plumber had offered him a quote of around ninety.

There were still around ten minutes left on my pay and display ticket when I finished, so I decided to walk towards the Grass Market and grab a little takeaway sandwich from a quirky cafe/restaurant I knew there. When I left the café, I walked back towards my van and noticed some rough-looking cocky builder type standing outside the Beehive Inn, smoking a fag while holding a pint of something dark and grizzly. Definitely not a rare sight to see men of all ages, sizes, and shapes loitering about Edinburgh's pubs in the early afternoon of a working week. But this one managed to get my goat up right away when a young and attractive office woman walked by. Just minding her own business.

'Aw right, sexy pants.'

She kept walking, blatantly ignoring the prick. What else could she do?

'Hey! Ye any gid et reverse parkin hen, aye?' he shouted after her. 'Well, why dae ye no back up ontae thus, eh?' He roared with laughter while swivelling his hips and pointing towards his groin. 'Dinnae ken whit yur missin, hen.'

The woman upped her pace, walking faster. She gave me the evil eye as she walked past. Must have thought I was mates with that fanny just because we wore similar overalls.

Soon it was my turn to walk past the cocky builder. I gave him the evil stare. He just glared at me with an arrogant grin.

'Whit the fuck ye starin at, ye wee poof?'

I took a deep breath and kept walking, focussing straight ahead. 'Cum oan ye fucker aye,' he continued. 'Spinnin me durty looks, ye wee radge. Cum oan then! Fuckin sae sutton ye cunt? Ah fucking dare ye aye, ye prick.'

I wanted to say something so badly. I wanted to do something. Chin the disrespectful Muppet. Head-butt his face. Smash that pint glass into the side of his neck, spilling his blood all over the pavement. But I said nothing. I bit my tongue, capped my rage, and kept walking.

'Aye, jist whit ah thought, pal. Jist whit ah thought.'

I kept my head straight and continued towards my van. I could feel my cancer shaking its head in shame. But what else was I supposed to do? Start a fight with him in the middle of the street?

***

I drove home in the early evening, thinking about that first long refreshing sip from a four-pack of chilled beer lying at the bottom of my fridge. I'd been looking forward to that first taste all day. When I reached the Burdiehouse estate, coming in from the duel carriageway, I witnessed more gangs of teens throwing stones and any other hardened objects they could find at the passing cars, buses, and lorries. Home sweet home. Where could I purchase a good old machine gun when I needed one for my next terrorist attack?

As I pulled into my street, two guys—probably not even drunkards—were urinating in the bus shelter that the gang of kids had cheerfully redecorated the other day. I had a good chuckle to myself, thinking about the potential faces of all those tourists in those hop-on-hop-off, open-top buses if they ever took a wrong turn into this shit pit estate one day. Edinburgh to Belgrade in a ten-minute bus ride.

Later that evening, Nikki messaged again. She wanted me to come and meet her on Friday night for a few drinks. Not one to play hard to get, I accepted her proposal.

Lying in bed later that night, I still couldn't sleep. It wasn't the beer and it definitely wasn't the cancer. Something else had been playing and probing away on my mind. Something I'd kept dark and hidden away in the filthy, foul, murky depths of my mind for many a year. Why was I thinking about that now? Why was I thinking about him? After all these years.

I remembered back around twenty-four years ago. Me as an eight-year-old sitting and playing in my mum's living room like any normal wee boy. It was only a year or so after my father had died in the Falklands. Sat across from me on the other side of the room was a rough and scruffy-looking man in his late twenties. My new stepfather, Richard. He sat in a comfy armchair watching the young me playing happily away. I remembered how he would sit so still there, just like a gloomy, grey statue, lacking in any noticeable emotion. Occasionally, he would sip from a can of warm beer. Then after a while he would light up a cigarette. He didn't always smoke it right away. Sometimes he'd just stare with a great chilling intensity at the burning tip but at least his eyes weren't on me anymore. When he got really bored, that's when the real fun would begin. He'd finally call me over.

'Liam! Come ower here.'

I tried to ignore the filthy bastard, continuing to play with my train set. Praying he would just go away or some magical, mystical force would make him disappear for all eternity.

'Ah said come fuckin ower here noo, ye wee shit. Dinnae make me ask twice, pal.'

I caved. His tone of voice and the fear of what he'd do if I didn't obey overpowered me. I stopped playing with my train set and moped over towards him. I always kept my head and eyes pointed straight down. Anything not to see that crazy drunken glint in his eye. More than anything I remembered the foul stench that surrounded him. A mix of sweat, booze, and fags.

'Try et, ye wee poof.' He shoved the can of beer right into my face.

I shook my head. Big mistake.

'Try et,' he continued with more intent. Shaking the can right at my mouth and nose.

'Mum wouldn't want me to,' I mumbled, opening my mouth but keeping my eyes firmly shut.

'Well, yur bludy ma's no here noo, is she son? So bludy shut et and drink.'

Richard forcefully planted the beer into my hands. Of course, I took it, raising it to my lips, still not wanting to look that crazy bastard in the eye.

'Drink et, ye wee poof, noo.'

I took a deep breath and sipped my first taste of beer. It tasted sour, flat, like stale cat's piss, but not as warm or as bitter as I suspected. I didn't swallow. Richard noticed.

'Swalley.'

Finally, I swallowed, making a loud gulping sound to prove how much hard work and effort it took to make it go down. I handed the beer back to him.

'Can ah go back to ma trains now, please?'

Richard gently nodded. But as I turned away, the bastard snatched my arm, pulling me back even closer. I couldn't help but yelp with pain. Richard looked calm, though. He took another exceedingly long puff from his cigarette with his free hand. I felt nervous and scared. Richard's burning glare turned to a mischievous grin. He yanked my little arm closer towards him. Then all casual like, still grinning, he put the cigarette out on my forearm like it were the most natural thing in the world.

It was absolute agony. Total and utter agony. I screamed and struggled wildly. The pain was too unbearable for one so young. I remembered it was the greatest pain I'd ever felt in my short life. Even to this very day. I continued to struggle but couldn't do anything, not a single damn thing, to stop this arsehole's sadistic actions.

He released me. Just like that. I didn't expect it so soon and fell harshly onto the floor.

'Noo!' he said, grinning all sleazy like, 'tak yur troosers auf.'

I could feel the tears trickling down my face as I unwillingly obeyed. Soon Richard's sadistic grin, followed by the rest of his smug, ugly puss, morphed to that of my doctor. The plump woman with the cute face who had informed me about my terminal illness.

'Maybe a year,' she mumbled, 'maybe less.'

I woke up. I'd fallen asleep after all and was sweating buckets. I sat up in bed and had a good feel of the bedsheets. They were absolutely soaked. Either I'd been sweating like a whore during a triple shift at the sauna on Rose Street during the festival or I'd well and truly wet the bed, and I hadn't done that since the days when Richard was my stepfather.

Cleaning myself up and wearing a new pair of boxer shorts, I sat huddled against the bathroom wall. I sobbed hard. I cried about a lot of things. Not just the cancer but about most of my wasted life. Nothing to show for it. No one to show for it. Thinking to myself that I was just as bad as, or maybe even worse than, all those other arseholes out there. The ones I saw every day, like the guys throwing their stones and vandalising things with nothing better to do. Things that didn't belong to them. The cocky man outside the pub, telling those women to their faces what he really wanted to do to them. The man throwing his litter onto the street without a care in the world. They were all just expressing themselves. Breaking free from society's rules and regulations. Maybe they were the ones who should be applauded and respected for doing what they wanted in the moment. Saying what was on their minds with no fear of consequences. Who was I to argue with that? Weren't those people supposed to be the happiest in life, the ones who could say, do, and act as they damn well pleased? No fear. No regrets. Was I missing a trick here or something?

I went to the kitchen window and looked out at the long row of six-story flats which surrounded the back of my house. Lights were on. Lights were off. Some people were up. Some were out. Some were asleep. I felt inspired to write another poem. It always did the trick of calming me down, taking my mind off everything. I sat down with a pen and paper at the window and wrote whatever came to mind. Usually, whatever was right in front of me at the time.

The people sit at their windows, doing their mundane tasks and things,
Oblivious to the people above and below them and all the other windows in between,
But I see them all, every trivial task they do, every simple move they make,
Some write, some sing, some cook, some clean,
Some just sit still in a grim, deathly, hollow silence.
Some walk around nude, some pleasure themselves, some fuck their wives, some make love to their maids.
Some play games with their children, some play games with themselves.
Some even look over towards me

I went back to bed. I felt better. I curled up onto the mattress, my eyes still wide open, yet I felt eerily calm. Tomorrow would be a new day.

Chapter 5

Before meeting Nikki that Friday night, I went for a quick session in the local sunbeds. I usually went twice a week to the studio on Lothian Road. Sometimes I liked to tease the cute girls who worked there about how they had hidden cameras in the booths so they could perv on all the hot guys who came in to work on their tans. It must have been a funny sight to see all those different shapes and sizes of naked tanners, striking their ridiculous poses just to make sure no white patches went unburnt. I remembered one of my very first tanning sessions, when I decided to up my cancer ray intensity to a whopping twelve minutes. By the end, I was so disorientated that I actually forgot to put my trousers back on when I exited the booth. Let's just say the tanners in waiting got more than their usual eyeful of UV rays that day.

Nikki wanted to meet outside Le Monde at 8.00 pm. It was now 8.15 and her last text was over an hour old. I didn't want to believe she was going to stand me up. I went inside and ordered a lager shandy. I sat in the corner and sipped it real slow while subtly checking out the local talent. At 8.30 she messaged to say that something had come up and she would be at least another hour. No other explanation. Screw it. I didn't even bother replying and promptly deleted her number. I had better things to do with my time than hang around waiting for a woman who acted like a flaky, disrespectful teenager. I downed the rest of my pint and left.

Outside, I didn't know whether to go straight home or head to another bar. Screw it. I'd text Babs. See what she was up to.

'What are you up to right now, sweet cheeks?'

I walked farther along George Street towards Hanover Street. The town was getting busier. More and more groups of half-drunk girls and guys were parading here, there, and everywhere. Heading to bars. Leaving bars. Heading to a specific club. Searching for a club. Sexy promoter girls, looking more like street hookers, offered fliers to anyone and everyone, even if they didn't want them.

'Sorry my love,' I cheekily grinned at one girl while making an imaginary force field around my body as she handed me her flyer. 'This a no-flyer zone.'

'What a comedian,' she said, shaking her head without a flicker of emotion. I turned into Hanover Street and approached Rose Street just as Babs messaged me back.

'Not much. Wee one asleep so watching Big Brother.'

I had had a Viagra pill in my wallet for the past year and was itching to use it on one lucky punter. The magic little pill had been given to me by an old tiler buddy of mine, Mikey, who'd been a bit of a sex addict himself back in the day. In fact, I remembered working with him on a bathroom refit a few years back. I'd finished stripping out the old bath, basin, toilet, and radiator, leaving Mikey to begin his three full days of tiling while our client went on a short, relaxing break to Loch Lomond. At some point during the second evening, Mikey had heard the neighbours next door frantically shagging their hearts out in a marathon sex romp. Remembering that I'd jokingly mentioned days before how the next door's loft could be accessed by climbing into our client's loft, Mikey attempted to test this theory for himself. He climbed into our client's attic, hoping to catch a sneaky peak of the rampant action next door. He did this by crawling, ever so carefully, into the neighbours' loft space and peering into their bedroom via a small crack in their ceiling. Mikey said that because the couple having sex were quite attractive, it was like watching a 'real-life' porno, so he decided to unfasten his trousers and jerk himself off into spunk fest frenzy. He got carried away, though, with too many jerky movements on the delicate ceiling plasterboard and ended up falling into the randy couple's bedroom below. Let's just say they weren't thrilled by the sight of his dirty little perverted, peeping-tom arse dangling from their rafters, his trousers around his ankles and his semi-stiff cock waving over their faces. As an apology, he ended up retiling their own kitchen and bathroom, walls and floors free of charge just to stop them from pressing charges.

Last year he had come across a couple hundred Viagra pills on the black market and I bought a few to try out and mainly impress a couple of first dates. Give them their fair dues. They worked a treat but sometimes the side effects were more trouble than they were worth. Excessive bloating, farting, constipation, then diarrhoea, and even making it difficult on some occasions to shoot your load.

I'd forgotten all about this last one, to be honest. Not that I needed it. It was just nice to have that wee special magic blue pill option as a backup plan once in a blue moon. Especially when you wanted to give that special sexy someone a rather good seeing to and, of course, ensuring she'd come back again for a less eventful second time.

If sexy Babs wanted to see me tonight, I'd take it on my way to hers. If our first session was anything to go by, she was going to be pretty damn insatiable for round two. So, the wee blue pill would be well and truly justified. Took half an hour to kick in more or less, so there was plenty of time.

'Fancy some company?' I sent my bold and upfront text right back at her. I continued walking down Rose Street and found a tacky little kebab shop. I was hungry, so I decided to buy a small donner. No sauce but plenty of salad. Made me feel pretentiously healthy to order it without the sauce.

My phone beeped. Babs had messaged again. 'You know the address, Mr. Plumber ;) x.'

Fucking bingo. Game on. I paid for my kebab and a bottle of water. I took out the wee blue pill from my wallet along with its year's worth of wallet sweat, dust, and fluff, and swallowed. Next I had to find a taxi. Boy, was Babs in for a good, hard treat tonight.

When I left the kebab shop, I walked out onto Frederick Street, looking for a taxi. There were a couple around, but none with their lights on. I had to make a choice. Stay where I was. Walk up and along George Street looking for one, and down along Princes Street, or keep heading along Rose Street towards Hanover Street. I opted to stay put. But after ten minutes, no more bastard taxis had come along. I felt a stir and twitch in my groin. The Viagra had kicked in early. I decided there and then to start walking towards Morningside from the city centre and chance my luck at catching a taxi on route.

Just then my phoned beeped. New message. I glanced at it. The message was from Babs again. I opened it. 'Sorry, but the wee one's playing up and won't sleep. He's demanding that I watch a movie with him. Sorry. Rain check?'

'You fucking bastard,' I raged. I wanted to slam my phone onto the pavement. Smash it to smithereens, but quickly refrained. I didn't want to lose Babs as a potential fuck buddy in the future by letting her know my real thoughts, so I sent back the nicest possible reply I could muster in my dire straits. 'No worries :) Another time then, sweet cheeks. Have a good night.'

Secretly I was half-tempted not to send the message at all and continue to her place anyway. Fake a 'dead battery in my phone,' then attempt to wheedle my way into her panties from her doorstep. Jesus Christ! I turned east and walked along Rose Street. I became hornier and stiffer by the second. At one point, I had to stop halfway along the street, adjusting my rock-hard cock to sit firmly tucked up behind the belt of my trousers while his purple head popped up towards my belly button. It was the best I could do without walking with a hunched back.

When I emerged onto Hanover Street, I stopped beside a bin. I contemplated my options for the rest of the evening. Head home for a late-night internet porn wankathon. Head back to meet Nicky and chance my luck with her again. Hit another few bars and clubs in the area and try to pick up some easy, loose, and liberal drunken lass who desperately wanted to get back at her cheating boyfriend, then give her a good seeing-to back at my place. Or spam text for a late-night booty call a few old shag mates, whose numbers I kept a hold of for moments just like this.

My train of thought was interrupted by the sound of high heels. I turned my head instinctively towards the George Street side of Hanover Street, half expecting to see, with my luck, some six-foot tranny. Instead I glimpsed the tall, sexy, curvaceous figure of a lass walking towards me on the opposite side of the road. She looked oddly familiar. I couldn't see her face right away because the street lights were so bloody dim. Council's fault for trying to keep Edinburgh in the dark ages, keeping the tourist board happy and playing on that eighteenth-century Gothic atmosphere feel. It took another few seconds to register just where the hell I'd seen the girl before. I couldn't believe my eyes when I realised. It was the girl from the bus stop. The girl with the pale skin, the deep, piercing eyes, the long, free-flowing, dirty blonde hair, the curvaceous figure. A vision of goddess loveliness if ever I did see one on the dark, grim streets of medieval Edinburgh. She looked so much taller with those high, high heels on. And that green silk dress that clung to every curve of her body. The last two times I'd seen her at the bus stop she'd been dressed so casual. Jeans, jumper, jacket. Even then, she'd looked good. But now, dressed to the nines like some classy glamour model stepping out onto her very own personal red carpet...wow. Just...fucking wow!

I watched her walk by in a hypnotic, lustful daze on the opposite side of Hanover Street, heading towards the National Gallery on Princes Street. She didn't even glance in my direction. And why would she? In that moment, who the hell was I to her? Just another random drunk layabout, kebab-munching loser on the streets of the new town. I kept watching. Jesus Christ, she had such a beautiful, delicious, sexy figure to die for. And that arse, which wiggled away from side to side through that skin-hugging dress. Man, I wanted a bite of those delicious cheeks bouncing and wiggling away, big time. And those breasts. What a spectacular pair of heaving bosoms if ever I saw a pair. She looked like sex on legs tonight, oozing so much sex appeal. So much so, in fact, that I could feel my rock-hard, Viagra-fuelled penis painfully throbbing behind my tight belt while stretching in epileptic bouts of ever-growing stiffness, trying to grow onwards and upwards, way past my belly button and up towards my chin if the laws of sexual physics would've allowed.

I continued to watch her walking down the street like David Attenborough stalking a rare and endangered Siberian tiger. Of course, I felt in awe of her in that moment, absolutely. I knew, just knew, that I had to go and speak to her for the life of me. Surely it had to be a sign. Three time's a charm. I had to go over there even if it meant dying on my arse. This was my moment. No buses, no traffic wardens, no interfering pedestrians. I had to know if she was my sign. I had to at least be sure. May the universe strike me down if I did not act upon this overwhelming vision of loveliness and feeling of pure lust that had just fallen into my lap. If I didn't do this, I knew it would haunt me for the rest of my damn short days. Persistence and perseverance would be key.

I hurried across the street and chased after her at a fast walking pace. A set of traffic lights was coming up where Hanover Street met Princes Street. A gathering of young student drunkards was noisily waiting to cross to the other side. I slowed down, thinking she would join the crossing herd. She did indeed stop but only to take a cigarette from her handbag and ask for a light from some young jammy swine waiting for the little green man to appear. Even the young man looked to be in utter awe of this angel. He gave her a light and watched her wiggle elegantly away, utterly mesmerised.

She continued past the first set of traffic lights, blatantly ignored the second set, and walked right on over Princes Street and towards the National Gallery's courtyard, which was wedged between the two galleries and East Princes Street Gardens. She continued towards the steep set of narrow stairs, Playfair steps, leading towards the top of the mound. I walked fast, closing in behind her. This was my opportunity. This was my chance.

I jogged up to her and tapped her shoulder. 'Excuse me, hey?'

She turned, startled at first, then smiled immediately. My heart pumped furiously, almost bursting from my chest. I felt proud of myself for getting this far without thinking about the outcome. Of course, I'd spoken to girls before on the street, but mostly just outside pubs and clubs, and only after they'd given me the eye, showing their interest first. This girl hadn't even known I'd existed until I put my hand upon her shoulder in that instant when she'd turned around to face me. Most likely half-expecting some homeless jakey tool looking for a few spare pennies. Or some ned bam-pot with a syringe in hand looking for an even bigger handout. She gave me a curious stare and waited for me to speak and state my case, if you like.

'This is gonna sound really, really crazy and I'm sorry to bother you and all but...,' I said, still catching my breath after chasing her so hard.

The girl continued to stare at me with her big, beautiful, deep, round, haunting eyes. Definitely the girl from the bus stop. Her eyes widened. She seemed curious and smiled politely. I think she could sense right away why I'd stopped her. And by her friendliness, she at least appreciated the gesture.

'…I think I saw you at two different bus stops on Morningside a few days back…'

Shit. Had I actually just said that? I sounded like a right lunatic stalker. I couldn't stop myself from speaking, though. My adrenaline was pumping in full flow.

'…and then, when I saw you again just now, I just, I just had to take a chance and talk to you, you know, or else, or else, I'd be kicking myself for the rest of my life if I didn't at least try and say something. So, hey, here I am. I just wanted to say hi. My name's Liam. That was it. That's all I have.' I stepped back a little, like I'd just performed my standalone theatre masterpiece in the middle of a packed fringe festival show and now awaited my rapturous standing ovation.

She looked a little subdued and taken back but she kept smiling, which was the main thing. She was beautiful. Even more so with her light makeup, yet still so pale with those beautiful, piercing blue eyes and pretty, sculpted cheekbones, gorgeous boobs, and a slim, curvy body that over-complemented them.

'You know, I really appreciate you stopping me. Liam, was it?' She spoke with a slight French accent, but her English was perfect, her French tone given away only by the odd under-pronounced word or two. 'But I have a boyfriend.'

'Don't say that. Jesus, I don't want to know about your personal problems already lady, geez,' I teased and she laughed. I ignored the boyfriend 'elephant in the room' for the moment. She seemed friendly enough and happier still to just talk out here in the middle of the street for the time being.

'Where are you from? I mean, where is that dodgy accent of yours from? Is it French?'

'You think I have a dodgy accent?' She chuckled. 'Yes, I'm from France but now I'm working here in Edinburgh, teaching French and English.'

'Nice. How long have you been living in Edinburgh?'

She hesitated. She gave me a blank look like she really had to go. The conversation was over.

'Come on, I really want to know. Just give me a few minutes of your time and then go. I mean, come on, I did run all this way just to talk to you,' I said, giving out my best charming smile.

'Okay. I will smoke a cigarette. We can talk, but then I have to go.'

That sounded like a fair deal to me. She lit up a cigarette and we talked out there on the street for a good ten minutes. Her name was Celine and she was a very artistic and creative-minded individual, indeed. She read books, and not just popcorn supermarket housewife trash novels either, but all the literary classics I'd read and loved myself. She knew authors even the Edinburgh libraries hadn't heard about. She knew Fante, Bukowski, and Hamsun, for Christ's sake. She could recite Walt Whitman and Rabbie Burns in the middle of the street. Something I bet most proud Scots still couldn't do, bar the New Year's anthem, of course. She liked to paint pictures and write her own poems in her spare time, which I, of course, took as a sure sign we were even more meant to be. Soul mates, ha!

I took great pleasure in telling her about my own attempts at poetry, which she surprisingly took a keen interest in, asking me numerous questions, particularly about my inspiration, which was usually the opposite sex. We both laughed at that. Christ, I could feel myself falling hard for this girl. She was quickly turning into everything I looked for in that unattainable dream woman, and then some.

She told me her age. I guessed twenty-two. She was twenty-seven. I couldn't believe it. She looked so good. I forgot about my sexual attraction towards her in a haze of passionate conversation. I didn't want this interaction to end. I felt like I could just talk and talk to this girl about anything and everything for a whole lifetime and then some.

When she smoked the last of her cigarette, instead of making excuses to leave, she continued to engage in our conversational bubble. 'So, what have you been up to tonight, anyway?' she asked, changing the subject. 'Partying with friends?'

'Actually, I was out on George Street.' Should I mention I was supposed to be on a date? Probably not. But what the hell. 'Actually, I was on a date.'

'Really. Well, good for you.' She seemed genuinely surprised I'd admitted that. 'So how did it go?'

Ha, I was wandering the streets of Edinburgh all alone. I'll give you one bloody guess how it went. 'Not bad, I suppose. But in the end, she wasn't for me.'

Celine smiled. I'd have given my life savings to have known her thoughts at that second.

'How about you?'

She hesitated. 'I was...out...with friends. Now I'm going home.'

I felt she'd just lied. Probably about who she'd been with. Maybe with her boyfriend and they'd had a huge fight, hopefully, but I didn't care. She was still here in the moment. That's all that mattered.

'So, what happened on your date? You just didn't click, huh?' Celine continued, stepping a little closer to me. She seemed happy and comfortable in my presence, still interested in conversing, not eager in the slightest to get away like when we had first spoke.

'Ha. It's a long story. Sometimes I just go after the wrong type of girls, you know?'

'That's because you're a man. And most men always let their penises have the final say.' Celine smirked. I chuckled. She was right, to an extent.

'Well, I'm in my thirties now, so not so young anymore, missy. And my penis is mature enough to let me have my own opinion every now and again. But mostly we just flip a coin.'

Celine laughed and gently punched my arm. Another good sign. She edged a little closer. Was she coming on to me? Flirting with her body? I wasn't going to question her new forward behaviour.

We continued to shoot the shit, neither one of us in any real rush to go anywhere. Celine continued to touch my arm every so often, whether she was laughing at one of my jokes or emphasising a point. Her touch felt good but deliberate. Like she knew exactly what she was doing and the effect her touchy-feelyness would have on me. It gave me the inclination that there would be much more to come this evening, just so long as I didn't say something stupid to fuck it all up. It felt natural to take this to the next level. So, of course, I asked her to have a drink with me somewhere nearby and continue our conversation in a warmer environment. To my delighted surprise, she eagerly accepted. Just like that. No hesitations or questions asked. I really couldn't believe my luck and timing.

We walked and talked while I led Celine to a cosy little bar I knew just on the other side of the Mound. The Wash Bar. Once inside, we sat at a cosy corner booth and ordered two vodka and cokes. Celine told me more about her future plans and how she was staying in Edinburgh for only another month before flying back to her home town of Agen in southwest France. There she would stay with her father for a month or so before moving on again and furthering her teaching career. Her dream was to live and work in Spain for six months, learning Spanish while teaching English and perhaps some French too. Afterwards, she'd return to France to finish her master's teaching degree before moving back to the UK again to search for a well-paid teaching job. She was only twenty-seven years old, so she had most of her life right in front of her.

I asked her to tell me about her parents and how they'd met. I always took great interest in how couples ended up together, past and present. Sometimes I heard the most wonderful and remarkable stories of chance encounters and small opportune windows of fate which often resulted in the magical beginnings and the bringing together of two families and future generations of siblings. All because a guy took the simple risk of building up the nerve to talk to a girl he liked.

Celine told me how her parents had met in her mother's hometown, Redon, in the north of France. It had been at an arts fair in the local town hall. Her father, coincidentally a plumber like me, had been contracted to do some renovation work there. On a rare day off, he wandered into the fair and saw his young, future bride-to-be selling her paintings and drawings and he fell hopelessly in love at first sight. But he couldn't find the courage right away to ask her out. Instead, he asked her to paint his portrait for a small fee and she agreed. It was only during the self-portrait that they started talking deeply and hit it off. After a brief, passionate, whirlwind romance, they became man and wife. Celine was born a year later. When she turned five they moved to her father's hometown, Agen, where his reliable working trade was a lot more fruitful.

After finishing our first round of drinks at the Wash Bar, we decided to head to another pub in the Old Town. On the way, we took a short detour stroll down the Royal Mile, towards the Cathedral and Parliament Square, which lay in its shadows. I was surprised when, halfway into the walk, Celine took my arm in hers. I tried to remain unfazed by her forward actions. Usually it was I who made the first bold move, but this was a nice, unexpected change to have the role reversed. I went with it.

As we walked around the Cathedral in a buoyant mood, we were soon playfully teasing one another like young children in a school playground who had crushes on each other. I made fun of her very polite, innocent, sweet English/French accent and mimicked the English words she over- and under-pronounced. To get back at me, Celine refused to speak English for five minutes and jabbered away in French. I mimicked this right back at her with my own outrageous French accent straight out of an old Monty Python movie, which, in all fairness, came out like utter gibberish. She laughed hard at my overly dramatic gestures and facial expressions, begging me to stop torturing her.

I offered to give her a piggyback, which she was reluctant to accept at first. When she finally clambered on board, I galloped around Parliament Square with her on my back like a demented pony to the bemused looks of the late-night tourists and drunkard passers-by. After a few minutes of this gallivanting, I halted on top of the Cathedral steps, slowly placed my head between my legs and gently tipped her over my back, lowering her upside down—to her playful screams—onto the pavement below. She laughed so hard that she struggled to get back onto her feet again. When she finally did, she playfully hit me right after I told her she was too cheeky to get a proper piggyback. When I turned to walk away, she pinched my bum and handed me my phone. I had to laugh. I hadn't even felt her take it from my pocket. I told her she was very sneaky and cheeky.

'I'm the cheeky, sneaky one?' She smiled.

I chuckled as a crazy thought entered my head. 'Do you know the difference between sneaky and cheeky?' I asked.

'I don't believe I do,' she said with a teasing look.

'You're the English teacher and you honestly don't know?'

'Well, I know sneaky. Is that to be devious or to sneak up on someone with naughty intentions?'

A mischievous thought of demonstration rattled around my head. Like a light bulb going off inside my mind, I had to show her the difference and, thus, immediately held out my hand for her to take.

'What are you doing?'

Celine took my hand and I pulled her close. Only a few inches separated us.

'Okay. Now close your eyes.'

She gave me a suspicious glare and grinned. 'No, I don't trust you. You might do something bad.'

'What? Like steal your phone?'

'Hmmm, that too,' she giggled.

'Just close your eyes.'

'What are you going to do?'

'I'm going to show you the difference between cheeky and sneaky.'

She paused in thought with an even more devilish grin before closing her eyes.

'Okay. So, this...is...cheeky.'

She looked so angelic in that moment when I leaned in towards her, like I was about to kiss her gently upon her soft and luscious red lips. She smelled absolutely divine and so freshly sweet, like an aura of deliciousness. Instead of kissing her, though, I lowered my hands over her curvaceous bum cheeks and squeezed hard. She let out a playful grin and opened her eyes.

'That was bad,' she giggled. Still, she didn't back away.

'Okay,' I smiled back, 'and now for something completely sneaky.'

'That wasn't the sneaky part?'

'Close your eyes again.'

She did what I asked and closed her eyes tight.

'Okay, now this...is...sneaky.'

This time I leaned in real slow. Right up close, until our faces and lips were millimetres apart. At the same time, I lifted my left hand and gently cupped it around the bottom of her cheek and throat, underneath her soft, flowing, dirty blonde hair. Softly, I kissed her red cherry lips. She never flinched in the slightest, and even better, her small, pretty, delicate mouth moved in unison with mine. The kiss lasted for a few warm heartbeats. Just as I felt the tip of her tongue brushing against the roof of my lip, I pulled away and opened my eyes to find her eyes still closed. She opened them and unleashed a radiant-yet-devilish, beaming smile. Lost in the wonderful moment, I'd forgotten all about my ferocious Viagra-infused hard-on still throbbing away, tucked in tight against the belt of my jeans.

'Well that was...unexpected.'

I smiled. She took my arm and we walked down the mile again in a comfortable silence. We made our way towards Hunter's Square and found another cosy dive bar down Blair Street, the City Cafe. I grabbed a table in the corner while Celine bought two beers.

We talked about cooking. She told me about some delicious French delicacies and cuisines like Foie Gras and Bœuf bourguignon, which I'd neither tasted nor heard of. Only the famous frog's legs and snails. She said she'd cook a French meal for me some time, although I thought she was just humouring me. Still, I couldn't believe my luck with this girl. The way she acted. Every word she said. It all sounded...too good to be true. I told her I'd cook for her some time, too. I was pretty handy with a wok and had been known to rustle up a few half-decent stir fries.

Then she asked a really out-of-the-blue question. 'Why do all men cheat? Even if they have the most perfect girl in the whole wide world and say they love you more than life itself! Why do their eyes still stray?'

'All men? Or just the ones you're attracted to?' I teased, trying to be smart. But aloud, those words sounded horrible. Thankfully, she seemed too tipsy to notice but still, I didn't know how to answer. By the way she'd sprung it upon me, it wasn't too hard to figure out that somebody somewhere, perhaps even recently, someone she'd loved dearly, had cheated on her and hurt her very much. I didn't want to go down this path of ex-boyfriends and past shitty relationships. I wanted to keep things upbeat and as positive as I could. So rather than discussing the obvious, I tried to explain my own theory. And not just regarding men, but women, too, who I'd felt had also become just as bad at fooling around and straying in this day and age as their male counterparts.

'I blame it on boredom. Men and women have become tired of each other. Especially if they've been together for an overly long period of time and are presented with the opportunity to stray. To spice up their dull and mundane lives with a little bit of excitement. The world is such an open and accessible place right now. We can meet new people every day and from all walks of life, people who might cater more to our ever-changing perverse tastes, needs, wants, and desires. Even just staying at home with the internet, there are so many more options, you know. We have shorter attention spans than people did in years gone by, which obviously contributes to our growing boredom with our partners. TV and social media have to take some of the blame, with their continuous expansion as hypnotic socialisers with thousands of channels to choose from within our own homes. Bloody commercials every ten minutes. A never-ending stream of information. I mean, when was the last time you were able to sit down in front of a TV for more than ten minutes without touching the bloody remote or glancing at your phone?'

'Does that include changing the volume and checking the interactive text?' Celine teased.

'Yes!' I smiled. 'And then when you watch most TV programs or movies nowadays, compared to the ones from fifty-odd years ago, Christ, you end up getting around a hundred-and-fifty various camera shots, angles, and edits. And that's even before the first fucking advert break. I mean, have you ever tried watching a movie from before the sixties or seventies? Back then you could go nearly twenty minutes with only one or two cuts or jumps in frame. Most people today couldn't handle that kind of focus and attention to detail. Their brains would constantly be searching for a distraction within the first few minutes. And I'm just as bad! I will happily stick on a movie while at the same time searching the internet and messaging on my phone or even doing the ironing or cooking a meal, all at the same time. Mental. And we do it like it's the most normal and natural thing in the world.

'And as for relationships and everyone swapping partners every five bloody minutes. I blame the likes of our favourite celebrities, movie and rock stars. We see these people gallivanting the way they do. Never out of the media for their social antics. Sleeping with anyone they like, dressing however they please, and acting however the hell they damn well choose, while most of us want to be and act just like them too.'

'I guess. But didn't men also cheat and stray before TV and the internet were invented?' Celine continued, grinning teasingly.

'Yeah,' I chuckled, 'of course...but definitely not to the extent of today's society. The 3D TV generation of right here, right now has to be the biggest, most easily bored, most pretentious fantasists our species has ever seen. We have so many material things, possessions, and gadgets dangled in front of our faces through media and advertising that our emotions are overloaded by this deeply embedded, lustful urge to want everything as soon as we bloody well see it. We want it all. Even if it's just slightly out of our reach. And then when we do finally get a hold of that precious little thing we want...'

'We quickly get bored and want something else,' Celine finished for me, 'and probably only because we saw somebody else with it in the first place.'

'Exactly! I mean, sixty years ago, was our society as fake, superficial, and pretentious as it is now?'

'I don't know,' chuckled Celine. 'Probably not. But I would need to ask my grandparents.'

I smiled, realising I was off on my own little raging tangent again.

'So, you really believe that TV is to blame for all the infidelity problems today?'

'Yes!' I laughed. 'And not just infidelity, our whole way of Western life. The way we communicate. The way we think, act, work out, eat, sleep, date, fuck. It controls our dreams, our passions, our inspirations. I mean, what inspired you to want to become a teacher anyhow?'

'Oooh, that's easy. Watching Michelle Pfeiffer in the movie *Dangerous Minds*?'

'You see!'

'But is that really such a bad thing?'

'Of course not! But the influence is there. Another kid might have been inspired to become a drug dealer or a gangster from watching the same movie. Who knows?'

'Who knows, indeed,' smiled Celine. We both laughed. 'So, what the hell did we do before we had TV, anyway?' she teased further. I couldn't tell if she was humouring me or really interested.

'Christ, I don't know...maybe people actually talked to each other. I mean, really talked. Face to face. Listened to each other with their full attention and understanding. Knew the first and last names of all their fucking neighbours and even their fucking postman and shopkeepers. Were part of a proper face-to-face community and not one where you hide behind four walls and a bloody LCD screen. Maybe they spent most of their days outside, physically interacting with the people around them. They probably read a shit-load more books and were generally happier people with their surroundings and limited basic belongings.'

'I'm sure more people go out into the world and travel today than even before.'

'Perhaps, on a ratio, yeah. But look at the world's population now compared to sixty years ago.'

'Hmm, maybe.'

I took a deep breath. Shit! I should stop before I ranted more tipsy nonsense. I should get back to a lighter topic before she excused herself to the bathroom and never returned.

'So...,' I smirked.

'So...,' Celine replied with a sly, lingering smile.

'Tell me, what's the craziest, most fucked-up thing you've ever done in your whole, entire life?'

Celine perked up a little. Her eyes glistened. 'Well...' she chuckled. 'Actually, I'm not too comfortable talking about that right now.' She grinned.

'A shy girl?' I teased.

'Well, why don't you ask me that question again tomorrow? Or perhaps the next time you see me,' she replied, leaning into me with a seductive whisper.

I couldn't help but grin devilishly right back at her. Jesus Christ, she had the most incredible fuck-me eyes. My loins stirred just thinking about what she meant by that 'ask-me-tomorrow' line. Was I in there? Jesus, my dick was still aching wildly and throbbing away behind my belt. If I could get her back to my place tonight before the effects of the Viagra wore off, it was going to be a wild one for sure.

Celine stood up. 'I'm going to the little girl's room. I'll be right back.'

She went to the bathroom and I watched her from behind as she walked away. Her arse looked even peachier in that dress and in the dim light of the bar. I imagined following her into the ladies' room. Hiking that dress right up over her waist, pulling her panties down to her silky-smooth thighs. Pushing her front ways up against the nearest wall and biting those delicious-looking arse cheeks before sticking my tongue deep inside her sweet, juicy wet patch. Devouring and savouring the taste of that fruity raw sexual wetness. She had one of those bodies and sexual auras that made you want to do the dirtiest and nastiest things to it. She made me so hard. Mentally and physically. Even without the

Viagra.

Chapter 7

We left the City Cafe and walked down another couple of side streets to look for a livelier venue. As we walked hand in hand down an old, dimly lit, narrow cobbled street, I spontaneously pulled Celine into a dark hidden doorway and pushed her up against the oak-wood door. For a second she just stared into my eyes with a wild and insatiable glee. God, I wanted this girl so badly and she knew it.

In the blink of an eye we were kissing passionately and running our hands all over each other's bodies like two blind lovers who'd never felt another's warm touch before. I felt my sexual urges skyrocketing to the boiling point. Surely, she could feel how hard I was, being so close together. I pulled away. I didn't want to get her too excited out here in the middle of the street. Better to do this back at my place, or hers even.

'Let's go back to my place...right now,' I said, bold and off the cuff.

She paused and looked at me with a sly stare. Gently she tapped my nose. 'Not. Just. Yet,' she said teasingly. 'I know another good bar up here. They do karaoke some nights. It should be fun.'

I grinned and pulled her away from the door, putting on my best enthusiastic pose. It was useless to sulk in the face of rejection. Especially in the presence of such a beautiful, sexy woman who could walk up to a man, any man, in any cafe, bar, or club around the world and have him. Oh, to possess such power. I wondered how many women I would have to ask blatantly, flat-out to have sex with me before one finally yielded. I shuddered at the thought, followed by all those slaps to the face and kicks to the balls.

'Let's go then,' I said, as upbeat as I possibly could, and dragged Celine out from the doorway.

We went to the karaoke bar. Celine begged me to sign up and sing a song for her. She'd even buy the drinks for the rest of the night if I did. I hesitated. The bar was only half full, and nobody had paid that much attention to the last singer who'd graced us with their horrendous and god-awful singing voice on the stage.

'What the hell,' I said, and strutted up to the stage to sing something. You only live once, huh? I settled for Bruce Springsteen, 'Dancing in the Dark.' I'd sung it in front of my bedroom mirror enough times while growing up, so it should be a breeze.

Halfway through the song I noticed some random, well-dressed hunk approaching Celine at the bar to chat her up. To my surprise, she blatantly ignored him, and rather coldly, too. In fact, I don't even think she acknowledged him the whole time he tried giving her his best chat-up lines and pattered shite. Instead, she continued to watch me from where she stood. Swaying her body in a sexy manner to the rhythm of the music. Dare I say, it felt as if she had eyes for only me? The guy went back to his table with his tail between his legs. I, on the other hand, felt empowered.

When I finished and went back to her, I mentioned that it was her turn to sing a song for me. She shyly refused and dragged me into a cosy little booth at the back of the bar. After another drink, I asked her if she was really looking forward to going back home to France and moving to Spain and then furthering her studies. Was it what she really wanted from life?

She hesitated, then said, 'Yes.' It was something she'd clearly desired from the age of eighteen, when she moved to Paris to study, but after two years she'd met a man five years older than she was. An ex-boyfriend by the name of David, who went on to become the love of her life. She described him as a bit of a smooth-talking rascal and con artist/drug dealer/bad boy/ladies' man (her words) who'd swept her off her feet one evening with his dominant and persistent dancing skills at a salsa nightclub. She became so infatuated that she dropped out of the university to work full-time as a waitress for five years while they lived together and she supported him. I had to chuckle. I wanted to meet such a guy, just one time. Just to see what kind of man possessed such powers to control a beautiful woman like her in such a way. Meanwhile, he bummed around from job to benefits to dodgy dealings and back again in one continuous circle. When Celine decided to go back to university a few years later and finish her degree, this guy talked her out of it. He made her feel like chasing her dreams was pointless and unfruitful (for him, perhaps). Worst of all, he belittled her into thinking she would make a useless teacher and that her time would be better spent looking after him instead; it would be more fulfilling to her in the long run and go a long way in making him very happy—thus, making her happy in the process. He belittled her so much that she forgot all about her dreams and ambitions and went back to working in a dingy old café, supporting her man, all in the name of what she believed to be love.

It took her five years to come to her senses and give this manipulative layabout the boot. He had consumed all her happiness, positivity, dreams, and savings while cheating on her with more women than I could ever dream of bedding in two lifetimes. And they were just the girls she knew about...there were certainly others. To get away she had to leave Paris and move back in with her parents. Again, working as a waitress, keeping to herself, saving as much money as she could while coming up with a plan. At twenty-six she decided to travel around Europe and at twenty-seven she applied for some French and English teaching posts all over the continent, using her bit part degree to nudge open some doors. Finally, she was offered a post teaching French in Edinburgh, where after only a few months, and because her English was so good, she was offered extra classes teaching English, too. And now, *voila*...here she was.

After another round of drinks, we had both hit the fairly drunk mark and were intimately snuggled up in the small booth at the back of the bar. It wasn't long before things started heating up again, and in no time at all we were touching, stroking, cuddling, and making out with an almost unrestrained and imploding passion. We just couldn't keep our hands off one another. After about twenty minutes of this, Celine said she'd never felt so comfortable with a man in such a short space of time. We had spent the last four hours of the evening together, which we both worked out was probably the equivalent of two dates.

I asked her to come back to my place again. She said she really wanted to, that both her body and mind were aching to do so, but not tonight. I was a little disappointed, but tried not to show it. I could tell by the way her body reacted to my touch, the way she softly moaned when I kissed her neck, bit her lips, ran my fingers along the sides of her thighs, that she wanted me badly and just as much as I wanted her. She must've seen the glint of disappointment in my eyes, though, because she immediately had a change of heart.

'Okay, Mr Poet. Write me a poem. Right now, right this very second, and I'll come home with you tonight.'

I felt shocked, flabbergasted. Under every day, normal, sober circumstances, this wouldn't have been too much of a problem. Just whack out one of my older poems and change it a bit. I felt so stunned by her proposal that I had to think on my feet.

'Really! Shit...really, fuck,' I replied, desperately trying to think of something, anything. 'Okay, I got it, I got it. There was a wee man who peed in a pan. The pan was too wee, so he peed in the sea. The sea was too wide, so he peed in the Clyde, and all the wee fishes went up his backside.'

Celine laughed from her belly and playfully slapped my arm.

'I mean a poem about me, silly.'

'Okay,' I smiled back. 'Just off the top of my head?' I had one. One I'd written but a good while back, yet for no one girl in particular, might I add. Lucky for me, the poem could be adapted universally for all women, worldwide, on the spur of the moment. Yet never had I wished for it to have more meaning for one particular girl than I did at that moment.

'Celine, so angelic, smart, and wild. Celine, with her devilish, sexy, yet secret smile. Celine, so gracious, warm, and bursting with energy. Celine, so pretty, captivating, magical, wild, and free. Celine, please, will you come home with me?'

Celine chuckled. I chuckled. I thought she liked it. Her face went bright red and she gently shook her head.

'Okay,' she grinned, 'let's grab some takeaway food and go back to yours.'

That was all I needed to hear. I grabbed her by the hand and led the way. We went outside and looked for a taxi. We didn't have to look very far. There was a trail of them all over the Cowgate. We flagged one down. Celine kissed me one more time with a slow, grinding passion before jumping into the taxi first and pulling me inside. Sitting in the back seat with her, I became infatuated. I couldn't wipe the big, fat, smug grin from my face. It was the first time in a long while that I'd felt such strong feelings for a girl, especially in such a short space of time. The feelings were amplified because it felt as if they were being mirrored right back at me. I was on cloud nine. Celine was everything I was looking for and more. But I also knew I had to be strong and keep my feelings in check and under control. I still had the tiniest inclination that something wasn't quite right here, that everything had progressed far too easily and smoothly for my own suspicious liking. I shook it off and put it down to paranoid reactions from too many dodgy experiences with beautiful-yet-flaky girls in the past. I had stopped believing in this love-at-first-sight, Hollywood nonsense a long time ago. Actually, it had been during my mid-twenties, when I started getting half-decent at meeting women, that I finally realised what pretentious and hopeful fantasist bullshit it really was. Love. True love. What a joke.

But this, with Celine, Jesus Christ. It felt like it might be the closest thing to it...well, the closest thing I'd experienced, for sure. It was like most of the things I'd learned over the years regarding women had been thrown completely out the window. I also assumed I was experienced enough to not jump the gun when it came to women and wear my heart on my sleeve like I'd done so many times in the past. Especially in my early twenties and teenage years, when I'd had my heart and soul torn to shreds more times than I cared to count and, thus, had said 'fuck you' to love and a big, fat 'hello' to casual sex and being more physical with a girl from the off and little else. Getting her into the sack as quickly as possible became the ultimate goal; then came dealing with all the love, emotions, and relationship bullshit afterwards. But in my early thirties, I'd become a hell of a lot more cautious. The body armour which protected my feelings became much thicker and sturdier than it used to be, or so I kept telling myself.

At Celine's insistence, we made a pit stop at a local kebab shop not far from my place. Once back in the cab, she asked me to recite the poem again like she was testing its authenticity, like I'd just read it off a leaflet pinned to the wall behind her in the pub. So, I recited it again, then again. Word for word, and she almost ate me alive. By the time we'd made the short journey back to my house, I'd already worked myself into such a sexual frenzy and horny state of mind, all I could think about was tearing that damn dress right off her sexy body as soon as we'd entered the front door. There was no way in hell I could make it through a takeaway meal in this horn dog state. My loins felt like they were on fire.

Once inside the front door, I threw down the carrier bag containing our kebabs. I turned, closed the front door, and turned to face Celine. She stood behind me and was in the process of taking off her cute brown leather jacket, left open to reveal her figure-hugging green silk dress and those beautiful breasts.

'Where can I hang my jacket?'

I stared at her with such an intense gaze of insatiable lust that I just knew, and she knew, it might be some time before the 'eating of any food' would commence. I put my arm around her waist, pulling her warm, curvy body towards mine. Our touches and kisses upon each other's lips were soft and probing at first. One little curious peck, followed by one longer peck after another, peppered with short, deliberate pauses. Like we were both feeling the other out. Then we just exploded like a firework! We began kissing with such angry, intense passion and fury that it would have taken a derailed freight train to break us apart. I turned and pushed Celine against the front door. I ran my hands all over her jumper and jeans, feeling and grabbing her gorgeous behind and those big, curvy, bouncy boobs behind her dress. She rubbed her hands all over me. Piece by piece, our clothing almost peeled itself off, departing our bodies and scattering to the four corners of my hallway.

Celine was down to just her purple satin bra and panties while I stripped to my jeans, which were opened at the button. Like a wild beast, I yanked those big heaving breasts of hers right out from their bra support, biting, sucking, and licking them with an immediate, insatiable desire. God, her nipples were so big and hard and tasted like heaven in my mouth. I sucked and gently bit away to the rhythm of her horny moans. Her hand reached down into my unfastened jeans, searching for my aching hardness. She didn't need to search very far and unleashed him from his cage while jerking him up and down with a vengeance. I continued to suck her breasts, which I'd guessed were implants by now. They were too goddamn round and perfect to be anything else, although I wasn't complaining. They were gorgeous. With my free hand, I felt my way inside her panties to search for that juicy, warm hole. Grazing my palm over her freshly shaven pubes, I found it in seconds. Jesus Christ, she was soaking. She must've been wet ever since we'd started talking this evening. I slid a finger inside and swirled it around. Shallow bursts at first, followed by harder, deeper, probing ones. She felt so warm and tight and wet in there that I found her sweet spot within seconds. Given away by the gushing release of her increasing, gasping wails, which she seemed to have absolutely no control over. I continued to focus my attention on her sweet spot as she wriggled and writhed around in the palm of my hand, gaining more furious and frantic momentum with every swirling motion I made. She tugged harder and faster on my cock. I wanted to be inside her so badly. I physically ached for her. But first, I wanted to taste that sweet wetness between her thighs that had haunted my fantasies this entire evening. I spun her around and pushed her breasts and stomach against the front door. I knelt and with the palms of my hands parted her legs a little wider. I gently spanked the inside of her thighs. Then, I pulled her inner thighs towards me and up so that her back arched and her gorgeous round buttocks sat right in my face.

Immediately I buried myself alive into those curvaceous round cheeks, parting them even wider than Moses and the sweet, delicious Red Sea to expose that hidden, juicy, wet treasure cave beneath. I couldn't contain myself and lapped her up, tasting and licking every last drop of her. This crazy lust and desire which consumed my body, mind, and soul had turned into a raging madness. I felt her entire body shudder. Her moans became louder and more intense. She banged furiously upon the front door with her fists as she came on my lips. I took a few moments to let her recover and gently bit and kissed at her beautiful buttocks, caressing and worshipping those plump mounds of flesh with my tongue and lips in a much calmer motion.

I stood to my feet, still rock hard and aching to be inside her. I had half a mind to just pick her up and carry her to the bedroom, but her sexy arse was still perking itself right up at me. Teasing me, taunting me. The way she'd sprawled herself against the front door, head rested, breathing hard, eyes closed, recovering from her orgasm, I knew I had to fuck her right there. Even though our moans and antics would be heard throughout the entire street outside. To be honest, the thought of anyone listening nearby turned me on even more. And to get one over on that music-pounding motherfucker next door, even better. I took my hardness, parted those gorgeous pale cheeks again, and gently guided him home. It felt like I had finally died and gone to heaven. Just how the hell had I ever gotten so lucky with this goddess?

***

With the extra wee bit of help from my magic blue pill, we screwed wildly for at least another three hours straight. We must have christened every single room in that goddamn house, trying every single position in every book ever written about fornication in the history of mankind before making up some of our own. I couldn't get enough of her. I had never fucked, or tried so hard to fuck, a girl before in my entire life. I dare say, my terminal dilemma played its part also. That could, after all, be the last time I got to make love to such a woman, let alone any woman. For once, I wanted to give her my best, my all, my everything. I wanted her to come back for more, much more. (If I've learned anything in life, it's to never take top-quality women like her for granted.) Because she was such a sexual turn-on to me, all I wanted to do was ravage her. She was my own living, breathing Viagra pill. And just when I thought she'd squeezed every last ounce of lust and desire from my deflated ball bags, it took only the slightest breath or movement from her wonderful heaving bosoms, or a wee devilish expression on her angelic face, or for me to momentarily glance at her wondrous curves as she reached over to drink from a glass of water lying on the bedside cabinet for my loins to stir back into action from the abyss of sexual desire and rise back up, standing to attention, ready for another tour of duty.

It was around 6.00 am when we finally managed to pry ourselves free from each other's genitals and other saucy bits and pieces. We munched through our reheated kebabs in a semi-naked, half-famished, half-exhausted bliss. I opened a bottle of red for us before we rested in each other's arms upon the living room couch. We engrossed ourselves in various music channels until our food had somewhat digested and our sexual organs gradually stirred and ached for more friction. Come noon, we were both physically and emotionally exhausted, sprawled across two opposite sides of my double bed like we'd landed there after falling all the way down from the moon.

***

By 1.00 pm Celine was in the shower while I made coffee. She said she had to be in school by 4.00 pm to begin preparation for an evening class. I wasn't proud of my next actions, but I still felt as if she was holding something back. Especially when I asked her to swap numbers. She said she'd take mine and give me a text later in the week. In the past, when a girl took my number but wouldn't give me hers, it usually turned into some kind of blow off. So, while she showered I had a sneaky wee rummage through her handbag. Bizarrely enough, I found a shit-load of condoms, along with a bottle of lubricant and tissues, which I ignored for the time being. I found her phone and gave my own mobile a little missed call. I also found a utility bill addressed to her. 51b High Street. I wrote it down and put her handbag back where I'd found it.

Sitting back on the couch and thinking about the wonderful saucy evening and morning we'd spent together, it occurred to me that she hadn't mentioned her supposed boyfriend once. Had they recently broken up or had a massive argument? Is that why she'd been so eager and keen to jump in the sack with me after only a few hours and a couple of drinks? I would keep my mouth shut and not mention the boyfriend thing again. I'm sure she'd tell me in her own good time.

Fifteen minutes later a taxi arrived. Even in the light of day, with little makeup and wearing her green silk dress from the night before, Celine looked naturally stunning. We hugged at the front door and kissed with a fading passion which lasted all too briefly for my liking.

'I'll call you later,' were her departing words as I watched her climb into the waiting taxi. I had the most horrible feeling I would never see or hear from her again. It was a feeling I could only relate to as one of complete unworth. Like I didn't deserve to have a woman like her in my life. Like I felt her to be completely out of my league, but not physically, just emotionally and intellectually. Yes, I'd been with beautiful, sexy girls before. Some even more physically beautiful than Celine. But most of these bleach-blonde, fake-tanned, George Street beauties were dead inside. Completely soulless and empty, with no real passion, purpose, personality, heart, ambition, character, or soul to their superficial and pretentious 'Facebook-and-Twitter' lives. This girl had more soul in one little finger than most of the shallow, meat-market women I'd had the displeasure of wasting my time chatting up on a Saturday night. More life and soul, in fact, than they would ever attain if they'd lived twenty-five lifetimes. Who would I need to be to win a girl like her? What would I need to do? I now fully understood the claims of warriors, kings, writers, and poets from ages past, who'd fought wars, crossed distant seas and deserts, and invaded faraway lands and kingdoms for women like her. Oh, how she had inspired me already, and without ever really knowing. Just the thought of being around her one more time was enough to inspire me to be a better person. Hell, a better man. Yet I couldn't rid myself of this feeling in the pit of my stomach that I would never hear from her again...if, indeed, it were left up to her to make the next move. Right after Celine left, I felt inspired to write another poem.

I saw you one day, heading for the subway train, I transformed into such a lovesick fool.
So I got off my stool and ran after you, deep down to the subway.
With moving bodies everywhere, I was thrown into deep despair, searching, searching everywhere...then I found you.
For one time-stopping heartbeat, you turned to me, smiling prettily and radiantly, but in shyness I turned away. What a fool.
When I finally found the courage to look back, all I could see was black, as your train began to move.
Goodbye, Ma Cherie.

I didn't like it. Lovesick nonsense shite. I crumpled it up and threw it in the bin, just like all the others. Still, I felt better for writing it. It was like getting her out of my mind by putting her onto paper. It made me pine for her less in the moment. Then to throw it away. I always throw them away.

Chapter 8

For the next few days I never heard a single thing from Celine. Nothing. Nada. Zip. I'd heard from Babs cashing in her rain check and asking if I fancied a cheeky late-night romp over at hers sometime. And, surprisingly, Nikki wouldn't stop texting me either. She wanted to see me again. She was sorry for not turning up on time for our date. She had popped into a friend's flat party on the way to meet me and lost track of the time. She wanted to arrange another date, but I ignored her. I'd completely lost interest in both women. I tried to do some plumbing jobs but all I could think about was Celine and why she wasn't contacting me. What had I done wrong? I felt positive that night had been perfect. We'd gotten on so well. Had so much in common. Physically and mentally.

On the third day of hearing nothing, I decided to not do any more plumbing work for the foreseeable future. I didn't even go to my specialist appointment at the hospital. What was the point? I had my painkillers and they were enough. I really didn't want to think beyond that just yet.

Almost a week went by and I still hadn't heard from Celine, so I caved and tried calling her. She never answered. No voicemail, just a continuous ring. I sent her some text messages, yet still heard nothing.

The next day I couldn't take it anymore and decided to pay her a visit at the address I'd written down. I felt like there was nothing left for me to do. I missed her a lot. Even though I forbade myself from wearing my heart on my sleeve. From falling head over heels for a woman of her calibre.

But my cancer told me a different story. Telling me that time was short. That I should wear my heart on my sleeve one more time and take that leap of faith into this now pretentious and superficial world. Where everyone assumed they'd stay young and healthy forever. Immortal in their own little private, cosy, bubbled lives. Well, that secret was out. Life *was* short. Too short for some unlucky few. Now it was time to make the most of it. Live by the sword, die by a hundred fucking swords.

***

I dressed casually, jeans and a t-shirt. I stood against my kitchen worktop, eating porridge and downing my third cup of coffee. The faint sound of heavy head-banging dance tunes could be heard coming from that prick next door. The fucker getting his own back on me, no doubt, for my late-night vocal antics with Celine a week prior. And, as always, my dishes in the kitchen sink vibrated along to the beats.

My phone rang for the tenth time that morning. Another jolly customer no doubt wondering what the hell had happened to me this past week. Wondering why I wasn't 'round their place like I'd scheduled, to start work on their new dream bathroom. Once the phone stopped ringing I listened to one of the fifteen voicemail messages from the past few days.

'Liam. It's Craig, man. It's nine-forty in the bloody morning, pal. Where the hell are ye? Ah thought you were starting ma new bathroom today. Av got the whole suite here crammed into ma hallway. Look! If yuv been in an accident and yur lying in hospital with yur legs ripped auf, or yuv a sledgehummer wrapped aroond yur skull, then ah apologise, man...'

I'm not really listening, though, and my eyes have refocused upon the kitchen sink. The dishes and glasses still jiggling away to the mambo number five. I could feel myself becoming more annoyed. I felt the rage building up inside again, but stronger and more intense than ever before.

'...Jist get yur bloody shite taegether and let me ken whit the hell's goin oan wi you man! Okay! Okay! Gid,' the recorded voice continued.

I finished the last of my porridge, sipped a little more from my coffee. The whiney voice in the background still going strong on the phone.

'And apologies again ef thir is sutton seriously wrong, man. Like yur lyin in bits and pieces all ower yur kitchen flare. Phone me back pal. Ta.'

I tried to enjoy the rest of my coffee but I couldn't help staring with deep agitation at the bouncing dishes. The pictures vibrating on the wall. That bass. Boom, boom, BOOOM. Thumping, thumping, thumping. Still nothing from Celine. The rage burned through my veins with even more vigour, searching for a release. Deep inside my head I could hear my cancer egging me wholeheartedly onwards. I closed my eyes. I could imagine that wee ned bastard next door sitting on his couch. Arms and legs spread wide again. Laughing his 'high-as-a-kite' wee head off. His banging bass merging with my own rage. Almost becoming one. Banging, thumping, boom.

***

I knocked loud and continuously upon my neighbour's front door. After a few seconds, it was answered by a rough, spaced, pale-looking teenager with one hell of an attitude.

'Aye! Fuck ye wantin, pal?'

I didn't have time for niceties. Just straight to the point. 'I want you to turn the music down. I can hardly hear myself think in my own house.'

'Whit the fuck dae tradesmen need tae hink aboot aye,' he said in a cocky, whiny tone. 'Hammer. Nail. Screw. Drill. Wash. Rinse. Dry. Repeat,' he chuckled.

In all honesty, I didn't expect the wee bastard to be so cocky and mouthy from the off. It was unexpected. I felt unprepared.

'Shid ye naw be at werk anyhoo wi aw they other working-class zombie retards naw?'

I held my composure well. 'Look, mate! I'm off work now. I just want some peace and quiet, all right?'

'Aye. Very gid. Av goat sum earplugs kickin aboot sumwhir ef ye wantae borrow thum likes.'

I clenched my fists hard. I could feel my knuckles burning white. 'Shouldn't you be at school, mate? Or doing something educational and productive with your life?'

'Am hame school, pal,' The teen grinned smugly.

'Of course you are!' I stepped away from the porch. 'Just turn the music down please, okay?'

There was a moment's silence. I walked back towards my house.

'Naw! Dinnie hink ah wul, pal. Cun play et us lood es ah wantae. Or et least until ma Ma geets hame. But ta fur yur concern neebs. Noo dae wan.'

The wee bastard slammed the door before I could turn halfway around to get in my reply. I took a deep breath and let the rage take it from there. I knew what had to be done.

Back inside my house, I casually walked into the spare room beside the kitchen where all my horded shite was stored from years gone by. It didn't take long to find what I was looking for. My Freddie Flintoff-signed, unwrapped and unused, deluxe cricket bat. Bought from eBay for one-hundred-and-eighty-five pounds.

This time I exited from the back of my house and into the garden. I hopped over the one-foot-high fence separating my patch of grass from the neighbours'. Without further delay, I approached his back door and booted it down. My rage had taken complete control. One ferocious kick and the flimsy back door was done for. I didn't even think about it. I just did it.

I entered. Music blared, filling the surrounding airwaves. The main source of it coming from upstairs. I assumed it had always been coming from the living room since it felt so damn loud and close to my kitchen.

I marched upstairs. Two doors were open on the landing, a

bedroom and a bathroom. A third door was shut tight and vibrating worse than George Best with the Sunday morning shakes. I didn't hold myself back and kicked open the teen's bedroom door with even more ferocity than I had the kitchen door. He lay on his bed smoking a joint and watching the bloody TV on mute while his stereo speakers shook the room. The music blared so loud that every step I took felt like I was making it in complete silence.

The teen saw me and sat upright on his bed, freezing in shock at the sight. And I must have been some sight. I stared right into his fearful eyes for no more than an overly long heartbeat before refocusing my attention upon his stereo sound system. I let loose. I went ape shit, smashing the hell out of the stereo and the speakers, then the TV, the Xbox, the PlayStation 3, followed by all the other electrical appliances that caught my eye, although the music had long since terminated. I kept smashing and smashing, anything and everything with my cricket bat. I couldn't stop myself even if I'd wanted to. The boy remained frozen on his bed. His mouth opened wide in a permanent state of shock, yet he couldn't get any words out.

Last but not least, I cracked open his iPhone 8 or 12 or whatever the hell the latest version was. It was now in electronic heaven, scattered to the four corners of this newly opened scrapyard. I lowered the bat to my side, breathing hard. All I could hear was the sound of my own crazy breathing. Finally, the teen released some sentences.

'Ye crazy...mother fuck. WHIT THE FUCK, MAN! WHIT THE FUCKING FUCK?'

In a heartbeat, I swung the bat right for the wee bastard's head but brought it to a sudden halt directly in front of his pishtified face. He screamed like a little girl before backing up fast and furious to the far corner of his bed. I, on the other hand, did not flinch one millimetre. I kept the bat pointed firmly at his face, still trying to gain control of my breathing.

'So then...fanny baws,' I finally spoke, 'about that music. You're going to keep it down from now on, aye?'

He nodded like a jack in the box. Trying to get some yes words out but nothing came through. I could see a small wet patch emerging on his light, faded jeans. It gradually became darker, bigger, wetter. Finally, he spoke.

'Absolutely, man! Ah swear. Nae mare music. Ah swear tae ma Maw.'

I felt like a huge weight had been lifted from my shoulders now that I'd been understood.

Back at my house, I had another cup of coffee. I called Celine again. No answer. Still ringing out. I decided that enough was enough. I needed to pay her a visit.

The time to act had cometh.

I drove into the city, approaching my favourite Gilmerton crossroads. Well, surprise, surprise, the lights were still red. I wasn't paying the slightest bit of attention, though. All I could think about was Celine. Her smell. Her delicious scent. The taste of her juicy...

I drove right through the red lights. I didn't give a fuck anymore. I wasn't doing red lights ever again. Within a minute, I found myself at another junction and another set of lights. From the corner of my eye I could see another car pulling out from my right. I still wasn't interested. I started singing along to the lyrics of Iona pop playing on the radio, my arm hanging out the window and catching the late-morning breeze. The car with the right of way turning into my lane from the right braked hard. I drove on past, still without a care, clipping the car's side bonnet with a nasty dent.

Looking back through my rear-view mirror, I could see the woman driver screaming and freaking in frustration, then letting loose on her horn like it was going to make me come back and apologise.

I parked my van down at Viewcraig Gardens, just off Holyrood Road. It was only a two-minute jaunt to the High Street from there. I lived around these parts a few years back when I first moved to Edinburgh after working up in Aberdeen, so I knew the layout along with some hidden gems—unrestricted parking zones. Especially along this well-hidden street. Only one problem. It was the one remaining ned and jakey district in the city centre and Old Town.

A few years back the Scottish government and the Edinburgh City Council had done a very discreet ned and jakey cleanse of the city centre (even though neither would admit to it), shipping off most those troublemakers and benefit cheats to the outer suburbs of the city, like Pilton, Niddrie, Burdiehouse, and Wester Hailes. Let the animals eat their own and fight amongst the scraps out there, away from the tourists, students, and general working class. Although you'd still find the occasional, resilient family of neds kicking about the centre from time to time. And those remaining stubborn few who found a way of staying behind always seemed to hang their trainers and tracksuits in the View-Craig and Dumbie-Dykes area.

I parked outside block number nine to eleven. I should've parked farther along but I was in a rush. It was in the back of my mind that some hillbilly neds were still living in the flats here. Particularly in block eleven. It didn't really vex me until I exited my van and a stocky wee middle-aged, toothless-grinning, gypsy, alcky ned bastard opened his flat door to give me the eye. I took a deep breath. He was probably going to have a good moan about my parking right in front of his home, but fuck him. It was a free country.

He stepped out of the doorway. Then a woman's gravelled, dragon-chasing voice screamed after him from deep within their humble adobe. 'Whit ye daen, Rab?'

'Am goan oot tae see sumwan, ye daft hoor.'

'Fur feck sake, Rabbie. Mind n clase the feckin door thus time. Et's feckin baltic oot thir.'

He closed the door behind him and approached me like he was ready for a fight. Without even flinching, I walked right on up to him and met him halfway. Jesus Christ, he was an ugly bastard up close. All his front teeth were either broken or missing, and I could smell the stench of a lifetime's worth of drink, pish, sweat, and vomit from his dirty, unwashed skin. He had a broad chest and shoulders, which surprised me. Usually, most of these jakey and neds were skinny wee runts, their bodies wasting away to nothing with a diet of cheap drugs and even cheaper alcohol from their benefit cheques. This one looked like he used to bench press once upon a time before he discovered those vices.

'Hoo much ye wantin fur yur wheels thir, pal?'

Jesus, that caught me by surprise. I was sure he was after a square go right out here in the middle of the street. But no. He only wanted to buy my van. Or so he said.

'I'm no selling it mate, sorry.'

'Aye, but hoo much *wid* ye tak fur et, pal?'

What was this guy up to? My gut instinct told me he was up to something shady. That he was only chit–chatting and biding time until the rest of his jakey followers turned up to assist his criminal cause. Then he got right up into my face, making me feel really uncomfortable. I retaliated and stepped right up into his face. Fuck his intimidating hard man shite. I was taller than him, anyhow, and with a slightly bigger build. He just had more fighting conviction because he was a street rat who didn't live life by the consequences of working-class society. A society I had been denouncing these past few weeks, myself. If we'd met like this a few months back, I would've just jumped straight back into my car and found another parking spot. Right now, though, I had more than matched the bastard for eye contact and dominant body language. Not backing down an inch.

After all had been said and done, he backed down first. I felt slightly relieved, but the scene was far from over. In silence, he walked around my van, giving it the eye. Then, after an excruciatingly long ten seconds, his wee nedette daughter wandered out of their apartment and over towards us. She looked about ten years of age.

'Whit ye daen, Da, fur fuck sake?'

Another ned jakey in the making. Already a mouth on her too, and with a father like that what chance did the little runt have in life?

The dad continued to circle my van, stopping once to shake it using the roof rack for grip. 'Aye, gid suspension likes.'

The girl copied her father but shook the van from the side doors because the wee runt couldn't reach the top. If this were an episode of The Walking Dead I would have pulled out my shotgun and blown both these jakey schemey zombie fuckers into buckfast heaven.

The dad then screamed at his daughter. 'Stoap et, Paris. Fuck auf back tae the hoose fur fuck sake, ye wee cunt ye.'

'Ah wantae see, Da.'

She stopped shaking the van. Surprisingly, I kept my cool as the dad continued to stalk my wheels. Memories of the recent conflict with my next-door neighbour lingered in my mind. This idiot had picked the wrong 'pal' to try his schemey shite on today.

'Dieel aye.'

I had no idea what the hell he had just said and I considered myself a local.

'What!'

He tried to slow his speech, which was amusing, as more spit shot out from his mouth like a hogmanay fireworks display.

'A deesil, aye?'

'Yeah. It's a diesel, mate.'

'M. O. Teed, aye?'

'About another nine months, mate.'

He kicked the tyres. I was getting tired and bored of this shite. I had a girl to go and see and win. The ned tried his hardest to intimidate me with this trivial macho charade. Maybe marking his territory, so to speak, for parking near his house. It worked to an extent. He knew I didn't live around here and therefore would never park around this way again given the choice after our little confrontation.

'Open the bonnet, pal. Les hear the cunt runnin thun.'

'Mate. I'm meeting someone. I haven't got time for this.'

He made his way to the bonnet anyway, completely ignoring me.

I sighed deeply, then opened the van and pumped the bonnet

from the inside. Anything to keep this twat amused. If I stayed on his good side, a confrontation would surely be avoided. Plus, I didn't want anything to mysteriously happen to my van while I was away trying to track down Celine.

The man stroked his fingers underneath the crack in the bonnet, searching, searching, searching. The stupid fuck couldn't even find the safety latch to fully open the bonnet. So, I went around and opened it for him. He glanced inside like he knew what the hell he was doing and looking for. I had a slight oil leak last year, which happened to be in a really shitty position behind the engine. Instead of biting the bullet and paying a couple hundred quid to get it fixed, I shoved in a bit of eight-millimetre copper pipe and filtered the leak into an empty Coke can, which I left fitted beside the engine.

'Thus es fir yur brake fluid, aye?'

'No mate. It's for an oil leak. It's a small leak. The copper pipe filters it through to the can.'

'Naw! Dinnae hink sae, man. Ah hink et's sutton tae dae wi yur breaks likes masel.'

'It's no for the breaks, mate. It's for an oil leak. I did it myself.'

He continued to inspect the engine, pretending to have a clue what the hell he was doing. I put my hand on top of the bonnet impatiently.

'Look, mate. I need to go.' Now fuck off, you jakey bastard, I continued inside my head.

He pulled his head from underneath the bonnet. 'Whits the rush, man? Whir ye auf tae likes?'

What the hell business is it of yours, you wee Pikey ned Cunt! That was how I really wanted to reply.

'Just going to meet a friend in town.'

'Few swallees tae aye. Ah geet ye, pal.'

Don't tell me this nipple was going to try and invite himself along. 'Nah mate. Maybe a few lemonades. Got to drive home at the end of the day too, you know.'

'Lemonade's fur fuckin poofs, ye cunt.'

I ignored him and closed the bonnet. The ned put his hand on my shoulder briefly.

'So, pal. Hoo much ye wantin fur et?'

'Like I said, it's no for sale, mate.'

He looked genuinely surprised. 'Really, aye!'

'Honestly, aye!'

'Fifty quid.'

I let out a chuckle. 'Mate, I could get at least two hundred from the scrappies for this.'

'Naw wi the day's prices, ye wudnae.'

'My mate got two hundred and twenty for his Peugeot a few months back. So, aye mate. I would.'

'Whir boots like?'

'In fife.' Jesus Christ, was I really having this conversation?

'Dinnae hink sae likes.'

What the hell bloody planet was this guy on?

'Look mate. I'm really running late. I need to go.'

'Nae bother then, pal. But ef ye ever change yur mind likes, ah stay et number nine jist thir.'

'Cool, mate.'

'Wan mare hing! Dae ye huv any pliers en your van?'

Bloody pliers. What the hell did this cunt want a pair of pliers for?

'No, mate. I don't have any tools with me today. Why the hell do you need pliers?' I was almost afraid to ask.

He stuck his finger into his mouth and wiggled one of his rotten teeth about. 'Wan uv ma tooth givin us gip like ken. Fuckin sare yin.'

I just shook my head, disgusted. 'I need to go.'

We shook hands. Then I walked off towards the High Street. Even though my gut told me to go back and move the van immediately, I didn't. My manly pride became a barbed-wire prison wall in the way. I kept walking. To move the van in his presence would show defeat of my alpha male persona. I tried to put it to the back of my mind, but it still niggled away as I walked farther towards the High Street. I just knew the fucker was planning on doing something to it while I was gone. Whether it was smashing a window, slashing the tyres, stuffing something up the exhaust…my mind sped on overdrive. I dreaded my return, when no doubt the bastard would be hanging around nearby and gloating when I couldn't get the bloody thing started.

'Buy et fae ye noo pal, aye?'

***

I found 51b on the High Street. I stood beside the large green oak door, pondering whether to ring the buzzer. She probably wouldn't be in, anyway. Maybe I should come back this evening when there'd be a better chance. Or perhaps I should bring my car around and park nearby, watching for her coming or going. But it was all single yellow lines down this bloody High Street. I convinced myself that it would be better to come back after 6.30 pm, when the wardens receded back into their filthy, dark cesspits. Plus, my recent encounter with that jakey ned bastard still floated at the back of my mind.

Just as I was about to turn and walk away, the large green door opened and a young man wearing a smart business suit walked out. Must've been one of her neighbours in the other flats. I grabbed a hold of the door before it closed and entered the stairwell, my mind made up for me by someone else's actions.

There were only six flats inside. A to F. So, B had to be on the ground floor. I guessed correctly. It was the first door to my right. I held my breath, preparing to knock. Shit! What if her boyfriend answered? I'd pretend to be the gas man or looking for a John or Adam or someone non-female. But what if his name was John or Adam, ha?

Screw it. I knocked, quick and hard. I held my breath, but there was nothing, not a single sound. Then I heard movement, the shuffling of feet, the clanging of keys. I stood away from the eyehole. I didn't want her to see me through a closed door and give her any reason whatsoever not to open the door. I didn't want to say what I had to say through a thick piece of secured wood.

The door edged open. Celine gradually revealed herself, wearing a sexy silk nightgown with very little else on underneath.

'You're early,' she said without making eye contact.

'Hi,' I limply replied.

She glanced up at me in a heartbeat. She looked well and truly dazed and confused. Then she froze. 'Jesus Christ! Liam. What the fuck?'

'Surprise,' I said, half smiling, half grimacing.

'How the hell did you find me?' she said in an angry whisper. 'What the hell are you doing here?'

'Hey, it's nice to see you too. Can I come in?'

'Absolutely not,' she snapped.

'So, we're gonna do this out here, are we? Right in the middle of your stairwell? With all your neighbours just a stone's throw away?'

'They're probably all at work, anyway.'

'Is your boyfriend home? Is that it? Do you want me to come back later?'

She looked confused. 'What boyfriend? I don't have a bloody boyfriend.'

'The boyfriend you said you had. You know, when we first met that night?'

She still looked confused. Then her eyes widened. 'Oh! Ohhh! Shit. Look—that's just my default line, okay? When guys come up to me on the street or in bars. I always tell them I have a boyfriend. It's quick. It's easy. It's painless. And a lot less rude and disheartening than a 'piss off, you smelly little pervert.'

That explained a lot. 'So, guys even try and chat you up on the street? Away from bars and clubs,' I said, shocked. I thought this had been my gimmick. I thought I was the one being unique and different from the herd. I felt hurt. Deflated.

'Yes, even on the street during the day. My God!' she replied. Still in shock. 'I can't believe you're here. How the hell did you find me?'

'I went through your handbag when you stayed over at my place the other night,' I said with a hint of pride. Proud that I had gone through with such a smart and sneaky tactic after all or else we wouldn't have been having this conversation right now.

'You went through my fucking handbag? Were you looking for money? Did you steal from me? I didn't notice anything missing,' she said, deadly serious.

'No way. What the hell do you take me for, Celine? I just wanted to find out a bit more about you, that's all. Since you were so reluctant to give me your goddamn phone number.'

'I took *your* number, remember?'

'Nice one, yeah. I've never heard from you since.'

Celine slapped the palm of her hand against her forehead a few times. 'Because...Liam. That night...that night...'

'Didn't you have a good time? It looked like you were having a good time from all the moaning and wriggling around you were doing.'

'Maybe I didn't want to hurt your feelings,' Celine replied sarcastically.

'You didn't want to hurt my feelings for eight hours straight? Even Anne Hathaway's not that good an actress.'

'Look, I had a good time, Liam, okay? I really did. You were a good fuck. You were a surprisingly great shag, actually. But for me...it was more of a sympathy shag, you know. I was just...you got me at a good time, that's all. I was down. I was pissed off. I had self-esteem issues. I still have them. You just got me when I needed some good, hard action the most. I guess you just got lucky.'

I didn't know what the hell to say to that. I kind of half-guessed this stuff already, but it took a face-to-face confrontation to really hammer it home.

'So, you don't want to see me again? Even for a coffee or a drink? Go for a drive in the country? Walk around a fucking museum?'

Celine glanced down. She hesitated. She wanted to say something, I could tell. Like a confession.

'Look,' I continued, 'if I really was some one-off shag for you, then surely to Christ you'd have just up and left right after you woke the first time that night. Perhaps without even telling me. But you didn't. We ate together, we drank some more. We talked, we laughed. We curled up in each other's arms and fell asleep watching early morning TV, for Christ's sake, before going at each other again like a combined Olympic wrestling and gymnast team.'

'Liam.' She glanced at me again with a stern, steely glare. 'If truth be known, I did like you, okay? You weren't just a good fuck with a nice cock. You had some good, deep chat and banter, too. But I don't do boyfriends, okay? Haven't done them for a long time now, and I'm definitely not going to be doing them for the foreseeable future.'

'Why not?'

'Because...' she said, tongue tied. 'I don't have to explain or justify myself to you.' She glanced down at her watch, 'Look! You just need to go, alright? I have some...some people and friends coming 'round. You can't be here when they arrive, okay?'

Now I felt confused. 'Why can't I be here when they arrive?'

'Because you just can't, okay?'

'Are you some kind of drug dealer or gangster?' I said half-heartedly. 'You're acting awfully suspicious for a language teacher, Celine. Do you have Al Capone's great-grandson coming round for a private French lesson?'

'No.' She took a deep breath and released.

'Then what?'

She placed her hands hard upon her hips.

'What, Celine? What's the big secret? An Ann Summers party? Illegal language teaching club? What?'

Celine let out another deep sigh. 'I'm a fucking prostitute, Liam, okay? Not a teacher. Not a student. I'm a high-class escort. A three-hundred-pound-an-hour fuck. Does that answer your bloody question?'

I was shocked. It felt like the whole of my insides were about to cave in. I needed fresh air. I just couldn't take in all this. How could someone so gorgeous and smart...be a fucking prostitute?

'So, my profession,' Celine continued, leaves zero room and zero tolerance in my life for any boyfriends in any form or capacity.'

I remained silent and perplexed. Celine cupped her hand to her ear.

'Oh! What's that I hear? The sound of your past eager interest scattering to the four corners of anywhere but bloody here. You're not the first man who's declared his heart and soul to me and then drowned in his own vomit and piss once I told him the truth.'

I felt sick. I did want to vomit. I couldn't stop imagining all those dirty dicks she'd sucked and fucked over the months or years. If she was, in fact, telling me the truth. Could still be a ploy to get rid of me. But Jesus Christ, all those dirty perverted men. I tried to remember if we'd used a condom back at mine. Then it dawned on me that I had terminal cancer and STDs didn't really apply to me anymore.

Before I could gather my thoughts, before I could even speak and finally say something, Celine went for the door. 'Goodbye, Liam. And don't come back here again, ever. Understood?'

She slammed the door in my face. As I stood there, heart-torn, a broken man, confused and distressed in her doorway, a sudden epiphany spurted into my mind. I knew that nothing would ever be the same again if I went through with it.

Chapter 9

Yes, Celine. I would come back for you again, my sweet. I would get in my ten-pence worth next time. But first I had to do a few things. Run a few errands, so to speak, before returning and running over my nudge, nudge, wink, wink, say-no-more, say-no-more proposition with her.

I walked back up the fairly busy and touristy High Street in the direction of St. Giles Cathedral and the George the Fourth Bridge/Mile crossroads. I checked my mobile phone, which I'd deliberately left on silent, only to discover another twenty-five missed calls. Why couldn't these people take a hint?

A few yards farther along, I saw a hairy-faced homeless man lying drunk and unconscious outside a kilt shop with his dog, close to the Jeffrey Street and High Street crossroads. I dropped my phone into the man's hat as I walked on by. Only the dog seemed to give a damn.

Walking farther along the mile with Blackfriars Street on my left, I noticed one of those traffic warden parasites leaning over the front of a small green Astra. A middle-aged MILF with two kids in tow stood arguing with the fat prick (and he was a fat one indeed), but it was no use. She'd turned blue in the face and the cunt still wasn't acknowledging her or paying the slightest bit of attention to her side of the story.

A motherfucker of all crazy ideas entered my head. I felt good. I felt like doing something radical. Making a change in the norm. Doing something completely crazy and out there. Within a swift second, my mind had been made up. I strolled up to the traffic warden, looking as happy as Larry's sniffer dog who'd just been given the task of smelling a line-up of one-hundred-and-one stinky, sweaty arse holes for hidden narcotics.

'All right, guys,' I said cheerfully.

The parasite didn't acknowledge me at first, too busy typing his little numbers and letters into his wee fancy ticket machine. His fingers were so fat and the buttons so small, it was no wonder he needed a full pelt of concentration. I let out a warm, friendly winking smile to the MILF, who seemed a wee bit confused by my presence. Then, quick as a flash and wasting no more time, I made a desperate lunge and grab, pinching the warden's ticket machine and small camera from his grasp. I sprinted off down the back end of Blackfriars Street like I'd just stolen the Crown bloody Jewels.

'Go! Get the hell out of here,' I shouted back to the MILF as the warden, baffled and flustered, then fully enraged, battered down the street to take chase after me. I didn't have time to look back again but I could almost feel the vibrations of the roller-ball warden bouncing down the concrete pavements after me. I imagined that scene from the beginning of *Raiders of the Lost Ark*, when the humungous ball of stone hurtles after Indy through the underground cave.

I'd like to think that the MILF took the opportunity to shove herself and her kids into the car and drive the hell out of town.

I turned a sharp right onto the Cowgate before taking another sharp right up the tight and narrow Niddry Street. A steep climb nonetheless, but it would eventually lead me all the way back up onto the Mile again. Halfway up Niddry Street, just passing the Hive, I made a quick glance back. The fat, round warden was already done for, huffing and puffing at the bottom of the street. He'd stopped to slaver some winded shite into his radio. His fat face looked utterly beetroot in colour. This walking heart attack was done for, toasted and ready for his butter and jam.

If he was radioing one of his nearby warden bitches to head me off, I'm sure it would take only a matter of seconds for the parasites to reach the North Bridge/Mile crossroads from one of the many side streets upon the Mile. With this in mind, I decided to take a little detour and get out of the open for a short while. Fuck heading onto the Mile now. I dived into Whistle Binkies instead, a dive music bar pretty much open 24/7. I remembered the bar had a staircase at the back which took you up onto the adjourning streets above South Bridge.

Emerging onto South Bridge like a bat out of hell, I continued bolting in the direction of Chambers Street, but not before flinging the ticket machine and camera right off the South Bridge and down into the steep concrete abyss of the Cowgate. I kept running but easily heard the two appliances smashing to smithereens at the bottom. I couldn't help but have a good, hard chuckle as I ran into the National Museum to cool down and hide out for a while. Job done.

In the museum toilets, I splashed cold water on my face. I chuckled again at the image of that fat parasite's clueless face when I took away his toys. And then the look of his fat beetroot puss when I ran back up the steep slope of Niddry Street towards the Mile once more. If only MasterCard did a 'Pissed off Traffic Wardens - Priceless.'

I grabbed a coffee to go from the museum canteen, then stepped casually back outside and continued west, past Bobby and down Candlemaker Row into the Grass Market and towards the Tollcross end of Lothian Road. Final destination: the glorious Bank of Scotland.

Joining the queue for the three bank tellers on duty, I deliberately timed it so I would be seen by the gorgeous and petite Sandra. I'd always had a thing for her over the years. We'd flirted, had a bit of surface chit-chat once in a while, but I had never actually bitten the bullet to ask her out. Probably because I couldn't face the humiliation of a frank, 'Fuck off, no.' And then having to come crawling back in there again to do my banking. Would be easier to just move to another branch altogether. Anyway, that was no longer an issue. Today would be my last day and final association with any bank on this godforsaken planet.

I sat opposite the stunning wee Sandra lass as she closed my bank account for good. When she politely asked why I was taking out all my money, I told her I was moving to Fiji and left it at that. She even got me a little bank purse for my nearly nine-grand's worth of savings.

'Well, that is your bank account closed for you then, Mr Walker,' Sandra said with those big, round, flirty, fuck-me eyes and that adorable dimple-faced smile. 'Will there be anything else today?'

I hesitated briefly, then let out the most mischievous smile and seductive stare I could manage. I knew I wouldn't trade this vanilla-topping sex-coned bank teller for my chocolate-chip-mint, caramel-fudge-and-strawberry dream sex cone Celine. But Celine wasn't a done deal yet. And I guessed it would be nice to have one or two back-up options for my new fun-filled adventurous life plan ahead. Just in case Celine told me to 'Get to France' again.

'Well you know, Sandra!' I replied, putting on my best flirty Daniel 'James Bond' Craig persona. 'If you don't mind my saying so, you have the most beautiful, angelic, dimple-faced smile I have ever seen.'

Sandra blushed wildly. 'Why thank you, Mr Walker. That's very sweet of you to say.'

'You know, every time I come in here, I've wanted to just, you know, what the hell...ask you out for a drink or a coffee some time and get to know you a little bit better. But I just never had the balls to do it. Well, not until this very second.'

Sandra still smiled, still blushed. She held up her hand to show me her wedding ring. 'I don't think my husband would be too enthused about that, Mr Walker. If I was single, I'd have to say, aye, why the hell not. But thank you for the compliment, Liam. You made my day.'

We both chuckled like a couple of teenagers.

'Worth a try though, no? The best ones are always taken, as they say!'

'Well, you don't get anywhere in life without taking risks, right?' Sandra replied with her own winking smile.

'You took the words right out of my mouth,' I half sang, quoting the lyrics from one of my favourite songs.

Sandra never cottoned on. I stood to my feet. So did Sandra. Even standing upright, she was so tiny. We shook hands. Hers were so small and soft. I loved her tiny hourglass figure. I'd never bedded a woman so petite. I guessed you could have a lot of fun in the bedroom with that. You could go from shagging Disney's Tinkerbell to the Munchkin Princess of Oz to Hermione in her school uniform, all in the space of one sex-fuelled bank-holiday weekend.

'Have a great life, Sandra.'

'You too, Liam.'

'You know, Sandra, I think I will.'

***

I made my way back down towards the Grass Market. I felt full to the brim with great energy, feistiness, and fun. Like the weight of the world was finally off my back and I had everything in life to live for again. I felt like I could do anything and be anyone and I wanted to share this newfound enthusiasm for life. I wanted my energy to be contagious in that moment. I wanted everyone to be infected by my new positivity and lust for life. Even the two average-looking office women walking towards me on West Port. One short and fat, one tall and skinny with a big horsey nose. I didn't care. I felt it was my duty to make them feel absolutely brilliant. I smiled wildly as I passed them. They looked confused as hell at my forwardness, but the little fat one duly smiled back.

'Good afternoon, my angels. Might I say how scrumptiously stunning you are both looking on this fine day.'

The two girls just looked at each other before turning back to face me. They must have thought I was high as a kite. But I was only high on life. The short fat one thanked me, still looking confused and still walking.

I came out with the exact same sentence for another few dozen passers-by. Some old, some young, some fat, some thin, some ugly as a battered raw fish. Some as beautiful as a Calton Hill sunset. Some embraced me like I'd really made their day. Some told me I was a perverted wee bastard or to go fuck myself. I guess you couldn't please everyone with genuine goodwill and positive compliments.

I didn't think anything could break my mood in that heavenly moment, I really didn't. But alas, one thing eventually did. As I entered the pleasant Grass Market strip, I was greeted by the sight and sound of my cocky builder friend from a week or so back. He stood outside the Bee Hive again, puffing away on a newly lit fag and sipping at his filthy dark pint. Still verbally abusing any women who happened to walk in his vicinity. I came to a halt, lingering beside a nearby bench, waiting for a fairly attractive MILF pushing her twin baby pram to pass him. As expected, the cocky builder's eyes were all over the hot lass.

'Hey-hey gorg-jaas! Whit a sexy wee erse ye huv thir, Missus. Gee's a bite?'

The MILF gave him the finger as she passed, but it only fuelled his fire.

'Oh, feisty yin aye! Why naw come back ower here and wiggle that sexy wee erse oan ma face, sweetheart?'

The MILF kept walking. Soon she'd be on King Stables Road and out of earshot of this mutt. I couldn't help thinking about what I'd love to do to this wido prick in a room without windows, where laws didn't apply. But should I really do something now? I wanted to do something. At least say something. But this arsehole wasn't going to listen to anything I had to say, that was for sure. No, this was definitely a case of 'Actions speak louder than words.'

I was still debating my actions when two high school girls walked towards the Bee Hive, making up my mind for me. This guy needed a serious education in manners when it came to the respectful treatment of the opposite sex. Without due cause, might I add. I mean, I'd be the first heterosexual man to hold up my hands and admit that I'd treated girls like sexual objects or pieces of meat in the past. And more times than I was proud to admit. But I'd always kept those feelings and fantasies just that— thoughts inside my head. It's common courtesy not to speak aloud the pure and utterly degrading filth I'm always thinking when I come into contact with the opposite sex. At the end of the day, I'm just a highly sexually active man. But I'll tell you right now, ladies, your man's a liar if the first thought in his head upon passing a girl he's never met or seen before isn't anything but a simple 'aye' or 'naw!' You would or you wouldnae. He makes the decision within micro seconds, mostly without any conscious effort on his part, and totally beyond his control.

The cute schoolgirls walked past the Bee Hive. Aye, I would, especially the slim blonde. But I'd kept that to myself, unlike some people around here.

'Awright, ma wee dolls,' the cocky man called after them.

At first they giggled to one another, then ignored him.

'Oh aye, ah wud breek the two uv ye lovely wee sexy skanks en fur free, darlins. Et wid be ma fuckin pleasure, dolls.'

'Fuck you, ye jakey fuckin creepster,' shouted back the blonde. Both girls gave him the fingered salute before hurrying off.

'Aye. Git back here, ye wee pair ov filthy skanks, ye. Al show ye where tae poke they wee fingers. Fuckin wee hoors,' he shouted after them.

I couldn't take it anymore. I couldn't stand by while this kind of mental abuse was handed out to the innocent female population of my glorious city. I swallowed my fear and walked casually up to the cocky builder, who was now making suggestive tongue movements in the girls' direction. I stopped a few inches shy of his beer- and fag-stenched odour. It took a moment for him to feel my presence, he was so absorbed in ogling the back ends of the young lassies still hurrying off in the distance. Eventually he turned, looking me over like I was pure and utter shite. Filthy dog shite, in fact, stuck in the cracks of the bottom of his trainers. I stared right back at the cunt. Still in half a mind about what to do next. Then, in flashes, it came to me exactly what I had to do.

The cocky prick remained silent. He stared at me and took a long, hard draw from his cigarette before throwing the remainder of it onto the already fag-littered cobbled street. Then he moved his face right up into mine.

'Whit. The fuck. Are ye. Staring at...ye wee poof?'

I casually let out the warmest, friendliest smile I could muster. Like I was just some random lost tourist who had happened upon him.

'Sorry to bother you, mate, but you don't happen to have the time on you at all, do you?'

The cocky twat looked completely confused and removed from all angry, aggressive thoughts. He'd bought it hook, line, and sinker, then glanced down at his watch. I could feel the adrenaline pumping through my veins at a million miles an hour. This was it. Do or die. I could quite easily just get the time from this cocksucker and be on my way. But even my cancer wouldn't let me duck out of this one so easily.

World. Better. Place.

He was still looking down at his watch. Even fiddling with the dial. It was an old-fashioned clunky piece of shit with Roman numerals splattered all over it. Probably a couple of euros shy of a five-euro note from some tourist marketplace in Ibiza. The dumb mutt couldn't even read the hands properly.

'Aye...et's, et's...hud oan.' He finally looked up at me, grinning and looking well-pleased with himself that he could read time. 'Ten tae two, pal.'

In a heartbeat, I unleashed my kneecap, solid as a rock, right into the cocky bastard's balls. He keeled over in even less time, cradling his crown jewels for dear life. His face turned fifty shades of pure red, his eyes squinting furiously while his mouth opened as wide as it would go. He hadn't even processed what the hell had just happened. He could only feel the pain and the shock of the moment. His mouth still opened wide. He hadn't even screamed yet. He could have been struck by lightning for all he knew. I wasn't finished yet, though. I raised my fist and, with all my almighty strength, I socked the cunt square on the jaw.

I both felt and heard the crack.

The bastard groaned as he keeled completely over onto the cold cobblestoned ground. My hand ached like a motherfucker.

I started laughing. I couldn't help myself. Not at the vicious deed of flooring this wanker, but of the floppy ridiculous state of him trying to breathe and gasp for air on the street. He looked paralysed. He looked like a fish. A paralysed fish. Exactly like the saying goes. A fish out of water. That's exactly what he looked like. A fish out of fucking water. And I couldn't stop laughing at his ridiculous puffing motions.

I knew I should've just left him like that. I'd done enough damage to him. But I kicked him in the guts, too. Just one last kick for good measure on behalf of all the women of Scotland. Or anyone who had ever endured such shite, pish, and dribble from pricks like him.

I saw movement in the pub from the corner of my eye. Could be his mates. Could be the bar staff. I wasn't hanging around to find out. I was out of there. Legging it up the Grass Market faster than you could say fanny balls, even overtaking the cute giggling schoolgirls as I ran. There was no danger of me ever looking back.

***

I made my way back to Celine's. I hung around the main entrance for ten minutes, hoping someone would enter or exit the building, thus letting me inside, but nobody did. So, I eventually bit the bullet and rang her buzzer. Surprisingly, Celine answered, buzzing me inside.

'Back again, I see?' Celine said, standing at her front doorway, waiting. Her arms were folded and she wore a cross look upon her face.

'Can I just come in for five minutes, please? Say what I have to say, then leave or stay,' I said with a grin. 'Whatever you decide once you've heard me out.'

Celine sighed and turned back inside her flat. Taking that as a homely sign of welcome, I duly followed, closing the front door behind me. I walked through the hallway, passing three more doorways, all of them opened and leading into other rooms. One was a dark red, seedy-looking bedroom with a large double bed. The second room was brighter, whiter, more virtuous and spacious, again with another double bed. The third room was a good-sized newly refurbished bathroom.

At the end of the hallway, I emerged into a spacious living room with a combined walk-in kitchen, which I guessed, once upon a time, had been two separate rooms. Everything was mostly cream in colour, from the couch and tables to the carpet and walls. I liked it. It felt very calm and soothing and tidy.

Celine headed straight for the walk-in kitchen and boiled the kettle sitting on the worktop counter beside the sink. For the moment, I couldn't take my eyes away from her perky behind. She still had that awesome sexy wiggle going on, even without the aid of high heels. Celine turned to face me, still crossing her arms while the kettle boiled.

'So, let's hear what you have to say, sneaky boy. Then you can piss off.'

Straight to the jugular yet again. I liked her style.

'Okay. I had a little think about the escort thing. I'll admit, it did take me just a wee bit by surprise at first.'

Celine raised her eyebrows, yet remained silent.

'Okay, it shocked the hell out of me. But I've had a good think about it these past few hours. And you know what? It doesn't bother me, Celine. It really doesn't. Life's too damn short for such petty and judgemental discrimination. It really is. And at the end of the day, you're just trying to make a living.'

I didn't know how I was expecting her to reply. Somewhere in between a smiling hug and a 'Get the fuck out of here' would suffice.

'Well, that's great, Liam. I'm so happy you went away and had your little mull and settled your demons. So, everything is fine again for you, yippee. You think we can be boyfriend and girlfriend now? Is that what you imagined?'

Hmm. I wanted to say yes. But maybe I'd been setting my sights a little too high.

'I don't know, Celine. I really don't. I just wanted you to know that I really don't give a flying shit about how you pay your way. I just want to spend some time with you. I want to get to know you in and out of the bedroom. And I wanted you to know that I'm fine...with everything.'

'You know, I've heard this speech once or twice before, Liam.

And you know what? It always ends in angry tears. Especially if you happen to be, say...accidentally here when a client comes around to see me. Or I have to cancel our plans because a good old regular who tips pretty bloody well wants to keep me for a few extra hours. You really think you could be impassive to all that?'

I let out the biggest beaming smile I could muster. 'Aye. I think I could.' And you know what? I really believed it.

'No, Liam! You couldn't. Trust me.' Celine turned back to the boiled kettle. 'Tea or coffee?' she asked, so relaxed and polite that I almost chuckled.

'Coffee, thanks.'

'With milk and sugar?'

'Black, one sugar,' I replied.

Celine poured coffee while continuing her rant. 'I know men, Liam. I know men better than they know themselves. And let me tell you about men. They are all the same at the end of the day. They all have the same jealous and possessive emotions. They're deceptive, disloyal. They will drop you like a hot poker for a younger, sexier, easier version of yourself, and at the drop of a hat, too, if they can get it.'

'We're not all like that! Some of us prefer older, sexier women.' I grinned.

Celine looked shocked.

'I'm kidding. Jesus! But aye, some of us can be good. Some of us can actually be loyal and faithful, believe it or not.'

'Well, when I want loyal, dependable, strong, and faithful, I'll just go and buy myself a German Shepherd. But tell me truthfully, Liam. How many other girls have you chatted up these past few weeks on the street like you did to me? Or gave your plumbing card out to for shits and giggles. Huh? Mr Loyal and Faithful?' Celine turned, handing me my coffee. She was so calm and gentle with the action that it seemed utterly bizarre when compared to her aggressive tone.

'Thanks,' I said, taking a sip of the coffee. It was good. 'Well, Celine, I'm still single as far as I can tell. I haven't made any commitments to anyone just yet. So, I can pretty much hand my card out to whomever the hell I please. And I'll eventually stop when I find someone who's worth keeping. Someone who makes me want to stop handing out my business cards to random women I happen to find attractive.'

'Well, please don't make that someone me, Liam. I already have enough problems in my life.'

'Too late,' I replied, grinning.

'I'm never going to date you, Liam. I can tell you that right now.

I'm never, ever going out with you again. And I certainly don't want you as my fucking friend. This is just a little courtesy coffee to let you have your say and get whatever you need to do or say off your chest.'

'Okay, so if you really don't want to see me again in an everyday, normal dating capacity, how about, for curiosity's sake...' I deliberately paused for my next suggestion, a card I knew I'd have to play sooner or later. I hesitated, then took a deep breath. Better to just come right out and say it without any further delay. 'How much would it cost to have you all to myself for, say, I don't know, about two or three days?'

Celine laughed hard, spitting some of her coffee onto her clean and shining laminate floor. She couldn't contain herself for the next few moments. 'What are you talking about, Liam? Are you on drugs or something? Is that where you've been these past few hours? Getting high as a bloody kite?'

'Absolutely not. So, tell me. How much to rent you out for a few days?'

I thought she might burst out laughing again, but she kept a cool face. Although she still had a glint in her eye like everything I'd said was just words from a mad man. Then she finally spoke.

'Well...much, much more...than you could ever possibly afford, mon ami, ma cherie.'

'Really! Try me.'

'Try you?' Celine set down her coffee cup and folded her arms again. I sensed that she might be enjoying this. 'Okay, just off the top of my head. For three days' work. Spending every single waking hour with you. Ten grand.'

I let out a weary glance. Damn, that was almost three times as much as I'd expected.

'Ten grand for three days' work! Jezzo, you're right, that is more than I can afford. I thought you were gonna say at least two or three.'

'Come on, Liam! Do I look like a cheap ride at the fairground to you?'

'Of course not! You're an angel,' I said so dryly that I knew it would be hard for her to tell if I was taking the piss or not. And I wasn't.

'You're so sweet, Liam. Such a charmer.'

'Look! I can only afford to give you around four or five grand now. I might end up needing the rest for other expenses. Like hotels and food and shit. But if I can't give you any more cash after the three days are up, you can have my damn work van. Even my house and all its belongings for all I care. I don't give a shit. Take it all.'

She had no idea that I rented my house and that my van was worth so much more in scrap than on the road. I did have some nice household furniture, though. Celine stared at me, totally confused.

'What is going on here, Liam? Are you taking the piss or are you actually for real here? Are you for real?'

'Just spend the next few days with me, Celine. That's all I ask. I guarantee it will be anything but dull.'

Celine edged right up close to me. Looking me dead centre in the eyes, studying my face, waiting for the punchline. For the piss-take smirk and smug grin that was never going to come.

'You are bloody serious about this, aren't you?' she finally blurted.

'Serious as fucking cancer to the brain.'

She squinted. Thinking hard. Very hard. Slowly but surely, I think she was coming around.

'And you'll give me the cash today. Right now?' she asked, still calling my bluff.

'Right now. It's all in my jacket pocket.'

Celine chuckled. 'You have four to five grand in your jacket pockets right now? You're playing with me, Liam, aren't you? You're such a funny guy. What the hell are you up to?'

I chuckled too at the ridiculousness of it all. Yet I was making it happen. This was going to happen. 'I'm not up to anything. I just want to hang out with you for a few days, that's all. Spend some quality time with a good, fun, cool girl like yourself. No strings attached. Let's see what happens. Let's see where it takes us.'

'Hmmm. Hang out, you say? And this cash you've just happened to acquire? You stole this money from whom?'

I let out a sly, winking smile.

'Just the last escort I propositioned this morning.'

Celine looked shocked. I think she believed it for a second. I actually think she didn't know what to believe anymore, to tell you the truth. This last ten minutes of conversation had been a bit above the norm.

I laughed hard. The worry on her face was priceless. 'I'm kidding, I'm kidding,' I said, easing the tension.

Celine leaned over and playfully slapped me on the shoulder.

'I just came into some money recently, that's all.'

'You'd better be kidding, mister, Jesus! Let me see it, then.'

I moved over to my jacket and pulled out the bag of cash filled with mostly hundreds and fifties.

'Take four or five grand for now. And whatever's left from the nine grand after the three days are up, you can keep that, too, if you like.'

Celine shook her head, grinning from ear to ear. 'You are absolutely fucking crazy.'

A short, comfortable silence filled the air. I didn't want to be the first to break it. I wanted her to dwell for a few moments on this plan of mine. I wanted it to sink in. After a few beats, Celine broke the silence.

'So where are we staying if we're spending the next few days together?'

'Well, if it's easier for you for things like hair, clothes, makeup and shite like that, do you mind if I just crash here?' I said. Hoping she'd go along with my suggestion without freaking out. I didn't want to go back to my place again, ever. I was done there. Plus, I was pretty sure my delightful next-door neighbours would have had the police around by now, looking for me. My next option would be checking into a nice hotel. Celine still hadn't answered my question, though, and seemed to be thinking hard. Finally, she just nodded.

'Sure, okay,' she replied, surprisingly cool with the idea. It was if she were trying to call my bluff. 'I guess that would make sense.' Celine grabbed her mobile and started dialling a number. 'I need to let my manager know first, though, okay?'

'Your manager,' I said, surprised.

Celine raised her eyebrows. 'Yes, my manager. He owns the flat.'

'You mean landlord?' I said, confused. She made it sound like she was some premier league football player.

'No, my manager. My pimp!'

Okay, so that made more sense. 'Oh, your manager. I see.' I guessed she had to answer to somebody in this line of work.

'Any more questions?'

'Yeah! I'm gonna take a shower. Do you want to come and join me when you're done?' I said, giving her a sly wink before backing away towards the bathroom.

Celine raised her eyebrows and watched me leave the room with a look of indifference, which I desperately hoped it wasn't.

Chapter 10

Ten minutes later I found myself taking the most enjoyably long and warm shower with Celine in her gorgeously oversized walk-in shower. I had my back turned away from her as she massaged my shoulders and upper back. She was good at it. Really bloody good.

'So, I take it you don't have a girlfriend or a wife hidden away somewhere?'

'I told you I was single when we met for the first time, didn't I?'

'I know, but you can't really take people at their word when you meet them for the first time in this day and age, can you? I mean, look how honest I was with you about my profession. Everyone tries to impress or make themselves look good when they meet someone new. Putting on their best face and persona. Hiding away all their dirty little secrets in the backs of their minds.'

'Well, only if they're worth impressing, I guess.'

'I suppose. So, when were you last with a girl, anyway?'

'As in, when did I last get a ride? Or when did I last have a girlfriend?'

Celine chuckled and gently slapped my bare arse. 'Your last girlfriend, cheeky boy.'

'Broke up with my last girlfriend about six months back now. Just been too busy with work and other things to find anyone else of interest or someone who'd have me.'

'Plumbing work, right?'

'That's right. You remembered. Same as your father. Unless you made that whole story up, too, about your parents.'

'No. That was all true. I only ever lie about my profession.' Celine massaged some shower gel into my upper body, then used a sponge to cleanse me down. It felt so good.

'So, you're not really an English teacher, then, or never wanted to be?'

'Of course I am. Of course I wanted to be. But the demand here, with my qualifications, wasn't too great. Plus, I still need to go back to university and finish my degree, like I told you.'

'And when do you plan on doing that?'

'I don't know.' Celine hesitated. I could sense annoyance creeping into her tone. Perhaps she felt like I was badgering her. 'I kind of fell into this line of work by accident, you know. It was meant to be a one-off to pay some bills. But the money turned out to be so bloody good and the work was...easy. I suppose I just became addicted to the quick money fix and lost sight of my main goals in life.'

I remained silent. I didn't want to ask her any more questions for the time being. I actually preferred it if she'd just open up to me on her own terms, but of course that would take time and trust.

The silence didn't last long, as Celine took her turn to question me. 'If you don't mind me asking, what are all these scars on your back and arms?'

I wondered when she'd get around to asking about them. Those dozen or so various cigarette burns on my back and upper shoulders. I still wasn't ready to talk to anyone about this yet, or ever, for that matter. I'd use the same default story/lie I always used when girls asked me about the strange burn marks upon my skin. Of course, most girls who had the luxury of seeing me naked were never that interested anyhow. Especially the one-night stands I'd never see or hear from again. Only those who were really, genuinely interested in me as a person. The contenders, as they say. They were usually the ones whose curiosity got the better of them.

'I don't really remember exactly. A childhood accident, my mother says. A firework hit me when we had a bonfire in the back garden one time. I was very young, so the memory didn't stick.'

Celine continued to scrub my back. 'Sounds like you came out very lucky. I guess it could have been a lot worse if it had hit your front side.'

Aye. Real lucky. I almost chuckled sadistically. I started thinking back to when I was a young boy. Playing outside in my mum's back garden on a gloriously hot sunshine day. Playing with toys I could barely remember.

I remembered him, though.

That sick bastard stood watching over me at the back door. Smoking away while mulling over various twisted, degrading, and sadistic acts he wanted to perform upon my young body.

'Here, ye wee prick,' I remembered him calling whenever he became board with just watching. It was always something distasteful and insulting he'd say to call me over. Never, ever by my name. He puffed the last of his cigarette, then flicked it onto the garden floor. Still burning.

'Geet yur skinny wee arse inside wee man, right noo.'

I desperately wanted to stay outside with my toys. I never wanted anything so badly in my entire life, I remembered that much. I wanted it even more than Christmas Day. But Richard's voice was just too damn powerful and overwhelming not to obey. The slightest hint of menace in his tone was enough to compel me, switching on something inside. Turning me into automatic mode. A mode that allowed me to bury deep my real feelings and emotions and that gave me the strength to turn around and face him. Although the fear of what he'd do to me if I made him wait any longer was even greater than what awaited me if I just obeyed.

Celine brought me crashing out from my brief flashback with even more questions. She'd bought my lie and thankfully drifted off onto another subject. 'So, why are you really wasting all this money on me, Liam? It can't be for the sole reason that you want to date me. I mean, you're a fit, handsome, funny guy. Surely there must be a few honeys out there who'd give you a second glance right about now, no? And all you'd need to pay for is dinner and a taxi back to your place.'

We both smiled at that. But she was right. It's not because I wanted to date you, Celine. It's because I think I'm in love with you, if the truth be known. In fact, I know I love you. From the very first moment I laid eyes on you, I just knew. But I want you to see and feel it, too, before it's too late for me. For us. Oh, Celine you captivated my very soul from the very first moment I saw you at that bus stop in Morningside. I'd do anything for you right now, Celine. I'd die for you in a heartbeat. Yet hopefully not before spending my remaining healthy time here on this planet with you. My very own 'Helen of Troy.'

That was what I wanted to say. But it was too soon for such romantic tripe. She'd just laugh it away anyhow. Maybe even call the whole thing off if I mentioned the L-word so soon. No, I needed time to work on her. She needed to get to know me first, the real me. I would tell her everything once the three days were over or the money ran out. Whichever situation presented itself first. But then again, how unfair and selfish of me would that be? To unload all my problems onto this poor girl and expect her to stand by me through the worst of it. Shite. What the fuck was I thinking? Now, the more I thought about telling her the real reason behind all this, about my terminal cancer...Christ, she didn't need that kind of shite in her life. Who the hell did? Maybe it would be a better idea to go our separate ways once our time together was up and the cash ran out. Yeah. That sounded like a much better idea. A few days of fun. A few days of making some good memories, then...adiós, amigo.

I smiled at Celine. She waited for me to answer.

'I just haven't got time to waste on chasing girls right now, you know. Especially with all the little melodramatics and twists and turns that come with it. Like when to call or text. How often to call or text. When to make your move. I just don't have the time or patience right now for any of it. But I like you, Celine. I had a good time with you last week there. I also respect your situation and your chosen profession, immensely. Like I said, I recently came into some money which I wanted to get rid of before...before I go away.'

'Go away?' Celine said curiously.

I'd nearly come clean without meaning to. Now I had to think fast. 'Yeah. I'm leaving. I have...I have an uncle in New Zealand. I was thinking about starting fresh over there in a month or two. Yeah, that's the plan.'

'Very nice. I've heard some good things about New Zealand. Scotland with sunshine, they say.'

'Yeah.' I smiled. 'That's what they say. So, this arrangement suits me just fine. A beautiful, sexy young lassie by my side for the next few days, one who doesn't play games. Throw in some good fun, banter, and naughty nookie on tap whenever I want it. It'll be like I've died and gone to heaven.'

'So, what about when the three days are over? Aren't you just going to be right back at square one again?'

'No, not really.'

'No! Why not? I'm still going to be an escort, Liam. I'm still not going to want a boyfriend.'

I couldn't help but let out a sly smirk. 'Because I'm pretty sure you will have fallen deeply and madly in love with me by then,' I joked.

Celine chuckled and playfully slapped me with the sponge. 'You're so full of yourself, aren't you, mister?'

I turned to face Celine. I pulled her closer so that we were both underneath the spray of warm shower water. Face to face, I stared right into her eyes, the windows to her soul. Her naked body looked so good as the water dripped and glistened down her soft, pale skin. Her warm body and round, firm breasts felt good against me. I felt myself stir. Then, in no time, I had a semi brushing against her thighs.

'You know, Celine. You ask far too many questions for a second date. It's like you want to be my bloody girlfriend already.'

Celine looked at me seductively. 'Comes with the job, I'm afraid! Plus, I'm making sure you get your money's worth.'

'You're still talking too much.'

'So make me shut up, then.'

I grabbed Celine firmly by her peachy bum cheeks. She squealed playfully. I lifted her off her feet. She squealed even louder, holding onto me for dear life. She wrapped her legs around my waist and her arms around my neck. I was fully erect, throbbing against her.

***

We started making passionate love in the shower and somehow ended up against the windowsill of Celine's bedroom. The brighter bedroom, not the seedy-looking punter bedroom opposite. I had no idea in the slightest how we'd ended up there in the heat of our passion. It must have been via every other room and piece of furniture in the apartment. I remembered taking her over the bathroom sink, the kitchen worktop, upon the living room floor, over the couch, in the hallway, against the front door. I couldn't even remember towelling myself down from the shower. But we weren't wet with shower water for very long. When we both finally came together for the second time, with Celine against that window ledge, I collapsed, still holding her in my arms, back onto her king-size bed, which we hadn't been anywhere near during our ravenous, round-the-house romp.

Celine rolled off my sweat-soaked body and onto her back. We lay together, facing the ceiling, utterly spent, just like our first adventure back at my place over a week past. Celine finally sat up and grabbed a packet of cigarettes, a lighter, and an ashtray from her bedside table. She lit one, then lay back down beside me and placed the ashtray by her side.

'Jesus Christ! I've never had so much fun standing up before in my entire life,' I said, still a little breathless.

Celine smiled warmly before stroking my stomach. 'It was good, Liam. You were really good.'

'Well I can't take all the credit, you know. I did have some great inspiration there to help me along the way.'

We paused for a few beats, both of us still trying to regain some control over our breathing.

'Hey! Is Celine your real name, by the way?'

Celine turned to me with a funny look. She blew some smoke in my face. 'Of course it is.'

'Oh! I just assumed all you...' I paused. I didn't want to offend her with the rest of that sentence.

'All us what?' Celine interrupted, feigning offence. Or at least I hoped she was.

'All you sex industry workers. Strippers, escorts, glamour models, porn stars. I just thought you all made up different names for your work, that's all. No offence like.'

Celine fell silent. She continued to smoke her cigarette while glancing at the ceiling. I really did enjoy joking around with her and winding her up.

'So,' I continued, 'if we were to stop our little arrangement right this very second, how much do you think our wee roll in the hay here would have cost me already?'

'Oh, Liam, you wild stallion, you! Why, I would have given you that one on the house.'

'Really! For real?' I replied, thinking she was deadly serious. Celine chuckled.

'This really is your first time with an escort, no?'

'How could you tell?'

Celine said nothing. She smoked some more of her cigarette, then sat up and stubbed it out. 'So, what do you wish to do now? Are you hungry?'

'Maybe a wee bit peckish, aye.'

'Do you want me to make some food for us? Or will we eat out in town somewhere?'

I didn't reply right away. I wanted to ask her something else that had been playing on my mind for quite a while. Something which interested me more than food.

'What have you always wanted to do?'

Celine glanced at me, confused. Still thinking about her food venture, no doubt. 'What?'

'I mean, if you could do anything right now. Anything at all this very evening. What would it be? What would you do?'

'Jesus Christ, Liam. I don't know the answer to that.'

'Come on! Just think of one thing. Tell me.'

'I don't know. Honestly, I don't.'

'There must be something simple you always wanted to do or try. Even some sexy, sordid little fantasy. Come on, tell me. In fact, it doesn't even need to be sexual.'

Celine still wouldn't answer. I think she knew the answer or had a rough idea, but deliberately kept stump. So, I jumped on her. I began tickling it out of her like a man possessed. She screamed hysterically, mixed with fits of laughter. She begged for me to stop.

'Okay, okay! I'll tell you! I'll tell you! Please just stop. Please. Just. Stop.'

I stopped, but remained on top of her. Holding her down. I waited for her to gather her breath and regain her composure.

'Okay, okay. I guess...one crazy fantasy I've always had was to dress up like a nun and make out with a really sexy hot priest inside a church. Or perhaps to get it on really hot and passionately inside the confession box.'

I couldn't stop myself from chuckling. I released my grip on Celine and turned back onto my side.

'Jesus Christ, Celine! Where do you come up with this shit? That is some really kinky-arse shite right there, no?'

Celine rolled over to face me. She had a new, excited glint in her eye.

'Well, you put me on the spot and it was the first thing that came to me.'

Suddenly, a thought occurred to me. I immediately jumped out of bed and searched all over the bedroom for any signs of my clothing. Celine stared at me curiously like I'd been possessed. Shite. I realised all my clothes were still in the bathroom.

'What are you doing?'

'I need to get dressed.'

'Why so fast? Where are you going?'

'I need to get my van and then we're going to take a wee drive.'

'Where's your van?'

'I left it over on the Dumbie-dykes estate.'

'You're a brave one. But we can just take my car if you like.'

'Na, let's take mine. I need to move it anyhow. If it's still in one piece, that is,' I half-joked. I left Celine in the bedroom and went to get changed.

***

When I reached Viewcraig Gardens and saw what had become of my van, my heart sank to the pit of my stomach. All the windows had been smashed in—front, sides, and back. The four tyres had been slashed to smithereens. The white paintwork all over the bonnet had been scratched and graffitied to hell and then some. The back door was slightly open, too. Upon closer inspection, I could see the doors had been forced, as the seals around the edges were all bent. I took a sneaky peak inside. Most of my tools had been stolen.

Mother-fucking jakey, ned, bastard, pikey, cunt ye.

'Buy it from ye noo pal, aye?' Those words echoed through my head like they'd been bellowed through a deep, dark, and silent Highland valley at the stroke of midnight.

I took a deep breath, let out a deep sigh, then realised I wasn't really that upset at all. I was going to get rid of the van eventually, anyhow. My tools...I didn't think I'd ever have used them again, to tell you the truth. I just wished I had something to drive around for the next few days, that was all. But not to worry. Celine's wheels it was. But first I wanted to pay my little jakey friend over there at number nine a wee visit. Just to see if he might still be interested in taking the vehicle off my hands and all. Fifty quid I'm sure he said, no?

I glanced over at his flat, number nine. The curtains were drawn but the lights were on. First I got into my van and made sure it was still running. I switched on the engine. Still ticking over. Still driveable even with the slashed tyres. Nice. I didn't have very far to drive anyway. I walked over to jakey central's flat and rattled the door with my fist. I heard movement inside. Thankfully, it was the jakey ned fuck who answered, with a can of special lager in hand, too, and not any of his brat bairns.

'Whits aw this bangin noise, man? Whits pure goan oan likes?'

'Sorry, mate. Did I wake you from your power nap slumber after a long, hard day at the benefits office, aye?'

He looked very confused. I don't even think he recognised me.

'Whit office ye talkin aboot, pal? Whae the fuck are ye like? And whit the fuck ye daen oan ma property, pal?'

Behind him in the hallway I clocked one of my tool bags. Fucking jakey bastard. Did this wido have no shame or tact?

'I'm here regarding our conversation from earlier this morning, mate. The one where you were interested in buying my van out there.'

The jakey fuck squinted his eyes, then stared over at my train wreck of a vehicle in the parking bay. He smiled that toothless ugly wee grin of his.

'Oh aye. That heap uv shite ower thir, aye. Ah wudnae gie ye ten pence fur that noo, pal. Haw haw haw,' he replied, chuckling away.

'Actually, mate. That's still a pretty fair price. You can have it for nowt if you want. I'm sure you could use it as a storage cupboard or perhaps even a spare bedroom for one of your wee brats.'

'Whit? Ye mean keep et en ma hoose?' he replied, even more confused and oblivious to the fact that I'd just insulted both him and his kids.

'Aye, in your hoose, man,' I said as cheerfully as I could. 'Just hold on and I'll bring it round for you, okay? No extra charge.'

'Whit ye talkin aboot? Et es roond. Ye cannae git it ne mere roond tae ma hoose than et awready es, pal.'

'It's no bother, son,' I said, turning to walk back towards my van. 'I'll bring it right on up to the door for you. No problem.' I stopped and turned back, my conscience niggling away at me. 'Is the rest of your family in the now by the way? Any kids or, heaven forbid, your fucking nedette of a wife?'

'Whit the fuck es ma burd and weans goat tae dae wi ye likes? Ye ken ma missus or sutton likes, huh?'

'No, mate. I don't know her. But is she in?'

'Naw! They're naw fuckin ins likes.'

'And your bairns?'

I could see his eyes rolling away as he thought furiously about why the hell I was asking such questions.

'The bairns are wi thir grandparents the night cunty baws. Whit the fuck es et aw tae dae wi ye like?'

'Awesome, pal,' I replied, climbing into my van. I could proceed with my plan. I started the engine and reversed out of the parking space. I drove all the way to the end of Viewcraig Gardens and spun the van around one-hundred-and-eighty degrees. It wasn't as hard to drive with four flat tyres as I thought it would be. The jakey cunt was still standing at his doorway grinning, watching, while sipping at his can of beer. I swallowed my fears and doubts, then just got on with it and drove, faster and faster towards number nine.

The jakey swine remained standing at the doorway, looking on obliviously at what the hell was happening right in front of him. I was up to forty, fifty miles an hour. I could hear the wheel trims and bearings scrapping off the concrete below. I could smell the burning rubber seeping in through the vents. The van was shaking like an old washing machine on its final wash. It felt like it was going to take off, up into the skies at any second. It flew up and over the curb, straight for the front door of number nine and towards that thieving gypsy jakey bastard still standing at the door like the demented dog he was.

Seconds before impact, the stupid prick finally gathered his senses and screamed. Terror seized his frozen senses when he realised this wasn't a hallucination from his recent drug-fuelled dinner. But instead of diving out of the way, the stupid fanny ran back into his flat and closed his front door. I would have laughed at his ridiculous antics if I hadn't been so busy opening the front driver's door and flinging myself out onto the front lawn shortly before impact.

As I rolled onto the ground, I heard the crunching, thunderous crash as the whole vehicle crashed through the front door, taking out half the front brick walls of the ned's flat with it. Most of the front side of the apartment crumbled to dust. Only the back side of the van stuck out from where the front door and supporting walls had been. From the demolished hallway radiator, dirty water pished out from all angles.

A few dozen people from the surrounding flats above quickly emerged onto their balconies to glance down at the bomb site below.

I stood to my feet and brushed myself off. I was about to walk away when I spied a full crate of beer lying behind the fallen right-hand wall where my van was now parked. It looked like it used to be some kind of storage cupboard. I stepped through the rubble and picked up the crate. I saw my drill box lying underneath a nearby table. Then the ned crawled out from a small opening in the rubble.

'The van's all yours now, mate. And thanks for the beer, pal,' I said with a wink and smile.

The ned continued to struggle up onto his feet. 'Whit the fuck did ye dae tae ma hoose, man? Ye fuckin radge, ye? Ma missus is gonnae go well mental noo man when she sees thus. That es me pure in her bad books noo like.'

I left it at that and went on my merry way. Aye, I thought, Celine's car it is, then.

Chapter 11

I drove through the one-way back streets of the Old Town in Celine's beat-up silver Ford Escort. For a working girl, she certainly didn't like to spoil herself or splash the cash on her modes of transport, that's for sure.

'She does me okay,' Celine said. 'What do I need a fancy car for, living in the middle of Edinburgh? I hardly use her, anyway. Shopping trips and days off spent driving around Scotland when I get the time.'

I drove up Blackfriars Street for the second time, then up onto the Mile. Left onto South Bridge. Then sharp right past the Tron and down Blair Street. I could swear to Christ I had seen a fancy dress shop around here somewhere once upon a time.

'What are you looking for, anyway? There's no churches around here,' smirked Celine.

I remained silent. I didn't want to ruin the surprise. At the bottom of Blair Street, we passed the blatant standout sauna on our left. I didn't think anything of it until Celine pointed it out. 'My manager owns this sauna.'

'Really?' I said curiously. Most Edinburgh locals were quite aware of Edinburgh's nudge-nudge, wink-wink, knocking shop saunas. I was pretty damn sure the majority of the male population had been in for a sly wee pumpathon, too, at least once in their lives.

'In fact, he owns quite a few of the saunas around Edinburgh and Glasgow, so I'm told. Casinos, too. Nightclubs, bars, restaurants. Strip bars. Drug factories.'

I made a right turn onto the Cowgate and drove towards the Grass Market. 'Nice, friendly, family-oriented, down-to-earth guy then, aye?'

'You're joking, yes? I've met him only once. I deal more with his right-hand man, Petrov. He's the one who runs the saunas and strip clubs in Edinburgh.'

'Petrov,' I said with a slight chuckle. 'That's not a very Scottish name.'

'Brad's Scottish. But most of his thugs, drug dealers, and pimps who hang around the saunas are from pretty much all over the place. Especially Eastern Europeans, and some Russians, too. They make good contacts for him in bringing more women over here and sticking them straight into flats and saunas around the country.'

'So, you've worked in those saunas, too, then?'

'When I first started, yes. But only for about a week. Petrov said that with my looks and physique I could be making better money working my own flat and charging a couple of hundred pounds an hour rather than fifty or sixty. Or even just escorting rich businessmen around town. I didn't believe him at first, since I'd never done this line of work before. But both he and Brad have a lot of upmarket clients, and I mean la crème de la crème. Politicians, judges, musicians, oil barons. You name it. I've never made so much money in such a short space of time and I'm not even sleeping with most of them. And I'm not saying my job is a good and moral one. Just, as far as making money goes, it can become quite addictive.'

'I'm surprised no one has actually closed these knocking shops yet,' I said, thinking out loud. Knowing that the Scottish government only tolerates these places because what's the alternative? Women walking the city streets at night with zero protection from the random men who pick them up.

'The word is that Brad has so many police, judges, and politicians in his back pocket that they just turn a blind eye. He has a lot of dirt on a lot of important people in this country. Or so I've heard. He's pretty much untouchable.'

'I've never heard of him. This Brad guy. What's his second name?'

'He doesn't have one. Or nobody could ever tell me. He's known as Brad to everyone, and that's about it. He keeps a very low profile. Yet lives like a king.'

'Was that him who you were on the phone with earlier?'

'No, I was phoning Petrov. He's the one who deals with my clients.'

'He's okay with you taking a few days off then, aye?'

'As long as he gets his share of the money at the end of my working week. He doesn't give a shit what I do.'

'But you have a good relationship with him, though? I mean, you're not forced to do anything you don't want to do?'

'Of course not, sweetie. I'm not one of his illegals he can just lock away and bring out again whenever he damn well pleases. At the end of the day, I'm legal here, and I'm my own boss.'

I smiled at that, but it was more just to humour Celine. I mean, the more she talked about these dodgy-sounding men she worked for, the more I started to get a really bad feeling about this dark and crazy underground world she'd gotten herself into. A world I had absolutely no idea existed in bonnie Scotland until now. And when it came down to the bare knuckles of it, was she really her own boss, like she truly believed herself to be? Or did these people she worked for just let her believe it to keep her comfortable? To keep her in line.

'You could just stop though, yeah?'

'What do you mean? Stop what?'

'Stop working. Like, if you wanted to just walk away from the whole escort thing tomorrow. You could just leave whenever you wanted? No questions. No ties.'

Celine hesitated before letting out a wry smile. 'Yes, I can leave. No questions. For sure.'

She didn't sound too convincing and turned to glance out the window at the passing gloomy Cowgate scenery. I was about to say something else when right at that very moment we drove out of the Cowgate and into the Grass Market. I saw exactly what I'd been looking for. My train of thought got back on track.

'Bingo,' I said, pulling into the next available parking bay. It was after 6.30, so single yellows were fair game to everyone in the city. I got out of the car.

'Where are you going?'

'It's a surprise, trust me. Stay here. I'll be back in five.'

I closed the door and made my way towards a wee, blink-and-you'd-miss-it fancy dress shop. Two pubs sat either side of it, which was the story of the Grass Market. Pub, shop, pub, shop, pub, pub, pub, restaurant, pub, shop.

The shop was closed, being after 6.00 pm. I made my way down through a narrow wee alleyway squeezed in beside the pub next door and the shop. I climbed over an ancient stone wall and jumped down onto the other side. I approached the back end of the shop. The sturdy door was made entirely of thick oak, so I moved towards the small window and tried to open it. It wouldn't budge. Looking down beside the outside drainage pipe, I noticed a loose metal grate, about the size of a DVD player. I picked it up and carefully smashed through the glass window. Easy-peasey. No alarm sounded, either. When I had scraped all the glass away from the edges, I climbed on in.

***

Ten minutes later, I made my way back to the car. I was getting more than my fair share of funny looks from various people walking up and down the Grass Market, but I took no notice. I could see Celine sitting in the passenger seat, keeping herself busy by filing her nails. I opened the door and climbed back in. Celine didn't look up right away. Still busy with her nails.

'Did you find what you were—.' She glanced over, then burst into a fit of giggles. 'Jesus Christ, Liam! What the hell are you wearing?' Celine covered her mouth, trying desperately to stop her laughter.

I was dressed in a full-scale Catholic priest outfit. Full-length black cassock with matching shirt, collar, and a black skull cap. Fake gold and silver chains with crosses around my neck. I stared at Celine with pure and utter seriousness, getting fully into my role.

'Please do not take the Lord's name in vain with me, my child. I bless you and absolve you of all your sins. Amen.' I made the sign of the cross in mid-air for good measure.

Celine continued to laugh, more in disbelief at my transformation than anything else. 'Oh my God! You are crazy, Liam. Really freaking crazy.'

I handed Celine a large plastic bag I'd brought into the car with me. 'Okay, my wee saucy Sister of Mercy! Shut the hell up and put this on.'

Celine looked confused as she took the bag. 'Please tell me this isn't...what I think it is...'

I couldn't for the life of me wipe the smug grin off my face when Celine peeked into that bag. She let out the most hysterical shriek of excitement I'd ever heard.

***

Fifteen minutes later, I pulled up outside a large church close to the Meadows. I thought I'd stop at this one since there happened to be quite a few cars parked outside. I guessed a Mass was already in process. I switched off the engine and turned to Celine, who sat wearing a convincing yet very, very sexy nun's outfit, complete with stockings and suspenders. Celine took a few moments to stare up in awe at the large, imposing church building directly in front of us.

'Liam! I don't care how much money you're paying me. There is no way on God's green earth that I am having sex with you inside that church, okay? NO WAY!'

'Jesus Christ, Celine! Who said anything about copulating on holy sacred territory, here? I do have some morals, you know. We're just here to have some fun and join in the service, that's all. Oh, and have a wee cheeky fun pray about, too, of course,' I said, winking.

We exited the car. I took Celine by the hand and led her through the small graveyard and up to the church. Some of the graves and tombs looked pretty impressive, and more importantly, very secluded. An ideal place, I imagined, for some sordid outdoors tomfoolery in the darketh of night.

'I'm not shagging you inside that graveyard, either. Do you hear me? No way,' Celine said, like she'd been reading my mind.

'Not even against that gorgeous-looking gothic tomb over there?' I teased. 'It would be something to tick off the bucket list though, no?'

Celine gave me an evil stare.

'Oh, Sister, have mercy! I'm just teasing.'

We approached the church. Celine paused suddenly at the main door before finally entering. She looked nervous. It was a big change, as she always seemed so strong-minded and self-confident.

'I cannot believe I'm actually doing this, Liam. I need to have my bloody head examined,' she said as her French accent strangely grew stronger.

'Hey. This was your idea, sweet cheeks. And WOW, by the way! Can I just say you look absolutely stunning in that outfit in this light?'

I could see Celine's eyes glowing with that compliment. 'Thank you. You actually look pretty damn hot and ravishing there yourself, Monsieur Minister.'

'Why, thank you for the compliment, my saucy and sinister-looking devil sister.'

'Oh, my pleasure, Father. Mon plasir.'

We entered the church. It looked well over half full, with all kinds of evening worshippers, old and young, sitting inside. This was going to be a lot of fun. I had planned to just sit at the back of the church for a wee while, you know. Listening to the sermon and fooling around with Celine. But now I was actually there in the moment. Fuck it. I had another idea. My adrenaline and confidence were skyrocketing. I wanted to attempt something a bit more memorable, risky, and adventurous. I would just wing it from here on in.

I let go of Celine's hand and urged her to take my arm instead. We made our way down the main aisle of the church towards the altar from where the Irish-accented priest conducted his sermon. As we walked towards the front of the church, I could feel and see from the corner of my eye more and more worshippers turning their attention upon us. Glancing with both confusion and curiosity at the odd priest and the sexy, curvaceous nun.

The real priest hadn't seen us yet and kept reading his boring, monotonous words. His voice sounded dull and mundane, like he didn't have his heart and soul in it anymore. I'd been here only a few seconds and already I wanted to stick my finger into my eye and swirl it around a bit from listening to the droning bastard. That's the problem with these churches nowadays. Too much textbook worshiping and not enough spontaneous and fun improvisation and lively interaction with the audience.

'Oh my God, Liam! Everyone in here is looking at us right now,' whispered Celine.

Just in front of us on the left, I noticed a young teen putting down his small handheld games console when another young teen beside him began nudging him hard to look up at this bizarre couple moving towards them. They couldn't take their eyes off Celine's sexy stockings, that's for sure.

I felt Celine grip my arm even tighter. 'I thought we were just going to sit down for a bit at the back, Liam?'

'Be strong, my child. You are in the arms of the Lord now,' I replied, slipping back into character.

When we reached the altar, the Irish preacher finally noticed us. He stopped his preaching immediately to glare over at us...well, more so Celine...in utter disbelief and pure, unadulterated shock. He fell absolutely speechless, though I could hear nonstop chattering and gassing from almost the entire congregation behind us.

I stepped farther up onto the altar with Celine. This daring act of movement into forbidden territory finally broke the priest's stunned silence. 'What in God's name is the meaning of this? How dare you interrupt my service! What the hell is going on here?'

'Forgive me, Father!' I replied loudly, so the rest of the church could hear me. 'This will take only a minute.'

Sensing the rage in the real priest's eyes, I knew we'd be lucky if he'd give us two seconds before bringing down the wrath of God upon us. So, I turned as quickly as I could to address the rest of the church.

'For this sister standing here before you now...' I pointed blatantly at Celine. 'IS A SINNER.'

Celine froze with all eyes upon her, trying to smile as politely and innocently as she could.

'I bring this foul and polluted beast upon you today so that you can all join together with me in harmony and matrimony and help suck out the very taste of sin and lust and impure thoughts infesting deep, deep inside this...this...' I gave the most wicked grin. 'This most damn fine and sexy impure creature I have ever laid eyes upon.'

I could see the priest had had enough of this charade. He shouted down to one of the altar boys who sat with a row of five other boys in the front.

'Patrick! PATRICK! Call the police, ma boy. Call the bloody police right now. Right this very second.'

The young altar boy didn't know which way to look or what the hell to do. He was clearly enjoying the show and reluctantly pulled out his mobile phone. Shit, I had to be quick.

'So, yes, my fellow sheep. I mean, worshippers. Act with your prayers and help me suck, suck it out, right out of her very dirty and polluted soul,' I continued, immersing myself completely into the spirit of this preaching shite lark.

'I'd like to suck something out of her,' commented one of the young altar boys at the front. An older woman behind, who I assumed to be his mother, clipped him hard around the ear. Some more children behind began giggling at this new drama unfolding.

The priest remained where he was, in a state of half-shock limbo. With little more time to spare, I pulled Celine hard towards me, into a very passionate embrace indeed. I heard a loud gasp of anticipation from the surrounding congregation. I looked deep and soulfully into Celine's eyes for another few heartbeats before sticking my tongue deep inside her mouth making out with her like two Highland cows on Valentine's Day, 'Gangnam style.' All tongues mixed with plenty of affectionate lust. It was a shockingly humorous sight, I imagined. Nobody knew which way to turn. Most, I could feel, were just holding their breaths, wondering if this was some kind of promotion for a local fringe production show in town. But the fringe festival had been over for months.

When I finished kissing Celine, I turned back to the crowd. The younger lot seemed to be smiling, chuckling aloud and enjoying the whole shebang. The older crowd, which seemed to be the overwhelming majority of people inside the church, looked as if I'd broken into each and every one of their houses and took a big stinking dump right in the middle of their brand-new living room rugs. They were absolutely mortified. The mother of the two teens had even covered her sons' eyes while Patrick, the altar boy, still hadn't dialled any numbers on his phone.

***

Celine and I ran from the church, hand in hand and laughing like a pair of crazy loons. What a rush. We made our way back through the graveyard and over towards the car. We were chased outside by a small crowd of the older churchgoers, headed by the enraged Irish priest frothing at the mouth. He waved a huge metal chalice in the air like he was conducting a witch-hunt in the Dark Ages.

Halfway through the graveyard, the priest stopped, completely out of breath. 'Aye! Run, you pair of Satan's fookin perverts, ye. And don't come fookin back, ya hear! Ya pair o mental fookin Egits, ye.'

Still laughing outrageously, Celine and I dove into her car and drove away as quickly as possible. As we headed back into town, we were still laughing and chuckling away uncontrollably.

'Oh my God, Liam! I am so wet right now with all this excitement.'

'You're wet! I almost peed my pants when that real priest came at us with his holy chalice. Nearly took my head clean off, the radge.'

'Not very Christian-like, was he?'

We were still giggling when we reached Lothian Road.

'You know, I honestly didn't think you'd go through with it, but wow...you made my fantasy come true, Liam. Thank you.' Celine reached over and kissed me long and hard upon the cheek.

We eventually parked down a side street just off Lothian Road. We were both hungry and wanted to grab some food and I knew a great wee Italian restaurant just around the corner. Still dressed in our convincing priest and nun outfits, we strode down Lothian Road, hand in hand, looking like we didn't have a care in the world. Both of us ignoring and lapping up the string of funny looks from our fellow pedestrians.

Entering the restaurant, we waited to be seated. Dressed like the higher-ranking members of the cloth we were pretending to be, I knew we would either be lynched by the Italian management or treated like the Pope himself. Thankfully it turned out to be more of the latter. And it was the manager, not the waiter, who came over to greet us.

'Hello, Father, Sister! And what brings you into my fine little establishment this evening?'

'Well...' I replied in my best upper-class English accent, 'my good Italian Catholic brother. The sister and I, we are visiting from out of town. Canterbury, to be precise. We're just taking in some of the local parishes, as one does with his free time and what have you.'

The manager looked very pleased. He was still smiling, so he must have been buying my nonsense patter. 'Well, Father, you will be made very welcome here in the best Italian restaurant in the whole of Edinburgh.'

When the manager turned away to check the seating area, I couldn't resist giving Celine a sly wink and a cheeky pinch on her backside.

'Well, thank you very much, my son. And bless you. May your family live long, fruitful lives and stay healthy for eternity'

'Thank you, Father. Thank you,' the manager said, turning back. 'Now, if you would follow me. I will place you at the best table in the house.'

We sat down. The manager hovered over us while beckoning

one of his waiters to take our drinks order.

'Would you like some drinks before you order?'

'Yes, we would. We really need it.' Celine said anxiously. 'A vodka coke would be awesome right about now. In fact, make it a double.'

The manager let out a curious stare before turning to me for approval.

'When in Rome, aeh? Oh, and just a beer for me, old chap. Or a pint of Guinness if you have it?'

The manager nodded to the waiter, who fluttered off to get our drinks.

'Just as well it's not Easter or it would be tap water all round, eh,' I joked.

I studied the menu, but was having a hard time deciding what to order. I could sense Celine struggling too.

'Any thoughts?' I asked her.

'Jesus, Liam. Everything on here looks so bloody good.'

I stared at the manager, taking in his name tag. Roberto. 'Roberto, my good man. Everything on here looks delightful. But tell me? Would it be possible to have, say...a little bit of everything?'

Roberto stared at me like I'd spoken to him in pure Scottish Gaelic. 'A little bit of...everything?'

'Si! A little bit of everything, Signor?' I threw a roll of fifties onto the table. His eyes glazed when he saw them.

'Yes! Si! I am sure...we could arrange...this for you, Father. And for you, Sister?'

'Oh, I'll have the same, thank you. But I'll just nibble on the priest's little bits and pieces when they arrive. Self-service buffet style, you know.'

I couldn't help but give Celine a very saucy look. The manager, too.

Celine chuckled. 'Oh, you know what I mean.'

Over the course of the next hour, an entourage of waiters and waitresses brought small samples of nearly every single damn dish on the menu. Everything tasted so deliciously fine that we just couldn't stop eating. And the six deserts on offer too. Mmm-mmm! Just exquisite.

Celine wasn't really in the mood for dessert and sipped away at a simple cup of delicious hot chocolate. 'You are just a fat bastard at heart, aren't you Liam? Where do you put it all?'

I couldn't reply, as I was far too busy filling my mouth with half a cheesecake and a spoonful of mint ice cream.

After another few drinks and finally squaring up the bill, which

Roberto was kind enough to discount by a good bit, being quite the religious man himself, Celine and I went for a nice wee stroll farther down Lothian Road towards the Castle and Princes Street gardens. At one point, I attempted to climb onto Celine's back, egging her on to give me an overdue piggyback since I'd given her one the last time we were out gallivanting around the Old Town. Celine was too busy laughing and giggling away to take any of my attempts seriously.

'Are you trying to jump me or hump me there, Father?'

I was about to make one more half-drunken attempt to board her when the lights and sounds coming from the approaching HMV picture house caught my eye. Seemed like they were having some kind of disco-themed party night themselves. Without flinching, I threw Celine over my shoulder to her playful screaming protests, revealing even more of her sexy stockings underneath her nun outfit. We then headed for the nightclub entrance. The bouncer seemed unusually cheerful for Edinburgh and let us in, no bother. Perhaps he was religious too.

For the next few hours we hardly left the dance floor. Busting moves like there was no tomorrow and dancing like we knew what the hell we were doing for most of our time there. Our fellow clubbers loved our fancy moves and outfits. Some even asked to pose for pictures with the priest and nun dancing couple. I'm pretty sure we ended up on a couple hundred Facebook newsreels that night.

Now, I don't condone drinking and driving, but we had to get home somehow. I felt only partially drunk, so in my book that was okay. We stuck the radio on full blast and sang cheerfully along to the Queen song rocking out from the speakers. Celine seemed a little more drunk than I was, so her singing sounded more annoyingly loud.

'That was absolutely wicked, Liam. Thank you so much for such a fun and awesome night out. Thank you.'

I'd never heard Celine speaking so sincerely, and it was probably just the drink talking, but I couldn't stop myself from turning to her and smiling warmly. I really had fallen head over heels in love with this girl. But when would it ever be the best time to confess that? 'Never' was the kindest and most brutally realistic answer.

Celine gazed back at me with an almost genuine and affectionate look of her own. Nevertheless, it was still contaminated by a drunken glow. I couldn't stop staring at her lips. Her beautiful and delicious, red luscious lips. I wanted to kiss her right then and there. So I did. I brought the car to a thunderous screeching halt right in the middle of the damn street. I pulled

Celine hard towards me, then kissed her with all the ferocious passion flooding through the fiery veins of my lonely soul.

Behind us I could sense two or three cars piling up behind us. One in particular was right up our arses. The bastard wouldn't stop honking away on his horn like it was some kind of competition. Some of the cars at the back just did the sensible thing and eased on around us. But that one particular twat right behind couldn't even do that simple task. He just kept honking and honking away like it was his goddamn given right to be an arsehole. I ignored the fucker and continued to enjoy my moment with Celine, kissing her, caressing her, holding her, almost oblivious to everything going on in the world outside.

The honking finally stopped. I assumed the irate knob jockey driver was about to drive around us. Then I heard his car door slam and the sound of his angry footsteps fast approaching. I was still kissing Celine, lost in my own wee world of magical glee when the baw-jawed fucker started screaming at us from my window. It appeared as though his perfect little magical world had suddenly come to an abrupt end, solely by the action of my bringing our vehicle to a halt right in front of his.

'OIHHH! OIHHH!' he screamed at the top of his lungs. Pure psychotic like.

Celine and I broke away from our passionate embrace and glanced up at the raging lunatic. Now that he had our attention, he engaged us with his little rant, like either of us gave a flying hoot.

'WHIT THE FUCK R YE TAE FUCKERS PLAYIN AT, EHHH? AH MEAN, WHIT THE FUCK! FUUUUCCCKKK!'

I wound down my window and stared at the raging bull for a few seconds. Celine turned to me, waiting for me to say something.

'WELL, ANSWER ME THEN, YE FUCKIN PAIR A CUNTS, YE! FUCKIN ANSWER ME, HUH!' the lunatic continued.

I casually turned to Celine with a cheeky smile. 'I think they let the animals get way too close to the cars at this zoo, darling.'

'YE FUCKIN ARROGANT WEE SHITE BAG, YE.'

I turned back to face the angry little man at the window. 'Hey, hey, hey! Listen, mate, and take a chill pill, okay? We just stopped for two minutes, that's all. All in the name of love. And if you'd only take a look around, you'll see that it's a reasonably wide road out there.' I gave Celine another wink before addressing the loon again. 'Just take some deep, deep breaths, man, and chill the fuck out, okay?'

'CHILL, AYE? FUCKIN CHILL AYE, YE CUNT? FUCKIN CHILL! MOVE YER FUCKIN CAR BEFORE AH RAM YE AUF THE FUCKIN ROAD, YE SMARMY WEE FUCK, YE.'

'Mate, please! There's a lady of the cloth present. Watch your language, okay?'

'MOVE YER FUCKIN CAAAAARRRR,' the angry man spat and sprayed before taking a few hard kicks at my driver's door, denting it pretty badly.

Celine, in her mildly drunken state, was about to shout at him to stop, but I interrupted.

'Hey mate, listen, LISTEN!'

The radge stopped and stared insanely back at me.

'Is that your car behind us, aye?'

'Aye! Et fuckin es, aye.'

In the blink of an eye I slammed our car into reverse and thundered into the front of his, smashing the entire front end of his bonnet. For a second I thought his eyes were going to pop out of their sockets. Then he made an insane lunge for me, right through the window.

'YA BASTARD!'

I was far too quick for the mentalist. Slamming the stick into first gear, I sped off like the Starship Enterprise entering warp speed.

'I don't think you should've done that Liam,' said Celine, staring back at the crazy man. I watched him through the mirror, scrambling back into his car like he had a chance of catching up with us. But in no time, he was speeding right behind. Shite. His car was still driveable.

'Bloody drivers in this country, aeh?' I said. 'They get all wound up over the most trivial things.'

Celine remained silent. She looked worried. Dare I say stressed as she glanced out the back window every few seconds.

'I'll pay for the damage to your car, of course, don't worry,' I replied, reassuring her.

Celine couldn't take her eyes off the oncoming mad man. 'Liam! He's coming and fast.'

'No worries, lass.'

I sped up to around sixty miles an hour in a thirty zone, heading in the direction of Meadowbank. I soon found myself whizzing past other cars on the road. Jumping red lights, then whizzing through a dirty speed camera. Fuck, I hated those things just as much as those bloody parasite traffic wardens.

'Note to oneself. Blow up and destroy a couple of speed cameras for shits and giggles.'

'What was that?' Celine asked, turning to face me.

'Oh, nothing! Just mumbling more rubbish to myself.'

I checked my mirrors again and saw the cunt right behind us. Jesus Christ, he wasn't going to let this one go, was he? He bashed our back end hard. I was of two minds about slamming on the breaks and letting the prick smash right into the back of me. I would have done it too if it weren't for Celine sitting right beside me.

'I think this lunatic is going to try and run us off the road, Liam. He's not going to stop.'

I continued to dart in and out of the light traffic. I ran through another set of red lights, utterly surprised that we hadn't come across any police cars yet. Most would likely be in the city centre, I guessed, keeping a watchful eye on the drunken weekend cattle herd.

To Celine's protests, I drove through the next set of red lights, narrowly avoiding more oncoming traffic. The Mad Hatter behind us wasn't so lucky, though, and rammed side on, right into an oncoming police car, of all things. Take that, you bastard. Ha! I couldn't stop myself from laughing in hysterics. That'll teach you to mess with a man with nothing to lose. Ha fucking ha.

'Holy shit,' I yelled mid-laugh. 'I feel like I can do anything right now. WOOOO! It's like I have some kind of crazy super karma on my side, you know? Take that, you crazy bastard.'

I was speaking to myself rather than to Celine. When I turned to look at her, hoping she'd be relieved and sharing in my joy of a lucky escape…well, let's just say she didn't seem to have the look of someone sharing in my newfound enthusiasm for life. Yep, she was definitely none-too-pleased with me, that's for sure. In fact, she looked more upset than any woman I'd ever seen.

'Pull over, Liam. Pull over right now!'

It's fair to say that her angry words took me by surprise. 'What! What's wrong?'

'Just pull the fuck over, Liam, and let me out, now.'

'You're kidding me, right?'

'PULL OVER,' Celine screamed. No, she wasn't fucking kidding.

'Okay, okay! I'm pulling over. Jesus Christ, Celine, what the hell is wrong with you?

Celine couldn't hold her rage inside any longer. 'WHAT'S WRONG WITH ME! WHAT THE HELL IS WRONG WITH YOU? YOU FUCKING ARSEHOLE, SELFISH PRICK.'

I brought the car to a screeching halt. I even used the indicators to pull into the side of the road, I felt so focussed.

'So, you know how to use them then, do you? Arsehole,' Celine said.

'Look, I'm sorry. I didn't mean to upset you with my driving skills, okay?'

Celine placed her hand upon the door handle, ready to leave.

'Come on, Celine! What are you doing? Where are you going?'
'Getting the hell away from you, you crazy psychopath.'
'Shit, Celine! I'm sorry. What do you want me to do?'
'Start acting like a responsible fucking adult, you bloody...penis.'
I couldn't help but laugh at her insult when maybe I should have been keeping a serious face.
'What's so funny, huh?'
'Celine, baby!'
'Don't you dare call me baby. I am not your fucking girlfriend, you dumb prick. I am your short-term business transaction, for which the contract has just been terminated.' She paused mid-sentence, shaking her head. 'I mean, what the hell is wrong with you, Liam, really! How the hell could I have been so stupid to do this with you tonight! How the hell do you expect to get away with this reckless, reckless behaviour? And how dare you! HOW DARE YOU! Put my life in danger like that.'
I let out a deep sigh. I'd never felt so bad in my entire life. I really had turned into an inconsiderate, arrogant arsehole that night. 'I'm sorry, Celine, alright? Truly, I'm really, really sorry. I just don't know what came over me, you know.'
'Is that the only excuse you have for this insane behaviour? That you don't know what came over you? Huh? How can you explain this crazy charade? Huh?'
I didn't know what else to say. I didn't feel ready to tell her about my cancer. This wasn't the plan. I'd just gotten carried away in the moment, that was all. I kept my eyes down and away from her. She looked so damn sexy when her blood boiled over like this.
'It's complicated' was all I could pathetically muster.
'It's complicated, yeah! Well, fuck you, Liam. Goodbye.'
Celine went for the door again, ready to leave. I couldn't help but grab her, panicking.
'Please, Celine! Don't go! I'm sorry. And I swear that if you stay with me until the end of our agreement, I will never take you for granted like that again. I was a damn fool back there and just got too caught up in the moment, that's all. I'm sorry.'
'Your bullshit apology isn't going to cut it, Liam. Now, tell me what's really going on with you. Really. All this money you're throwing away. The crazy, reckless behaviour.'
I glanced away from that insane look burning in her eyes. Drilling into my lost soul. Maybe it was time to fess up. She looked pretty mad.
'Look, okay! If you want to know the truth...' I turned back to face her. I was trying to be as sincere as I possibly could. I let out a deep sigh. 'I'm dying, Celine, okay?'

Celine looked at me in utter disbelief. 'You're what? You're dying!' She let out a false chuckle. 'Oh, please. Is that the best you can do, you fucking arsehole?'

I grabbed a tight hold of her arm. 'Look, it's the truth, okay? I swear. I was just so fed up with my boring, miserable, pathetic existence that I wanted some careless, no-strings excitement in my life for once, you know? Before my boat comes in.'

She looked to be of two minds, but most of her still seemed convinced that I was nothing but a lying sack of shit.

'You're making this crack up now, aren't you, Liam? You're playing me for the fool here again?'

'No, I swear, okay? Please...I swear I'm not!'

'But you look fine to me. A picture of health. You're not even pale, weak, coughing, sickly! How long do you have left to live, for Christ's sake? Fifty goddamn years?'

'I don't know. I really don't. A year, maybe less. With all this excitement, maybe only a few days,' I replied with a stupid grin that was totally the wrong play again.

Celine let out another false laugh. 'A year! A few days! Oh, piss off, Liam. Goodbye.'

Celine shrugged away my hold and left the car in a burning whirlwind rage, slamming the door shut behind her. She looked so angry, I think she even forgot that this was actually her car.

I got out too and gave chase. 'Celine, wait, please! Celine, please.'

Celine turned sharply to face me as I approached. 'Liam! You need help. You need a good fucking psychiatrist along with a good, hard, swift kick in the balls.' Celine opened her purse and grabbed a roll of hundreds. 'Here! Take this. Take what I have left of your money here and go get yourself a really good psychiatrist, okay?'

I grabbed her hand filled with the money and pulled it away from her purse. 'Celine, I don't want the bloody money back, alright? Burn it if you don't want it for all I care. Give it to charity. It's worthless to me now. Worthless.'

I pulled her hands right up to my chest. I looked her dead in the eye. I could see her tears swelling. She tried to dart her glance away. Anywhere but right at me. I shook her. Shook her really hard until she looked me right in the eyes again.

'Celine. I am fucking dying. And that's the God's honest truth, okay? In a few months' time. Definitely less than a year, I will cease to exist on this shit-pit planet. I have inoperable cancer of the brain. Spreading deeper and deeper inside by the day. My old life as I knew it is over. While my new 'I-don't-give-a-fuck-one' is only just beginning. So please believe me and trust in me when I tell you this.'

I could feel my eyes burning into Celine's pupils with all the sincerity I could summon from my soul. Celine hadn't looked away once since I'd started talking, so I took that as a good sign. Even though she was more than likely studying every tiny movement of my face, every creasing wrinkle, every darting of the eye, for any kind of deceit.

'Just stay with me Celine,' I continued. 'Just stay with me for the next few days or until our time together is up, please. That's all I ask. That's all I want.'

Celine remained silent, still studying me hard. I could see her eyes moving ever so slightly. Her brain taking everything in and processing it.

'Please, Celine! I'm begging you here. Please. Stay with me.'

I could see tears forming in her eyes. If this showed one thing at all, it showed she cared. Even if she never wanted to see me again, her tears spoke a thousand more words than anything that would ever roll off her tongue.

Still she didn't speak. After what seemed like an eternity, I held my hand out for her to take. It was the sincerest action I could think of. She turned from me, breaking the tension. She ran her fingers through her hair and took a deep breath. She was clearly thinking hard. Contemplating everything that had happened. Trying to make a decision.

'But you just said you don't give a fuck about anything anymore...'

'Aye, I know.' I smiled. 'And I did, I mean, I don't...well, not until I met you,' I replied, tongue-tied.

Celine shook her head, then wiped away her tears.

'Celine, I made a mistake. I got caught up in the moment, but you made me see the error of my ways. So, I promise that if you stay with me, everything I do now within your company will be completely legal and legit. I understand that my life is fucked. I know that. But that doesn't give me the right to fuck up yours, too.'

The next few moments were the longest and most excruciating of my life, I swear it. Just watching her. Looking this way and that. Glancing in any direction bar mine. I had absolutely no idea what she was thinking. Her body language was all over the place. One second she looked like she would run a mile. Another, I really believed she was about to punch or kick me swiftly in the balls, then run a mile.

Finally, she sighed, closing her eyes. She reached out and took my hand. I felt a great wave of overwhelming relief. It felt good. It felt really good. I could've stripped naked there and then and jumped around Meadowbank Stadium with sheer joy. But I restrained myself. I kept it all bottled up inside. Only the glazed look in my eyes gave any hint of my real emotions.

'Okay, Liam. Okay. I'll do it. I'll spend the next few days with you.' I wanted to hug her. To hold her close and pull her tight and never let her go. I wanted to at least say thanks. To show my appreciation of her decision. But somehow nothing seemed appropriate. I definitely didn't want to ruin everything again by saying something more stupid. So, I held her hand and led her back to the car without saying another single damn word.

***

When we got back to Celine's place, we still hadn't spoken to each other. Emotionally exhausted, we both headed for the bedroom and fell down beside one another on the bed. Then, after a short while, we turned and hugged each other, really tight, and for a good long while too. It felt good. Just holding, cuddling, lightly kissing, and caressing in complete silence. I had no idea how long we spent kissing and touching and stroking and feeling each other. And I mean really feeling each other out. Not the sleazy, groping kind to which I'd become quite accustomed these past few years. For the first time I could remember, I began to make real, slow, passionate love to a woman. No kinks, no rough stuff, no spanking, no biting, no pulling hair, and certainly no dirty, filthy sex talk. We just made love. Pure and simple. Real slow, quiet, burning love. Burning like a newly lit cigarette left abandoned on an ashtray to filter itself out.

Only the sounds of our rhythmic breathing and beating hearts echoed around us. Our eyes locked in unison as our bodies entangled themselves, becoming one. It was the most beautiful thing I'd ever been a part of or experienced in my whole, entire, shallow life.

Afterwards we just lay in bed for another long while. Still neither one of us speaking out to break the silence. We just enjoyed the moment together. Only when Celine finally left the bed, heading into the kitchen to fetch us some water, did we finally let words come between us. Bursting our cosy little bubble of silence.

When she came back from the kitchen, I could see it in her eyes right away. I could sense something playing on her mind...my cancer. She wanted to speak about it. She wanted to talk about it. She wanted to understand. She looked at me with those big, deep, beautiful, wise eyes. Then she spoke.

'So, when do you start your treatment? Or have you started it already?'

'I'm not starting any treatment.' I replied instantly, shrugging it off like she'd just asked me to change the TV channel.

'But this is what people do, no? Do they not? To fight. To try and make it better.'

'The other sheep, you mean. The ones who spend what little time they have left on false hopes and promises. Trying every new medication and treatment under the sun to give them a few extra months of life.'

'If there's at least some sign of hope, then yes, sure. Why not?'

'I'd rather end it all right now, thank you very much, than cling to life by a single ball hair. Drugged out of my eyeballs. Rotting away in some darkened room or a godforsaken hospital bed with barely any of my own conscious thoughts remaining.'

'Surely you have to at least try some kind of hospital treatment, Liam?'

'Why should I?' I replied stubbornly. I'd already made up my mind. 'I'm not wasting what precious little time I have left on a soul-destroying treatment which has a zero-point-two percent chance of success.'

I glanced away from Celine for a few beats. I really didn't want to think about this. Any of it. Christ on a bike, I'd been avoiding it for so long. Pushing the cancer questions to the bowels of my mind. Why did people always have to ask questions to satisfy themselves? Why couldn't they just be content and respectful of other people's wishes and inclinations?

Celine would be the first person I'd opened myself up to. Even if the opening was only a tiny little crack. Why couldn't she understand how damn hard it was to talk about this? To be forced to confront death? Look him dead in the eyes. Oh, the mortality of life.

What did she want to hear? That I wished beyond all sense and reason that this was happening to somebody else and not me? Selfish, I know. Horrible, disgusting, to say the least. But these were my thoughts. That's what I wanted. Somebody else to suffer and deal with this decease rather than me. Anybody, in fact. In this second, I would've gladly passed my affliction on to a newborn baby if it meant I could live an extra ten years. No, shit. I didn't really mean that, did I? Did I? But if given the choice...?

'So, what happens when your health starts to decline or you don't feel like getting up in the morning anymore? Then what?'

'Then I'll just end it. I'll end it right there and then.' I was serious, too.

Celine felt it. She sat upright. Looked at me hard. Raised her hands and turned my head towards hers. 'Liam!'

'What?' I replied, eventually yielding to her strength. I looked her dead in the eye.

'Don't say such a thing.'

'Well, if you want the cold, hard, honest, and brutal truth, Celine, then it's pretty much what I'm going to do. I mean...when it gets really bad...eventually.'

My secret was out. I knew it had been dwelling there this whole time. I'd done my best to paper over the cracks. I hadn't even thought about it in depth or spoken it aloud until this very second. Something I wanted to avoid until the last possible moment. Then I'd let it pour over me. Consume my soul. Engulf my fight for life. My reasons for living. I'd do it. No questions asked. End it. End it all. Better to burn out than fade away.

'Oh my God, Liam. Really! This is what you would do?'

I turned onto my side, facing away from her. It felt easier that way. Not to have her in my sight. Not to look her in the eyes anymore and feel her shock, her pain, her concern...her warmth.

'Liam?' she continued. Demanding an answer.

'My mind's made up, Celine.' And it had been for some time. 'I just think it's the best thing to do. When the time eventually comes. Fuck living out of hospitals, tubes, drips, medicines, and bottles of pills.'

'And how do you plan on ending it, Liam, huh? How?'

I nearly chuckled at the sincerity of concern Celine voiced. It felt good that someone was worried about me for a change, showing emotion.

'I don't know, Celine. I haven't really thought too long and hard about the dirty deed just yet. Jesus! Let me live as much as I can first, eh, before I start worrying about that shite...'

Celine fell silent. I felt I owed her an answer for her concern at least. Keep it humorous, though.

'I don't know, maybe jump off a cliff somewhere up the coast. Or jump from the top of that Walter Scott monument, ha. He was a good guy, that bloke. A great fucking writer, too. That would be a fitting end for anyone.'

'You have to pay seven pounds to climb up that monument, you know.'

I did a double take at her reply. Was she taking the piss or being serious? I chuckled. I laughed out loud and couldn't stop myself even if I wanted to.

'And so what? You think I'd seriously reconsider at the last minute if they charged me to go up there? Seven fucking pounds to top myself. Sounds like a bargain, if you ask me.'

'I just meant...I don't know what I meant. I'm not thinking clearly.

An image came to me of you going there, that's all, trying to get in. But they asked you for money and you didn't have your wallet.'

'And why wouldn't I have my wallet with me?'

'I don't know, Liam. Maybe because you're about to fucking kill yourself. Why would you take your wallet or any other belongings?'

'Then I'd just jump the bloody barrier,' I replied, half teasing, half serious. 'What would they do? Call the police on me? I wouldn't be coming back down to face them, that's for sure. Well, at least not the way they'd be thinking.'

Celine kept quiet. What a ridiculous conversation. Funny, though. Even if she'd never meant it. I chuckled and couldn't resist turning around to cuddle her. When I studied her face, she looked scared and sad. It made me want to laugh even more for some strange reason. I'm sure she meant well.

I thought about a suicide story from donkeys back. A man who killed both himself and his dog. I pondered whether to mention this to Celine. I should at least say something. It might cheer her up.

'You know, there was this one guy who checked into the Balmoral Hotel with his little Jack Russell a few years back. He insisted on having a room high up with views overlooking Waverly railway station. He ordered a delicious, top-notch, three-course meal. Hired a top-of-the-range female escort for a few hours of extra dessert. Afterwards, he showered and shaved. Dressed himself in a full kilt attire. Picked up his wee dog. Stepped out onto the window ledge overlooking Edinburgh's Old Town. Then flung himself and his dog down onto the glass roof of Waverly train station and the busy railway platforms below.'

Celine looked horrified. Disgust and outrage swept over her face. 'That's not a nice story. Why the hell are you telling me something like this?'

'I dunno. I always thought it was funny, that's all. Just imagining the look on everyone's faces down on the platforms as this guy wearing a kilt and clutching a terrified dog landed in front of them.'

'It must have been horrific for the poor dog.'

'Funny how everyone always commiserates with the dog, huh.'

'Well, he wasn't hurting anyone. I'm sure the dog didn't want to fling itself out of the window to its imminent doom.'

'But don't they say that dogs adapt emotionally to their master's feelings and behaviourisms after some time?'

'Shut up, Liam. Just go to sleep.'

I paused, deliberately holding back the end of the story. I unleashed a beaming smile. I whispered into Celine's ear. 'The dog survived,' I lied.

'No, he did not,' Celine replied, almost turning to me in

desperation.

'I swear. It was in all the newspapers at the time. Nobody knows how. Everyone called him the miracle dog. One of the passengers who witnessed the whole thing ended up adopting him.'

Celine smiled in satisfaction, then cuddled closer. She stroked lightly at my shoulders and hair as our breathing unified. No more words were spoken between us that night. We soon fell into a deep, sound, and relaxing sleep.

Chapter 12

I woke up naked. For some reason, I felt surprised by this until I remembered that I hadn't bothered putting my boxers back on after exercising my passion with Celine the previous night. It felt like late morning. The curtains were drawn, yet I could see and almost feel the strength of the sun's glare trying its damnedest to break in through the dark, thick curtains. Even before turning to face Celine, I knew she wouldn't be there. I could sense the open space beside me before I saw it.

I noticed, for the first time, a medium-sized map of the world stuck upon one of Celine's bedroom walls. For some reason, my eyes drifted and re-focussed upon the North American continent. The United States of America and Canada. Canada seemed so huge and superior in land mass to its US neighbour. How the hell could the mighty United States let so much land mass slip away from it? And to Canada, of all places. Surely the States could've owned that entire North American continent at some point in its history, if it indeed was the all-out powerful nation it would have you believe it is. What had stopped it from conquering?'

Well, I didn't have access to the all-knowing Google right now, so I guess that particular knowledge would have to wait.

I got out of bed and found my boxer shorts underneath the chair beside Celine's bedroom desk in the far corner of her large bedroom. I put them on. Some neatly organised books sitting at the back of her large oak-wood desk caught my eye. *Post Office*, *Factotum*, *Women*—all by Bukowski. *Ask the Dust* by Fante, one of my all-time personal favourites and possibly the greatest tragic love story I'd ever read. Then I noticed some French books, *Betty Blue* by Phillipe Djian, another tragic classic. Raymond Radiguet's *Devil in the Flesh*, Jean Cocteau's *Les Enfants Terribles*, Knut Hamsun's *Pan and Hunger*, more of my favourites. Jesus Christ, it was like looking through my own personal bookshelf back home. I had a sly chuckle when I saw some Irvine Welsh books. Ha, the maestro himself. Then Alasdair Gray, Robert Burns. I liked that she had taken an interest in Scottish writers. The poets—Walt Whitman, Robert Frost, followed by a few dozen more. Last but not least, one of my own personal favourites, Jacques Prévert.

I picked up the collection of Prevert's work and skimmed through the pages. I hadn't read anything by him in years yet I knew some of his work by heart. I put the book down and walked towards the closed bedroom door. I felt like having a nice, long, warm shower.

I wondered what Celine was up to. The apartment sounded so eerily quiet.

When I opened the door, a delicious wafting aroma of cooked meat engulfed my famished senses. Someone was cooking. I entered the combined living room/kitchen to find the delightful sight of Celine cooking breakfast, wearing only a T shirt and a thong.

'Bonjour, mon cher,' I said, remembering one of the few French phrases I'd picked up in high school.

'Bon Matin,' Celine replied in her perfect French. 'Comment avez-vous dormi?' she continued, instantly losing me.

'Oui' was the embarrassingly best I could muster in response.

'Comment aimez-vous vos oeufs? Douce ou dure?' Celine went on.

'Oui, oui,' I replied, letting out a clueless grin.

'Dure il est! Prenez un siège. Et je vais vous versez un peu de café.'

Nothing. It all went over my head.

'Par-lay voo on-glay or Ecosse?' I replied, butchering her language even more. Celine smiled warmly at my utterly shite French. Finally reverting to her second or third language, English. 'Take a seat and I'll pour you a nice cup of coffee.'

I sat down on the couch. Celine took a break from the frying pan and poured me a black coffee with one sugar, then handed it over.

'Merci. So, what did I do to deserve such a delicious-smelling feast?'

Celine made her way back to the gas cooker. 'Who said it was for you?' she said with a grin. 'Well, it did get a little bit iffy there last night after such a fun day together. I suppose I just wanted to start this new day with a fresh slate. That was all.'

'Wow! I guess I don't know what to say then.'

Celine took the frying pan away from the hob. She placed a couple rashers of bacon, eggs, and sausages onto a plate already filled with bagels and beans.

'Do your talking with your appetite,' Celine said, putting the plate down in front of me. It would be my first home-cooked meal in a long time. It looked so good.

'Okay then, I will.'

As I got stuck in the tasty feast, Celine poured herself a cup of coffee and sat down beside me.

'That's a nice wee collection of books you have in your bedroom there.'

'Thank you. I have so many more back at my parents' home in France, even the exact same books. I just...I just get so damn bored sometimes, you know, and head out to the old book stores around town from time to time, picking up some of the same old familiar copies again and again.'

I looked Celine deep in the eyes. She stared back at me with a curious gaze before I threw one of my favourite poems at her for shits and giggles.

"Some say the world will end in fire. Some say the world will end in ice...'

Celine smiled, nodding her head in approval. 'So, you know Frost too.'

'Yeah, but this is my own, naughtier version.'

'I'm impressed. So then, please do continue.'

"Some say the world will end in fire. Some say the world will end in ice. But from what I've tasted of desire. I hold with those who favour fire...that fire in your eyes...that fire burning and raging, deep down between your thighs...'

Celine chuckled and playfully slapped my thigh. 'You are bad.'

I stared hard at her again. 'An orange on the table. A dress on the carpet, and you on my bed...'

Celine quickly joined in with my recital and we finished the poem in unison. 'A delicate present of the present. The coolness of night...The warmth of my light.'

We both smiled and then laughed, sharing the moment. It was a good moment.

'And you know my Jacques Prévert too? Double points.'

Celine stared deeply into my eyes with the utmost seriousness.

'Trois allumettes une à une allumees dans la nuit. La première pour voir ton visage tout entier. La seconde pour voir tes yeux. La dernière pour voir ta bouche, et l'obscurité toute entiere pour me rappeler tout cela, en te serrant dans mes bras.'

I slapped my head, frustrated. 'Shit, I wish I'd paid more attention to French back in high school. Who was that?'

'One of my favourite poems, actually.' Celine grinned and shrugged her shoulders dismissively.

'Tell me.'

'When you learn some French, I'll repeat it again. Until then, you'll never know.'

I shook my head. What a tease.

'So, what are our plans for today then, monsieur? Steal the Scottish Crown jewels from Edinburgh Castle? Streak through the Scottish Parliament while the First Minister debates live on TV? Maybe bungee jump off the Forth Road Bridge?'

I just grinned. 'All very good ideas, Celine, but I actually have a few of my own.'

I drove Celine's car all the way over to Eyemouth on the East coast of Scotland. It took over an hour. I'd never been to any of the beaches in Scotland or really taken a good look at the seas surrounding her. Wasn't this what countries like Spain and Greece were for? Now I wanted a look, though. A burning urge and overwhelming desire to feel and see this great Northern Sea at work overcame me.

The sea approached. It looked...unreal. Unnatural. Now that I had the focussed chance to take it all in without distraction. And it wasn't just a passing piece of oblivious scenery on my way to somewhere more important to my needs at the time. This was the sea. One of the most magnificent beasts and forces of nature in the world. What a beautiful and remarkably deceptive creature she was. Working in unison with all the other seas and oceans of the world to keep our planet alive and flourishing. How insignificant she made everything else feel and look. Perhaps that was why I avoided her. She always made me see and think about the bigger picture whenever I laid my eyes upon her. And before the cancer, that was the last thing I wanted to think about.

We found a secluded beach a few miles shy of Eyemouth. The sun half shone from above and behind a relatively cloudy sky while a breezy wind gusted all around. I took the car off road and along an old dirt track fit only for tractors and four-wheeled drives. The ground seemed dry, so I wasn't too worried about getting stuck. I drove as close to the beach as I possibly could without stranding the vehicle in the soft sand.

We'd discussed the matter on the way and agreed about what we wanted to do as soon as we arrived. 'Best to get it over and done with quick and fast,' giggled Celine.

I'd heard rumours that the North Sea wasn't the warmest nor friendliest of seas in the world, but what the hell. You only live once.

As soon as I switched off the engine, Celine and I raced each other like two overly excited children, seeing who could undress the fastest. We swore we'd take everything off. Every last piece of clothing imaginable. Once the underwear, pants, bra, and boxers had been stripped off our bodies and discarded in the back seat, we knew there was no turning back.

In a bout of invigorating giggles, we exited the car and ran like a pair of loony streakers as fast as we could. Over the cool, dry sand, down onto the low-tide mud and weeds. Lady bits and man parts jiggled away for the whole world to see. Then boom—our pale, naked bodies collided with the crashing and surprisingly welcoming grey North Sea waves. As soon as that cold rush of intense sea water smashed into my stomach, I dived head first into her murky waters, beating her at her own game. It was bloody freezing, yet felt simply amazing. When I rose back up from her murky depths, whipping my head from the water, I couldn't wipe the lottery-winning smile from my face. I'd never felt so alive. And Celine was alive in that special moment with me.

For a few long beats, we steadied ourselves up to our chests in the sea water and glanced, beaming, at one another. We didn't need words or thoughts to describe our feelings in that wonderful moment. Our body language and smiles painted that particular picture quite well.

I wish we could've remained trapped inside that tiny shrapnel-sized bubble of time forever. In that moment, we represented everything I imagined the best of life to be. Freedom. Joy. Love. Completely and utterly present in the moment. Letting go. Even if it were only to be the calm before the storm.

When we finally walked out from the sea, hand in hand, laughing like a bunch of happy and lovesick teenage fools, we barely noticed the family of five who had stopped enjoying a quiet picnic only a few dozen yards away. Or the dog walker and jogger, who'd also stopped in their tracks to do a double take at the crazy naked couple who'd just skinny dipped into the North Sea. We were so focused on each other that we never really noticed anyone at all.

***

Driving back into Edinburgh, I heard on the radio that Scotland was playing South Africa in rugby at Murrayfield. That match would be kicking off in just over an hour in Edinburgh's west end and there were still a thousand or so tickets available at the seventy-thousand-seat arena. I couldn't help but turn to Celine and unleash a huge, devilish smile.

'Do you like rugby?'

'I'm French. Does a bear shit in the woods?'

'A polar bear doesn't.'

Celine shook her head, grinning. 'Of course, I adore rugby.'

Just then Bastille's 'Pompeii' came onto the radio and we both started chanting and singing along at the exact same time and at the very top of our voices. It was another nice moment.

The traffic on the west side of Edinburgh was absolutely bedlam. So chaotic, in fact, that we had to abandon the car on the border of Gorgie and Fountainbridge and make our way on foot with the never-ending swell of crowds. Once we reached the stadium, we purchased tickets for the lower southeast stand and made our way inside. The game had just kicked off, which suited my new plan of action just fine.

'You're sure you wish to do this?' Celine cried over the noise of the crowd, half of them still singing another verse of 'Flower of Scotland' for the umpteenth time. 'It doesn't seem like too much fun. I mean, you're going to have those humongous players and security gorillas chasing after you once you get onto the pitch. Are you really that fast?'

I removed my jacket, soaking up the atmosphere while reminiscing over my past rugby-playing days in my late teens and early twenties down in Melrose. A small, rugby daft borders town in south Scotland where my mum had moved after splitting up with that bastard Richard. I was actually not a bad wee player, to tell you the truth, and still thought from time to time about how much of a playing career I might have had if it hadn't been for breaking my leg in three places during a Scottish cup semifinal during an awkward scrum down battle. Ten minutes away from reaching a final to be held right here at Murrayfield Stadium. It was the closest I ever came to playing at the national stadium and still something that haunted me to this day.

'Celine, please! I was one of the fastest players in the top league before I broke my leg back in the day. And besides, apart from making out with you...' I winked at Celine,'...mothing on God's green earth would give me greater pleasure than scoring a try at the national sporting stadium of my country. So, I have to at least give it a go.'

'Okay. I just thought it might be more fun to stand here and watch, that's all.'

'Do you know how many rugby games I've been to at this stadium where I've just stood here and watched?' I asked, handing Celine my jacket.

I waited for the nearest steward to turn his back before making my way down towards the front row of seats. Celine had already made her way towards the nearest crowd stewards. There was only a shallow stone wall separating me from the seating area on the pitch, so I waited for Celine to approach the two stewards, distracting their attention, before I made my move.

'Excuse me. Hi. Can you tell me how to find my seat please?' asked Celine, waving her ticket in their faces.

This was my window of opportunity. I jumped over the small wall and onto the field. Some of the crowd around my eyeline glanced at me but said absolutely nothing. I jogged towards the closest ball boy along the perimeter of the pitch and picked up one of the spare rugby balls lying beside him. Now or never then, I guess.

'Hey! What are you up to, mister?' cried the boy, noticing me at the last second. But he was too late. I was already jogging onto the pitch to begin my play, setting up the distant rugby posts of the north stand as my final point of destination.

From the corner of my eye I could sense some of the nearby players and coaching staff who were eagerly warming up on the sidelines but who had now come to a halt and were glaring in my direction. The gradual sound of gasps and grumbled anticipation from the surrounding crowd flooded the field as they, too, focused on this random nutter jogging onto their field of play. As I approached the first set of players with their backs towards me, I broke into a full-scale sprint and ran, just bloody well ran, as fast as my legs would carry me, directly for the opposite try line.

The match ball was still in play at the other end of the field. It was quickly brought to a grinding halt as more and more players focused their shocked, then angry, attention upon me, along with most of the seventy-thousand-strong crowd.

From the sidelines, I heard the faint cries of 'Stop him. Get him off the pitch. Bring him down.' And from the corner of my eye I could see the security guys and stewards flooding onto the pitch too, from all corners of the stadium. Running straight for me. This new pitch invasion from the officials spurred the rest of the standing-in-awe' players to make their moves and charge after me too.

'Get orf the fackin field, you stupid arse,' raged one South African player as he desperately tried to tackle me to the ground. A tackle I easily side stepped no bother, which some of the crowd lapped up. Another three players gave chase as I entered the second half of the field. My body ached to its very core as I urged myself to gain more and more speed and momentum. More than I had ever dreamed I had left in me. Every ounce of blood, muscle bone, and fibre in my being went into absolute overdrive. An underlying depth reserve I never knew I had. I would give my everything now to make my goal a reality: placing that rugby ball down behind that Northern Stand try line.

I could feel the crowd really getting into it when I sidestepped another oncoming player, then shrugged off a tackle from a third. Making him look like the overpaid fool he was. The crowd roared even louder. I felt I finally had most of their support during this 'lone-wolf' pitch invasion.

I sensed more and more players chasing me. Must have been at least a dozen from the thirty already on the field. All of them foaming at the teeth for my blood and guts. Yet the try line was almost in sight. I could taste it. Feel it. My speed and momentum were at their peak. I ran on the fiery fuels of my heart and soul and very little else. I was going to do it. I was going to do it. The try line was there. Right fucking there. Right in front of me.

Shite!

From the corner of my eye, I saw them. Two huge fullbacks coming directly from my left. The closest two obstacles blocking me from reaching my goal. They looked to be in a furious rage at the disruption I'd caused to their game.

Somehow, I managed to palm off the first player before making a crazy, spontaneous, diving roll underneath the second as he put in a crunching tackle to my midriff, which miraculously vanished from his line of sight. One more player was coming from my right, but I was just a little bit too quick for him and skipped his tackle while continuing towards the try line to the cheers and delight of the still-roaring crowd.

I was inside the try zone and could've placed that ball down anywhere I liked. But right behind the posts was where the real secret feel-good factor waited. And there was no one around for yards to stop me from doing so. I made my glorious and overly dramatic dive behind the posts and relished the moment of slamming that white leather oval-shaped ball home and hard into the grass and mud beneath me. Of what I could remember about the short and vague series of moments afterwards, half a dozen huge and beefy rugby players dove right on top of me. Everything after that faded straight to black.

***

When the police were finished with me, they led me out of the cells and down towards the main front desk of the police station. Celine sat waiting and rose to her feet when she saw me coming. Before I could even greet her, two uniformed officers had me sign some paperwork before informing me that my court hearing date would be sent to my home address via post some time in the next few weeks.

'Brilliant! I look forward to it,' I replied a little too excitedly, just relieved that they hadn't pinned anything else on me yet. Like the road rage incident from last night, vandalising my neighbours' home, assaulting the knob-end builder outside the pub on the Grassmarket, assaulting a traffic warden, damaging public property, leaving my van parked inside some ned's kitchen...was there anything else?

I turned to Celine and we embraced each other. She smiled wildly, her face filled with pride. She touched my face which was still covered in bruises, bits of mud, and crusted blood.

'Are you okay?'

'Yeah, just a little stiff and sore. But I'm good.'

'Wow! You were amazing out there today, Liam. Really, just fantastic. I was so proud of you.'

We both laughed.

'I've never seen or heard anything quite like it in my entire life,' Celine continued. 'Even at the Stade de France.'

'It felt so amazing, Celine, you know. Words can't describe. I mean, did you hear the roar from the crowd when I went past that last player to reach the try line?'

Celine and I laughed even more as we left the police station hand in hand.

'This has been one of the best days of my life, Celine. Absolutely amazing.'

Celine sighed. 'Surprisingly, I can almost say the same.'

'And you know the best thing about this being such a great day?'

Celine glanced at me, confused. 'I don't know. What?'

'The day's not even over yet.'

On the steps of the police station, I took Celine into my arms and kissed her with a vigorous passion.

***

We parked up on Waterloo Place and I led Celine down towards the beginning of Princes Street. I still had one more surprise for her that night and I had a feeling she would really lap it up. I led her by the hand along the front pavement of the Balmoral Hotel before sharply turning onto the steps of the front reception. Celine paused for the briefest of moments, looking very surprised.

'What are you doing? Why did we stop here?'

'This will be our new home. Well, at least for tonight.'

'You're kidding. You know how much it costs for a room here, right?'

'A room.' I chuckled hard. 'Have you ever tried buying just a drink? But don't worry, it's all courtesy of my good old friend here, cold hard cash.'

Celine chuckled. 'It's a beautiful place though, no?'

'It looks like a big goddamn palace.'

We made our way into the reception and booked a room on the top floor for two nights. I signed all the necessary paperwork under a false name, just to be on the safe side. The last thing I wanted was for my spontaneous little sideshow adventure here with Celine to come to a crashing end once the authorities finally upped their game.

'We're definitely not here to top ourselves though, are we, Liam?' Celine teased as the receptionist turned to find our room key. 'Like the kilted man and his little dog in your story?'

I grinned. 'Do you see me wearing my kilt the now like?'

The receptionist interrupted our little moment and handed me our room key.

When we exited the lift on the third floor, I lifted Celine up and over my shoulders. She playfully kicked and screamed as we made our way towards the room. When we entered, I threw Celine down onto the king-size bed before jumping right on top of her. The devil in me took over and all kinds of naughty, raunchy hell broke loose.

A few hours later we both lay naked on the bed, entangled in each other's arms, in the afterglow of our most recent lovemaking session.

'I still can't believe you scored a goal at the national stadium.'

'It's called a try, Celine. It was a try.'

'Well! You still scored. Those players were so funny chasing after you, and those security guys and stewards.'

I smiled, reminiscing over the memories. It had been a good day. Quick, but good.

Celine turned onto her side to face me. 'You know, Liam. I actually have my own tiny little confession to make.'

'Oh yeah?' I curled onto my side, mimicking Celine's body language. Our faces were only centimetres apart.

'Remember yesterday when you asked me if Celine was my real name?'

'I do, aye! But go on.'

'Well, my real name is not actually Celine.'

'Really!' I chuckled. 'So, what the hell is it, then?'

Celine smiled seductively. Her words lingered in the air.

'In fact, to tell you the truth, I don't even want to know. I love your name. You'll always be Celine to me. So forget it.'

'Good.' Celine chuckled. 'Because I was about to say that I don't trust you enough to tell you yet.' Celine poked out her tongue at me. She looked so cute when she did it.

I just grinned and shook my head. I took a deep breath. She didn't trust me enough yet, but she was getting there. I couldn't hope for anything more than that, I supposed, after only a few days together.

'So, what do you want to do now? It's still early in the evening, no? Although I don't mind if you just want to snuggle up here for the rest of the night. '

'Well...' I paused. 'Two things come to mind, actually,' I said, acknowledging her will to change the subject.

'Oh yeah! Two things, really?' Celine replied, teasing, edging closer to me.

'Number one is to definitely stay here and make more, much

more, crazy, passionate, wild, and invigorating love.'
'And the other?'
I paused again before unleashing another devilish smile.

***

We entered the busy karaoke bar in the city centre. One singer was already in the middle of blasting out a half-decent version of Alice Cooper's 'Poison'. I signed up to sing my own karaoke song while Celine went to the bar to get in the drinks. Once I'd signed the dotted line, I headed over to her.

'So, what song did you choose?'

'It's a surprise.'

'Come on. Tell me.'

'No,' I continued, determined to keep her stumped while giving her another of my best mischievous looks. 'Now let's find a table.' I took her hand and led her into the crowd.

Twenty minutes later I downed another whisky and coke and slammed the empty glass beside five other empty glasses on our table. I was still waiting to be called up onto the stage. The entire bar area appeared full to the brim with at least a hundred people, all of them there to watch their friends participate in the late-night karaoke competition.

Celine took a gentle sip from her second cocktail of the evening. She could sense how nervous I was from the start and stroked my upper back, calming me down. 'Jesus, Liam! You really are nervous.'

'Like you wouldn't believe.'

'But you already sang the other week there when we were out. And you didn't seem that nervous at all.'

'That was a small, grungy, wee bar, Celine, in the early hours, with half a dozen or so people hanging around who didn't really give a shit if it were me or Rod Stewart belting one out.'

'After everything you've done. Running naked on a public beach with your meat and two vedge dangling for the whole world to see. Disrupting a church service. Staging your own pitch invasion at your national stadium and scoring a try in front of thousands of people. Even after all that adventurous, exhausting sex with me.' She grinned. 'And singing here makes you more nervous than anything else.'

'I'd like to think that I'm good at those other things, Celine. But this terrifies the shit out of me. Which is why I've always avoided it like the plague.'

When I was eventually called up onto the stage, I downed the rest of my newly bought pint in seconds.

'Go on, Liam. You can do it,' said Celine, encouraging me with all her enthusiasm.

I sneakily grabbed her cocktail and downed that too before she could say or do anything about it.

Celine looked playfully shocked at my actions. 'You cheeky bastard.'

'I'll buy you another one when I come back, I promise.'

'You mean when you come back with the prize money?'

I staggered nervously onto the stage. To say I was feeling tipsy was putting it mildly. The round of applause I received felt way below average compared to the applause the previous participants had gotten. I could hear Celine cheering at the top of her lungs from somewhere amongst the crowd, which gave me a wee extra boost.

There was an awkward pause as I approached the microphone and stared out at the vast crowd all around me. Every one of them looking right back at me like I was about to reveal the real, true meaning of life. And then...the stage fright consumed me. Jesus Christ, it was a big crowd. I immediately withdrew into myself. It was the damnedest thing. I wanted to leave, walk off the stage, just get the hell away from there at all costs. Head back to the comfort of my hotel room where everything would be nice and sound.

'Go on then ye fanny, sing,' cried some random voice from the crowd.

'Come oan then,' cried another.

'Geet oan wi et, ye nonse,' went another.

The host who'd been introducing the acts came up from behind me. He whispered into my ear, breaking the trance I'd cast upon myself. 'You all right there, mate?'

Shite. I had to do this. Fucking had to. 'Yeah! Yeah, I'm good,' I replied. 'Let's do this.'

As soon as that first musical tune hit my ears from The Killers' 'All These Things That I've Done', my nerves evaporated. I immersed myself into the song head first. The crowd seemed a bit dubious at first, but somehow and from somewhere I managed to tap into a stage presence and live energy performance that Freddie Mercury would surely have been proud of. I was loving it. Where the hell was that stage fright now? I was never going to see any of these people again, so what the hell did it matter how well I sung up there?

This was my moment.

By the end of the song, I had the whole goddamn crowd squeezed into the palm of my hand, chanting 'AV GOAT SOUL BUT AM NO A SOLDIER' over and over again. It was spine-tinglingly amazing.

Celine had been up on her feet the entire time. I could see her clearly going crazy with excitement along with the rest of the crowd just as soon as I'd finished singing. For a brief moment, I thought she might get too carried away, rip off her top, and start swinging it around her head. I left the stage to rapturous applause. Celine held out her hands, greeting me back into her arms with a passionate kiss.

'I want you to take me home right now, Liam, and fuck the living hell out of me,' she yelled, still caught up in the excitement of the moment yet for everyone else around us to hear in the process.

'Okay,' I chuckled. 'I can do that.'

***

Celine and I walked hand and hand back down along the North Bridge, overlooking the gardens, the castle, and the gorgeously lit Balmoral Hotel and clock tower that we would call home this night. In my other hand, I carried a bottle of honey-flavoured whisky that I'd won for finishing third in the karaoke contest.

Instead of turning left towards the hotel, I led Celine back up Waterloo Place, past our parked car and up to the very top of the deserted Calton Hill. We made our way towards a bench situated against the old observatory west walls, with the most magnificent and breathtaking views of the whole of Edinburgh's Old and New Towns.

'I've never been up here at night before,' Celine said softly, stuck in an awe-like trance at the breathtaking view.

'It's the most beautiful sight ever, no?' I replied, unable to take my eyes from the gothic lit castle and the surrounding Old Town landscape stretching out in front of us.

'Edinburgh looks even more stunning at night from up here than it does during the day. How is that possible?' Celine continued, smiling.

'I have no idea.'

'It's like being transported back in time. Even the distant street lamps down there in the city look like old burning lanterns.'

'Edinburgh's just one of those rare cities, I suppose, that looks utterly amazing and breathtaking during both the day and the night.'

For a long time, we just sat there, staring out in awe at the beautiful, dimly lit landscape before us. Eventually Celine broke the silence, peeling her eyes away from the breathtaking scenery to speak.

'What do you want, Liam?'

'What do you mean?' I said with a slight chuckle, confused by her question.

'If you could have anything in the world right now, right this very second. What would it be?'

'Honestly.' I knew exactly what I wanted. I picked up Celine's hand and held it in my own. 'A few more days with you would do me just fine for now, mademoiselle.'

'That's it? That's all you want?'

'Well, that and a new clean, healthy brain.' I grinned. 'I'm a simple man, Celine, and I value the simple things in life most of all now.'

Celine turned to face me with teary eyes and a look of complete love. I pulled her close, hugging her tight.

'That's all I want. Just to spend a wee bit more time with you. Just like today. Doing something. Doing nothing. But tax free and without a receipt, of course.'

Celine giggled while gently slapping my shoulder. She fell completely silent while looking at me with the utmost sincerity, more than I'd seen from her. Curious about her serious expression, I was just about to ask her what was wrong, what was on her mind, when she finally spoke.

'I want us to find a place together, Liam, and move in.'

Wow! What an unexpected shock. But a good one nonetheless. A really fucking good one. Jesus! It actually rendered me speechless for a few beats.

'Where the hell did that come from?' Are you serious?'

'Will you? First thing tomorrow or whenever we leave the hotel! Can we just look for a place together, somewhere? And just spend some time doing something or nothing. Just like we've been doing these past few days?'

I hesitated, more through sheer joy and elation than anything else. My mind had completely rocketed into space. This was more than anything I had ever wanted in my whole damn life. Yet still I just couldn't believe it.

'Hello! Liam! Are you still in there?' Celine said, playfully tapping me on the head with her knuckles.

I came out of my trance and gave her a reassuring glance. 'Yeah, sure thing. Let's do it. I'll move in with you or you with me. Whatever you want, Celine. I'll do it.'

I felt distant. Flashes of a future Celine and I could never have raced through my mind. Future holidays. Travelling the world. Building a home. Having children. Raising a family. Growing old.

'What is it, Liam? What's wrong?'

I shook those thoughts away just as quickly as they came to me. I changed the subject. 'I just…I just don't know how long I'm gonna have left, Celine. And I don't think you fully understand how bad this situation is gonna get in the next few months. Maybe it's not quite such a good idea after all for us to keep seeing each other after tomorrow, you know?'

'Are you fucking kidding me, Liam? Don't you think I should have at least some say in the matter, no?

'Of course I do. I just...I just don't want you doing anything rash or in the heat of the moment. Or maybe do something out of sympathy because you feel sorry for me or because you feel fucking guilty, or because you feel you have to.'

'Fuck you, Liam. I'm doing it out of love. And if you say you love me too, it's a done deal as far as I'm concerned.'

'You're doing it out of love?' I replied, surprised, shocked, yet slightly smiling at hearing such words from this steely girl who only yesterday had told me to fuck off out of her life and never come back.

'Yes,' she replied softly. She turned her head and rolled her eyes down and away.

'This is the same Celine who didn't want any men in her life right now. Refused to get involved with anyone because of her work. Even pretending to have a boyfriend. Who wouldn't give me the time of day until I put money down for her services.'

'It wasn't like that, Liam. I did like you. I liked you right from the very first time you chased me down the street and made me talk to you. I wanted to give you a chance. I wanted to see if you were like all the rest of the arseholes in my life who were just after one thing. I wanted to see how far you'd go to pursue me without my doing a damn thing to help.'

'So, you were kind of playing with me, then?' I said, but not feeling the slightest bit upset. We all play our silly little mind games in life. Everyone does, every day.

'I just wanted to push you away a little and see how far you'd go to come back, that's all. Like I said, it was only a stupid, selfish game. I didn't realise how serious you were until you came back with all that money.' Tears trickled from Celine's eyes. She sniffed and wiped them away with her sleeve. 'I'm sorry, but these past few years I've been a very tough nut for anyone to crack.'

'But you do crack,' I said with a smile. I pulled Celine right up close to me, hugging her hard. She wrapped her arms tightly around my body.

'Yes! I do crack, but only for the right person,' Celine replied with her face buried into my chest. We both fell silent for a long time. I enjoyed the feeling of her hugging my body. I gently ran my fingers through her hair. Soothing her and caressing her, over and over again, as I continued staring out at beautiful Edinburgh town in silence. It must have been a good twenty minutes before either one of us spoke.

'So, what do you want to do with your life, Celine? I mean, where do you see yourself five years from now?'

Celine looked deep in thought, pondering the question very carefully as she continued to lay against my chest.

'I mean, do you want to be an escort forever?'

Celine smiled wryly. 'Of course I don't! I mean, I intended on doing it for only a few weeks at first, you know, but...once I started getting all that cash in hand. The feel of that quick easy money in your palms...I guess I kind of got seduced by it all. To tell you the truth, when I was little I always dreamed of growing up and becoming a lawyer rather than a teacher or an escort.'

I was genuinely surprised by her admission. 'Really! Wow! That's different. I thought you were going to say a pop star.'

'No, it was my father's fault. Always making me watch those bloody awful law dramas on TV, ' Celine said as I ran my fingers through her hair for the millionth time. 'So, what about your mum and dad?' Celine continued. 'You've never really spoken about them.'

Shite. Talk about being wrenched right out of the moment. Richard came to my thoughts immediately. My gruesome stepfather. I could see him standing inside my bedroom, standing right in front of me. He yanked my small arms towards him and forcibly placed my hands upon his belt buckle.

'Take et auf! But slowly...very slowly.'

'Liam!' I heard Celine calling from afar. I came out of my daze. I took another long, hard swig from the whisky bottle lying half empty on the bench beside us.

'My mum...she lives in Melrose now. It's a little old town down near the borders.'

'And your father?'

It pained me to think and speak about this even more than the cancer. So many goddamn bad memories. I could barely remember anything about my father.

'My father. He died a long time ago. He was a soldier. He died in the Falklands War a few years after I was born.'

'I'm so sorry.'

'We used to live outside Edinburgh at the time on an army base. So of course, after he died we had to find another place to live. We ended up in a small town outside Edinburgh called Musselburgh, which was where my mum met my stepfather.'

I stopped there. That was all Celine needed to know. Nobody

needed to hear any more than that.

'But he's dead now too,' I lied. I had no idea if that scumbag was still living or dead, but something was nagging at me to find out. 'And then in my early teens, Mum moved us down to Melrose.'

'Where you started playing rugby?' Celine said warmly.

'Yeah,' I said, smiling back. Celine hugged into me. I took another swig from the whisky bottle. Celine took a long, hard swig, too.

'First thing tomorrow, Liam, we'll find a new place together or I'll move in with you until we do. I promise. Then I'm quitting my job. You are officially my last-ever client. Congratulations.'

'And what about your manager?'

Celine looked a little uncomfortable. 'I don't have to see him anymore. I'll grab my things from the flat tomorrow. Leave what money I owe and then I'm all yours.'

I couldn't help but smile at that. This was an absolute dream come true. 'So, does this mean I get a refund for the money I gave you?' I said with a grin.

Celine laughed hard. She took another swig of whisky. When she put the bottle down, I pulled her onto my lap and kissed her hard. Celine broke away, glancing left and right along the dark, secluded path leading around the observatory from either side. Nobody else was around. 'So, you don't want to wait until we get back to the hotel to ravish me?'

'I remember saying I wanted to try and bring out my more adventurous side too at some point, did I not?'

Celine kissed me hard, clearly turned on. I could still taste the delicious hint of the honey whisky on her breath, tongue, and lips.

'I like adventurous,' she said between kisses. 'And it's been such a long time since I've done...outdoor adventurous.'

We kissed passionately. I felt myself stirring, getting harder. Celine began grinding on top of me. Pushing herself deeper and harder against my hips. She moaned and moved quickly for my belt. I wanted to move us away from the public path, so I stood up and carried her in my arms as she wrapped her legs around me. I carried her over towards the observatory wall, shielded behind some thick trees and bushes, yet with the stunning views of gothic Edinburgh still very clear behind us. Our passions overheated as I lowered her to the ground.

I desperately wanted to take her from behind, up against that cold, hard stone wall of the observatory.

I pushed her back. She looked a little taken aback by my dominant gesture, but welcomed it. Her eyes glazed. Then I turned her around and pushed her even harder against the wall, making her spread her hands against it. I yanked down her trousers and panties. God, her arse looked so peachy in the dim lights coming from the city below. But in all fairness, it would look good in any light. I just wanted to stand and stare at it forever. Feeling it, caressing it, touching and running my fingers all over those smooth, silky curves again and again. But I couldn't take it anymore. Especially now that Celine was begging me to take her. Begging me to put my hardness deep inside her.

Teasingly, I slid myself in slow and deep with ease. I was so turned on that I wanted to explode right there and then. Exploding deep inside her with my first stroke. But no, not yet. Not yet. Instead I bit down hard upon my lip and restrained myself.

God, I fucking loved this woman. I'd never been so turned on before in such a short period of time. She started wriggling away wildly and uncontrollably against the wall. Her moans were so loud. Loud enough for the whole of Edinburgh to hear on top of that hill.

Finally, I took her more roughly and for as long as I could hold on and bear it. Then, hugging into her for dear life, I put my hands underneath her shirt, grabbing her breasts and squeezing them. My ears were engulfed by her pleasurable moans. It felt so good. She felt so good as I continued my deep long strokes inside her. This was my heaven. This was my ecstasy. And with the dim city lights of old Edinburgh town shining up at us from my below...it felt so perfect.

She cried out that she was about to come. It was a good thing because I wasn't sure how much longer I could hold on myself. When she finally moaned that she was coming, I sure as hell couldn't hold on any longer and gave myself to her in that moment too. Exploding my seed deep inside her. Wild horses couldn't have stopped me in those last few seconds.

I collapsed against her, forcing her even harder against the stone-cold wall.

Neither of us spoke for quite some time.

We just stood there. Resting against the other. Holding each other. Warm skin against warm skin. Trying to regain some civilised control over our breathing and senses. If anyone had walked along that path in those past few minutes, we sure as hell didn't notice or even care, for that matter.

***

Later that night, back in the warmth and comfort of our hotel bed, we made love again. Afterwards, I held Celine tightly against my stomach as she fell into a deep and tranquil sleep. After an hour, I still couldn't sleep. Something was niggling away at the back of my mind. Something I would have to take care of very soon. Something that could change everything. Especially anything I was ever going to have with Celine. But once again, I put it to the back of my mind. Right now, here with her, I felt like I had been in a dream these past few days. Just one big wonderful, crazy dream.

I wanted to write something else, another poem. Inspired yet again by this beauty by my side. I imagined waking up with Celine in the morning. Lying next to her pale, naked body in the aftermath of our love. Watching her sleep. Gently running my fingers with smooth feather-touch-like circles down the small of her back, then up towards her beautiful, pale, and fragile feminine shoulders.

Darker thoughts invaded my fantasy and I imagined that Celine was married or had lied about a boyfriend after all. Perhaps stuck in a loveless rut, which could easily be interpreted as just another metaphor for the life she'd chosen to live. There was just something more poetic and tragic about it that way. I imagined us seeing each other behind his back. Long, secret walks in the countryside and forest. Holding hands. Hide and seek. Playful sword fights with sticks. Picnics in the long, silky grass. Making ferocious and passionate animal love against a thick tree trunk. The feel of the rough bark against our skins. But would she ever leave him for me? It would drive me insane to be with a girl like her and know she'd be going back into his arms again and again. Night after night. Both of us sharing our seed with her.

The urge to write something, anything, utterly filled my senses and I grabbed for the hotel's printed notepaper and pen lying upon the bedside table.

You lie naked on my bed, in the aftermath of our love,
Glowing beads of sweat roll sweetly down your bosom, your
hips, your thighs, your belly button.
Your sex tasted so sweet last night,
Like a fresh, juicy, cool peach on a warm summer's morning,
To lick you, taste you, bite you, kiss your moist peach lips,
Be inside you, heart, body, soul, flesh, and skin,
Oh, what it is to have such feelings within.
I watch you now, sleeping, so beautiful, raw, and naked in your
silence beside me,
You're perfect in this moment, a moment you shall never know,
but only ever see through my eyes, if I allow it,
And then tomorrow, you'll go back to him,
and all I'll have left to remember you by is just a fading taste...

I wouldn't throw this one away. I would keep this one for her. Let her wake to it tomorrow morning. Now, though, I felt tired. Sleep had her firm silk grip wrapped tightly around my neck. Writing my thoughts down on paper had done the trick. Within minutes, sleep had throttled me into a soothing pit of tranquil darkness.

Chapter 13

The sun crept slowly up the back of Calton Hill as I shaved quietly in the bathroom of our hotel room. I'd left Celine sleeping deeply in the king-size bed next door and didn't really want to wake her until I was fully ready to leave. There was something I had to do today...in fact, *needed* to do. Something that had been playing on my mind for so long now, yet I knew it had to be done and couldn't delay it any longer. At least not while I was still fit and able to go through with it. Even though it would probably jeopardise any remaining short future relationship plans Celine and I had together. I just couldn't ignore it any longer.

With only a tiny portion of my face left to shave, I thought for a second that I'd carelessly cut myself with the razor when a slight trickle of blood dripped from my nose and spilled into the sink. It was soon followed by another spot of blood, then another. Then a great throbbing pain in the side of my head overwhelmed me and I quickly tilted my nose upwards to stop the bleeding. It worked, yet the pain got worse.

I needed to take my medication to stop the headaches or at least dull them until I realised that I'd stupidly left all of them back at my place in my sudden anxious rush to leave. Shit, how could I be so stupid? I felt dizzy and sat down upon the bathroom floor for a short while. The pain inside my head was still severe, yet almost bearable. I crawled into the shower cubicle, switched it on to a warm setting, and sat inside the cubicle. The warm water felt like a godsend as it poured all over me, massaging my head, through my hair, and over my skin. It felt damn good and relieving. After twenty minutes of this, the bleeding eventually stopped while the headache began to fade significantly.

Finally, I exited the shower, drying and dressing myself as quietly as I could inside the luxury bedroom. It still wasn't quiet enough to keep Celine from stirring in her sleep and awakening to find me fully dressed, freshly shaven, standing over her, and ready to leave.

'What are you doing, Liam?' Celine yawned and smiled at the same time. 'What time is it?'

I crouched beside her. I placed my hand gently upon the top of her forehead and stroked my fingers through her silky smooth, dirty blonde hair.

'It's early Celine. It's really, really early.'

'Come back to bed, Liam,' Celine replied, snuggling into me and trying to pull me back inside the warm and cosy space beside her. 'We've been asleep for only a few hours.'

'I can't. Not yet.'

Celine opened her eyes wide. She looked concerned and sat up suddenly to face me. 'What's wrong?' she said, cupping my face. 'Is everything okay?'

'Everything is fine, I swear. I just need to do something by myself for a few hours today, that's all. If I leave now I can hopefully be back by midday, okay? And when I come back we can start our new life together. I was even thinking we could just leave here for good, you know, later today. Drive up to the Shetlands or Orkneys and hole up there for a while.'

'Or we could drive down to my parents' place in France if you fancy a few weeks away,' Celine replied excitedly. They have a nice little guest cottage beside their house. There's a lake, too, and a really beautiful forest, great for long, relaxing walks with nothing but nature surrounding you. My parents would give us all the space we needed. They're very liberal.'

I tenderly kissed Celine's hand. She really did want to be with me. Last night's declaration of love and affection wasn't just the ramblings of a drunk, emotional, and insecure young woman. She really was sincere in her confession. And when I thought about the extreme things I might have to do that day to settle my demons, I figured that moving to another country and hiding out for a while might not be such a bad idea. I mean, Christ, they'd have doctors and medicines in France, too, no?

'Okay. We'll discuss it when I get back. Hopefully by this afternoon. Just wait for me here until I get back, okay? Then we'll come up with a plan.'

'Just answer me one thing, Liam. Whatever you're going to do today...is it legal? Is there a chance you might end up in jail or even worse...dead?'

'Absolutely. One hundred percent. No!' I lied, reassuring her with a warm smile. I leaned over and kissed her upon her forehead. Celine took a hold of my hand and gently caressed it while wearing a blank, oblivious expression, like she secretly understood that this could be the last time we ever saw each other.

'Now get another few hours' kip, all right, m'lady? I'll be back before you can say brain cancer.'

Celine winced at my sickening choice of words and gently shook her head. 'Just promise me you'll be careful, Liam, okay? Just...whatever it is you're going to do out there. Please come back to me in one piece.'

I smiled and kissed her forehead again. She fell back onto the mattress and closed her eyes. As I rose from the bed, I gently laid the poem I'd written upon the sheets beside her.

I really hoped she'd like it...

When I left the hotel, I felt good, in a boisterous and mischievous mood. Even though I was dying, I felt utterly full of life. Even when a thuggish-looking skinhead gave me a hard stare from a nearby bus stop right outside the hotel, I didn't let it spoil my mood. And when I walked towards him to cross the street, he quickly turned the other way.

I made my way onto Rose Street and approached the most expensive-looking suit shop I could find. Most of the shops weren't open yet, it was still so damn early. But when I spied an old-man tailor behind the window, busy arranging his displays for the approaching opening hour and day ahead, I knew I'd found my winner.

At first the old man was reluctant to let me in. 'Come back at eight-thirty,' he kept shouting from behind the closed glass door. It wasn't until I pulled out my big wad of fifties and waved them around like a geisha's fan that he finally caved. He sighed and turned the lock and key to let me in.

An hour later I emerged from the suit shop wearing a very smart, snugly fitted, expensive black Armani suit. Part one of three of my plan was complete.

I found another secluded little shop just farther along down Rose Street. It was an antique store that sold everything from retro household furniture to typewriters and walking sticks. It was the old handgun replicas on sale behind the counter which interested me most of all. All I needed was something that looked remotely the part. The best the store had on display turned out to be a cool steel magnum handgun that, when the trigger was squeezed, shot a lighter flame from the barrel. Awesome. Part two completed. Part three of my plan would require me to take a taxi ride up to the Porsche garage at Newcraighall in southeast Edinburgh.

Ever since I was a little boy I'd wanted to drive and own a Porsche 911 Turbo, black in colour. I remembered receiving a collection of different toy Porsches as birthday gifts over the years, all in different colours. I even had a picture of the 1989 version on my bedroom wall, right up until I left home. I'd never had the chance to own one myself, let alone drive one. The older I got, the more it became a fading dream. Forever out of my grasp. Over time the dream finally faded away like a last gasp of hazy smoke from a burnt-out cigarette. But today would be my day. I felt the part and looked the part. I was going to get my car and by any means necessary

I walked into the Porsche sales office and took a slow stroll around the various cars on show. I could see my 911 Turbo, the latest model on display. It looked beautiful. Like a dream. The only slight annoyance was that it was silver and not my preferred black, but that was a minor niggle. I stepped closer and admired her for a long moment. She was absolutely stunning. I prowled around her territory, admiring her gorgeous and perfect silver bodywork while gently running my fingertips all over her smooth and electrifying steel skin.

From the corner of my eye I could see movement from the sales office in the far-right corner of the showroom. It was a middle-aged sales rep who had an uncanny resemblance to the porky, pre-generation game show host comedian Jim Davidson. He wore a cheap suit and glasses and quietly approached me from the side, looking far too eager and confident for his own good.

'And what a beautiful little harlot beast she is you have your eyes on there, sir,' said the sales man with a huge false grin.

I half turned towards him, pretending I'd only just realised he was there. He looked and sounded like a right pretentious twat, but I guess that came with the job. So, I let out a pretentious chuckle of my own. 'Yes she is,' I replied, upbeat. 'And she's dressed in a rather delicious outfit, too, but is she available in a sexy black?'

'What a good eye for colours you have there, sir. And why, yes, she can be made very available to you in the black, sir, just not on this particular day. But final delivery, you can have any colour your heart doth desire. I'm Harry Mortimer, by the way, sir.' Harry the salesman extended his hand for me to shake. I smiled and took it.

'John Walker.'

'Nice to meet you, John. And what is it you do, Mr Walker, to enable you to wear such a stunningly fitted suit, might I ask?'

I almost chuckled aloud again. What a charmer. It was like he was actually hitting on me.

'I'm a banker in the city, Harry. Working for RBS, actually. And I've just earned myself a sweet little bonus for all my hard work this year. A very sweet bonus, indeed.'

'Oh, very nice,' Harry replied. I could see the cha-ching glee in his eyes. That lizard-like lick of the lips. The subconscious rubbing of his hands that told him he was onto an easy sell here with another cocky banker through the door.

'So, I thought, what the hell, eh? May as well treat myself for my troubles, no?'

'Why the hell not?' Harry chuckled.

'You only live once, right?'

'Exactly.'

I gazed at the silver fox car. I ran my fingers along her body again. She felt good. Really good. I wanted her bad.

'And you know what, Harry? As soon as I walked through that door and saw her sitting there like this and our eyes met, it was like love at first sight, mate, you know? Like it was just meant to be.'

'Oh, I understand exactly what you mean, Mr Walker. So how about a little test drive for you then, sir, to get you settled in? Get a little feel for this beautiful lass.'

'You know what, Harry? I thought you'd never ask.'

***

I accelerated the Porsche with a ferocious jolt up onto the A1 slip road before roaring out onto the never-ending duel carriageway ahead. What a beast she was. What a noise coming from that engine. So easy to manoeuvre and glide between the other cars. It was like cutting through warm butter. To Harry's murmuring distaste, I was having a great time taking her up to speeds well over the national speed limit, then easing her back down the gears again whenever I saw an approaching speed camera.

I could feel Harry becoming more nervous and tense the faster I made her go, along with the more cars I overtook. He grumbled a few times about speed limits, insurance, and other gripes. But between my whoops of delight, the blasting 'Viva La Vida' Coldplay song from the radio, and the superb roar of the engine, I couldn't really hear a damn word he said.

We roared past the quiet country town of Tranent, which lay on my right while, directly opposite, a glorious side view of the doom-and-gloom, apocalyptic-looking coastal power station of Cockkenzie lingered on my left. I felt amazing and even lowered my driver's-side window to let in some warm, fresh air.

Suddenly, Harry switched off the radio.

I gave him a quick side glance and smiled. He looked annoyed. I knew it was coming, yet had expected it well before we'd passed Tranent. He was going to have one heck of a long walk back to the garage.

'Okay, Mr Walker. I think we've driven quite far enough for one day. Time for the drive back then, I suppose? Then we can go through your paperwork.'

'Sure thing, Harry. Sure thing.'

In the distance, I spied an approaching lay-by just off the hard shoulder. I slowed down and pulled over almost instantly. The brakes on this beast were just as impressive as her acceleration. I turned to Harry with another grin and waited for him to say something. He wore a very confused look upon his face. I had to bite my tongue to stop myself from laughing.

'What...what...are you doing, Mr Walker? Why are we stopping here?'

'You know, Harry, it's been really nice making your acquaintance today. Really lovely, in fact.'

Harry's confused glare quickly went up a few gears of its own. 'What...what are you talking about, Mr Walker? We've got to drive all the way back to the garage now and get your details set up, right?'

'Wrong, Harry! Now get the hell out of my car.'

'What?' he replied, utterly astonished, yet still not moving an inch.

I pulled out my gun and pointed the hard, steel barrel right at his forehead. 'Get out of my car, Harry.'

'Mr Walker!' Harry replied, jumping erratically and raising his hands in defence. 'What the hell is this?'

'Get the hell out of my car, Harry, as in right bloody now.'

'All right, all right. Just stop pointing that thing at me, okay?' Harry exited the car, then turned to face me. 'What's wrong with you? Why the hell are you doing this, Mr Walker? I don't understand.'

'When I figure that one out, Harry, I'll send you a nice wee postcard to explain.'

'But you'll never get away with this.'

'Well, I'll certainly give it a big enough try. Now throw me your phone.'

Harry groaned before reluctantly chucking his phone at me.

'Now close the door, old chap,' I said in my best Roger Moore.

Harry complied. I pulled a pair of sunglasses from my suit jacket pocket and put them on. I was about to drive away when Harry tapped gently upon the window. I pressed the button to lower the tinted screen so I could hear what he was trying to say.

'I never brought my wallet with me. I don't even have any money for a bus or a bloody taxi. I could be walking out here for hours without my phone...'

I had to chuckle at his audacity. What the hell did this have to do with me? The more time he took to get back to the garage, the more time I had to see out my plan.

I was about to just drive off, back out into the quiet motorway lane, leaving the dust from beneath the tyres lapping in his face when I realised that I did indeed have a little special something for my new friend Harry. A parting gift, so to speak. I dug deep into my trouser pockets and pulled out a ten pence coin along with one of Celine's cigarettes I'd taken from her handbag that morning. I put the fag into my mouth and lit it with my lighter gun. Harry looked furious, but said nothing. Not that I gave him a chance to mind.

'Here's ten pence, Harry. Go and call someone who gives a shit, pal.'

I flipped the coin at him while speeding away. I never got the chance to see if he'd caught it.

***

I took the next turn off on the A1 and headed directly for Melrose. I was going to see my mum for the first time in as many years as I cared to remember. Because of everything that had happened with Richard in my distant past, I'd begun to distance myself more and more from my mother. And it wasn't because I blamed her for what happened. Absolutely not. Well, I did at one point, but definitely not anymore. I realised now that the abuse I suffered at the hands of that sick bastard was no more her fault than was my cancer. And when she had finally discovered what was happening to me at the hands of Richard, she kicked that dirty hound to the road once and for all, upping and leaving with me immediately to start a new life down in the borders. She never did report him to the police, but I think this was more for my sake than hers. I'd been through enough ordeals and even back then the idea of taking his sickening actions any further never really appealed to me. To have everyone around you knowing the full facts of the things he had done. The police and social workers plying me with question after question. Doctors and psychologists studying every square inch of my body for evidence. The inevitable court case, judges, lawyers, a jury, then me standing in front of everyone to give evidence. In front of him, even. No, seeing that prick again was too much under any circumstances, and I wasn't brave enough to go through all that drama and emotional turmoil at such a young age. Neither was my mother. So, it was just as much my decision to run away and start anew as it was hers. We would try and forget but never forgive. Start again. A clean slate.

The older I got, though, especially when I hit my twenties, the more I started thinking 'what if?' What if? Maybe I should have done something after all. Maybe *she* should have taken the lead and done something. What were the consequences of taking no action? How many more innocent children had suffered at his dirty, filthy hands throughout the years because of my lack of courage and conviction? And with the growing guilt gradually infesting my soul and building up in the back of my mind over the past ten years, I had to get away from my mother's sight. The more I saw her or spoke to her, the more I was reminded about that monster and what he had done. What he got away with.

I pulled up outside Mum's house on the quiet and dull-looking housing estate on the northern outskirts of Melrose. She lived in the end house on a row of six council houses. I didn't waste any time exiting the car and walking towards her front door with all kinds of wild emotions running through my head. When I knocked, she answered within seconds. The mixed look of shock, confusion, and surprise on her face was itself worth the journey. It was only when I saw her like this, face to face, that I quickly realised she didn't know about my cancer. I put it to the back of my mind for the moment. It really wasn't at the top of my priority list to inform her of my imminent death, as selfish as that seemed.

'Liam! Oh, my boy. What are you doing here?' She chuckled with joy before throwing her arms around me.

I tried to hug her back. It felt difficult. Awkward. I managed to wrap and rest my arms upon her back before stepping away. Christ, I couldn't even remember the last time I had told her that I loved her. I didn't even think there had been a time. I did, though. I loved her immensely. As much as any son could love his mother for giving him the gift of life, but saying it to her face would be the most difficult hurdle I could hope to overcome. Even more so than fighting the cancer decaying at my core. My emotions were so stubbornly set in their ways, so deeply embedded and rooted into my soul, it would take a monumental effort to say those three little words.

I...love...you.

I could feel my body tensing and twisting inside just thinking about it.

'This is so unexpected, Liam. Please, come in, sit down. Let me make you some breakfast or a cup of tea. It's been so long.' She had already turned back into the house and was halfway down the hallway, assuming I would follow. In my vision of this meeting, I hadn't planned on staying around for a friendly chat. Just get what information I needed and be on my way.

I stepped into the hallway and called to her, halting her in her tracks. 'Mum! I'm not staying. I'm sorry, but I don't have time. I just came here for one thing from you right now and one thing only...I'm sorry.'

It was the firmness and meaning in my voice that stopped her, right on the edge of the hallway. Her left foot freezing upon the beginnings of the living room carpet, just one more step away from her comfort zone. She slowly turned back to face me. Even before I saw her face, I knew that she knew the exact reason I was here. When she finally turned all the way around to face me, her expression was filled with utter despair.

'Oh Liam. Oh please, no!'

'Tell me where he is, Mum.'

'Liam. What makes you think...'

'Just tell me, Mum,' I roared like a starving lion facing down an injured wildebeest. 'Everything you know about him...tell me. The last place you saw him. The last place he worked. The last place he stayed. Where his parents are. His brothers, sisters. Tell me everything. Right now.'

There was a long, tense, silent pause made even more unbearable in the moment by my mother, who had seemingly aged another twenty years in that moment. Her look, her posture, everything that portrayed her to the outside world. It was like the memory of this monster had crippled her within the last few beats of her heart.

'He stays on a caravan park up in Dunbar. Belhaven or something like that, I think.'

She wouldn't even look me in the eyes as she said it. My stare must've been more intense than she'd felt in her life. Even more steely than Richard's when he'd no doubt denied all the accusations against him.

'How reliable is this information, Mum? How old is it?'

I expected her answer to be at least within the ten-year mark.

'Less than a year.'

I felt flabbergasted. How was that possible? Don't tell me she was still in touch with the sick fuck all this time.

Before I could utter a sentence of disgust, she answered for me. 'I was shopping in Edinburgh last January for the sales, you know. I think I even phoned and messaged you that day too, just to say I'd be in town, but you never answered. You never answer me anymare! That day in and out of the shops alang Princes Street he was the farthest thing fae my mind. It wasn't until I reached Primark when a very auld mutual friend of ours fae our courting days recognised me and approached me in the women's department. I was in all kinds of shock. All I could think about was to get away fae her as quickly as I possibly could. All those auld memories bombarded ma mind again. I mean, I didnae even ask her anything about him at all. She just volunteered the information willingly, alang with half her bloody life story. Christ, I even lied about where I was staying now just in case she relayed everything back tae him, you know.' Mum paused, taking a deep breath.

I was getting more annoyed with her storytelling ramblings. I felt the rage burning up inside. I just wanted her to get to the bloody meat of the answer. 'Mum! Please? Where is he?'

'She said he was living in some auld caravan park out in Dunbar,

Belhaven or something similar. He's married again. Third time now, apparently. He has children of his own now, tae. I'm so sorry, Liam.'

My stomach turned. Mixed emotions of rage and queasiness brewed inside me. I felt like throwing up. I felt like lashing out at something or someone. Instead, I bit my tongue and stood calm.

'Thank you.' I stepped back, half turning to leave.

'Liam!'

I stopped and turned back to face this old lady standing in front of me whom I barely even recognized...my mother.

'Please! Whatever you're thinking about daen...please dinnae, son. There must be...some other way.'

'His last name was Hunter, right?' I replied, ignoring my mum's pleas.

'Yes, aye, but Liam, please...think about whit your daen, son.'

It was too late for me to rethink things. The rage had taken over and fully consumed my body and soul. This was going to happen. My mind was made up. I was going to finish this today or die trying.

***

I drove into the BnQ car park at Galashields. Inside, I bought some thin rope and a crowbar, then placed them into the front boot of the porches. Within another ten minutes I was on my way to Dunbar, weaving erratically in and out of morning traffic like Ayrton Senna, flying recklessly through speed camera after speed camera, almost double the speed limit at times. At this rate, I'd be there in no time. With a calmer head, I really should have taken my time driving out there. I mean, anything could have happened. The police could've chased me. I could've crashed, putting both the lives of myself and other, innocent drivers in mortal danger. But being so self-obsessed in that moment, I didn't care. The only thing on my mind was him. Finding him, confronting him, then...then the rest would surely take care of itself. And the sooner I did this, the sooner I could drive back to Celine. Back to my beautiful, wonderful Celine. The love of my life. The new flicker of light in my flameless, fading soul.

Once I hit Dunbar, the caravan site was easy enough to find. There were a few parks scattered around the area, but only one by the name my mother had mentioned. I had no idea how the hell I was going to find him once I was inside that park, if indeed he was still living there. He could be at work, on holiday. He could've moved on. He could already be in the ground.

As soon as I drove through the gates and saw the main reception and the caretaker's trailer, I had a feeling it might be easier than I'd first thought. I'd envisioned parking outside the main road leading into the trailer park, clocking and studying every last resident who came and went. Or knocking upon every single damn door. Asking neighbours and fellow residents if they knew a Richard Hunter. Surely somebody would know that cunt, whether he was here or long gone.

In the end, it was a polite and flirty middle-aged female receptionist who quite willingly told me everything I needed to know. In short, Richard was staying at number sixty-one.

The road leading into the trailer park was a one-way system all the way back around to the exit/entrance. The numbering system on the trailers was fairly simple and obvious to follow. Row after row of pale green livable trailers. Even numbers on the left. Odd numbers on the right. Sixty-one fell on the right, just over halfway along on the inward curving circular part of the park with some spectacular views of the North Sea and the surrounding cliffs and hills.

There was a car in the driveway. Some old clapped-up banger of a Volkswagen. Someone was home. I pulled the silver Porsche to the side of the driveway. I immediately clocked a shadowy figure behind the net curtains, peering through to inspect this out-of-place vehicle and the well-dressed man inside, now parked in front of the trailer.

This was it. Now or never.

I exited the car and forced a happy demeanour across my face, as happy and as salesman-like as I could make it. I walked casually to the trailer's front door. Those damn memories haunting me again. Racing through my mind from all angles. Richard touching me where he shouldn't touch. Hurting me against my will. I grinned, forcing it. I knocked hard. Let's do this.

I took a deep breath. Shite. What if he answered? What if he did still live here? Could I control myself? Could I keep my anger and rage under wraps and see my plan through to its bitter, final end? Or would I completely relapse and release all this pent-up hidden anger upon hearing the sound of his voice? Would I spontaneously unload my uncontrollable rage from every fibre of my mortal sinned being and just beat the living piss out of this piece of dog shit? Beating him to death with my own fists and feet, right where he stood.

The door opened. At first I saw a grumpy old man with bad posture and a beer gut. Shit. Wrong man. Wrong house. After a blink, my gaze steadied and I knew it was him. It was fucking him, all right. He looked older. So much older. Jesus Christ, he must be nearly sixty yet he looked eighty, defeated and deflated by life. His skin was old, wrinkly, and yellow with thousands of thin blue veins. That big beer belly made him look pregnant. But Jesus Christ, those eyes. That glint, that look. It was unmistakeably him, alright. He dressed almost the same too, even now, green vest, old ripped jeans. Still a fag in one hand and a can of beer in the other. The same brand of beer, too, for Christ's sake, after all this time. The memories overwhelmed me. I felt lost, faint even, and utterly speechless. I had to take a step back and rub my eyes to compose myself. It felt like a dream. Some sick, fucked-up dream or hallucination. I held my breath. What the hell was I doing here? I saw Celine. She smiled back at me wildly while we danced in the sea together. My rock, my angel. Her image did the trick in calming me and refocusing my senses on the task at hand.

'Mr...Mr Hunter?'

'Whae the hell wants tae ken likes?' Richard replied. The aggression in his tone was more gravelly and bitter than I remembered, yet unmistakably him.

'Mr Richard Hunter, aye?'

Richard looked even more annoyed, if that was possible. His posture straightened. He took a threatening step forward. His body tensed, his arm muscles bulged. The image of the younger, stronger man he'd once been echoed faintly throughout his entire frame.

'Ah said! Whae the hell wants tae ken, pal?'

He was right up in my face now. I felt deterred for a second. My guard fell. I felt scared, nervous, anxious. I felt like that wee innocent and defenceless little boy again, unable to take a stand for himself. I couldn't even look him in the eye.

'Sorry, I...' I gathered myself. Be strong. Be strong. You can do this. 'I'm a...I'm Harry Martin...from the postcode lottery, you know...in association with the Porsche garage in Edinburgh.'

Richard's expression turned to one that looked confused as hell.

'Yur wi...whae, pal? Fae whir?'

'I'm with the national lottery, sir. You do the lottery sometimes, aye?'

Jesus Christ, I pleaded inside. Please have heard of the bloody lottery, you dumb fuck.

'Fuck naw. Bludy waste uv beer money that pish ef ye ask me, ken.'

'How about...the scratch cards? You must have done a scratch card once or twice before, sir, no?'

Richard paused. He was thinking long and hard. Sizing me up. I could feel him building up to push me off his doorstep and slam the door in my face at any second. He glanced at the car I'd pulled up in. That beautiful, gorgeous, slick silver fox. Those wonderful, shiny curves. He looked my suit up and down, then breathed.

'Mibbe ma wife does, ah dinnae ken, though. Hud oan. MARY! MARY!' Richard yelled back into the trailer. 'Geet yur arse oot here, woman.'

A nervous-looking woman, pale, skinny, in her mid-forties and with darting, anxious eyes, emerged into the hallway. She looked like a bundle of fear and nerves, almost deliberately keeping her head down. Not wanting to make eye contact with me or her husband.

'Whit, whit's wrang?'

When she glanced up at me for the quickest of beats before glancing down again, I could see that her face was battered and bruised. She had a fading black eye, too, from what I could see.

'Thus snobby wee prick et the door wants tae ken ef we buy fuckin scratch kerds.'

'Naw, never,' she replied, quick and anxious. Then, catching me by surprise, a nervous-looking young boy and girl also emerged from the other room to stand behind their mother with sad, curious eyes. Neither of them could have been any older than ten or eleven. When I stared at the boy, all I could see was myself as a young boy, looking right back at me. It hit me for six.

'You...you have kids, too?'

Richard snarled and clenched his hands into fists. He stepped right up into my face again. 'Aye, ah huv kids...'

I backed away just a touch. The mixed stench of alcohol and sweat coming from his body made me want to vomit.

'N al mak sure yul never huv any uv yur ain in aw ef ye ever come anywhir near ma hoose again, ye cunt.'

I snapped from my daze and backed away. His tone reminded me of the sexist, angry man outside the pub whom I'd floored only a few days earlier. Was it just me or had Scotland always been full of this many angry, aggressive, lowlife men? What had made them all so angry and full of hate? Was it just a sign of the times? A sign of the new, bitter, and cruel world we lived in? Where so much was possible and achievable, yet no one lived up to their full potential. Or made something good of their lives and lived out their happy dreams. No. Most of us were already burnt out by the time we reached adulthood due to uncontrollable hardships, turbulent upbringings, and soul-destroying jobs. If you were lucky enough to find one. And then what? Motivation sucked out of you one cancerous draw at a time. Dreams shattered to a billion nightmarish pieces. Then we quietly faded away out of our miserable existence.

Half turning and half apologising for the inconvenience, I pretended to head back to my car.

'Sorry for the inconvenience, sir, I was only looking for a Mr Richard Hunter at this postcode address, that's all. I wanted to give him his prize since his name came out of our postcode lottery last Friday. Again, I'm sorry to have bothered you, sir. I'm not here to cause any bother, sorry.'

I turned fully towards the car just as Richard twitched and called out to me in protest. I could hear him stepping out from beyond his front door threshold, out into the world. Out into my world. The little fish was taking the bait.

'Hud oan a minute thir, pal. Whit ye talkin aboot prizes n postcodes and bludy lotteries fuck sake?'

I stopped where I was. I took a deep breath. I wanted to let out the slightest of grins, but refrained. The stupid fish had been hooked just like I predicted he would be. I turned to face him, relishing the moment.

'Whit prize?'

'The car, sir.' I half turned, gesturing towards the silver beauty parked behind me.

'The car! But whae the hell's machine es that? Es that whit yur drivin, ma friend?'

'No, mate. Not anymore.' I could finally release the grin I'd been holding back the whole time. 'It's what you'll be driving from now on, Mr Hunter, if you can just show me some ID.'

I had to make it a wee bit official and less suspicious, you know.

Richard glanced at me in a stunned silence. He gazed back at the car again, then back at me, then back at the car. For a second I thought he was going to drop right down onto his knees and start bawling his eyes out.

'Am sorry, pal...' he said, shaking his head in disbelief, unable to comprehend the situation. Unable to take in that a life which had dealt him nothing but shite all these years, and mostly from his own making, had now given him something he believed he'd always deserved. 'Sae whit yur saen es. That thus mean fuckin beauty uv a drivin machine right here. Right fuckin thir before ma ain eyes...es mines. Ets fuckin aw mines?'

'Aye! I mean...yes, Mr Hunter.'

Richard ran his fingers through his hair, back and forth, back and forth. He started jumping up and down and yelping in sheer joy and excitement. Sadly, he was the only one doing so.

'Holy shite, man! Av never won anyhin befare en ma entire puff, ye cunt. Ah mean, es thus fur real aye? Es thus fur fuckin real aye?'

I glanced past the overly excited figure of Richard and towards the front door of his trailer. His wife and two kids had moved even closer to the doorway. They weren't smiling, sharing the excitement, or joining in with Richard's newfound joy. In all honesty, they looked like broken people watching as their tormentor was given a second chance in life. Broken souls with nothing in common or able to relate to this elated man dancing up and down on their lawn.

'YE FUCKIN BEAUTY YA!' Richard screamed to the heavens.

'Come on, Mr Hunter. Jump in and I'll give you a wee test drive before we sign the paperwork.'

Chapter 14

I let Richard drive for a while up the scenic east coastline towards North Berwick. He looked so happy and overjoyed. He even seemed like a new man, the way he never stopped talking in an upbeat manner the whole time we drove. Mostly, though, he spraffed a lot of shite about his hard life. How difficult he'd had it all these years. How nothing good had ever happened to him ever since he was a young boy. Married three times in total. No job. No savings. A born fucking loser, but not anymore.

Like I said, I wasn't really paying that much attention. I was more concerned with finding a good spot along the passing scenery of the high and low cliff coastline to execute the final part of my plan.

Richard was talking about how much he could get for a car like this when we passed the most perfect spot I'd seen yet, so I motioned for him to pull over in the next empty lay-by.

'Just pull over up there for a minute and I'll show you what's underneath her bonnet. I think you'll be mightily impressed.'

'So, ah huv tae take the car though, aye? Ah cannae jist take cash instead, naw? Ah mean, dinnae get me wrang, likes. She's a fuckin stormin beast ken. A real beauty. But yuv seen ma situation ken. Cash wud be a lot mare handy right noo.'

'Mr Hunter.' I smiled as he pulled into the lay-by. 'When you sign for the car, you're supposed to keep a hold of it for at least six months. After that you can do whatever the hell you like with it, mate.'

'Shite. Six months, aye...shite.'

I could almost hear the wheels and cogs inside his head spinning into overtime. Most likely thinking how the hell he could ever keep such a stunning car in such good nick or keep it hidden from the local vandals and thieves for the next six months. And then, after that, how much could he get for it?

Richard brought the car to a grinding halt, stalling her in the process.

'Now pop the bonnet and the boot for me.'

Richard looked clueless, so I showed him how to pop the bonnet from underneath the steering wheel. I took the keys from the ignition and pressed the button to release the back boot, which was situated upon the key ring.

'Simple enuff, eh!' Richard said, grinning.

'Go and take a look underneath the hood for yourself. See how beautiful she is down there.'

We both exited the car.

'I'm just gonna grab something from the front compartment.'

Richard headed for the popped rear bonnet and lifted it high before fixing it to the latch to hold it upright. Meanwhile, I made my way to the front boot, where the rope and crowbar awaited. I took the crowbar and tucked it neatly into the back of my trousers. The hard steel against my skin was cold and uncomfortable, but it was going to be only a short and minor discomfort. I left the front boot open and headed back around to Richard at the rear of the car. He leaned over the engine, tucking his head down and hovering his gaze all over the sparkling-clean machine. His hands and fingers rested upon the edge of the engine frame, supporting his posture. Another idea occurred. Perhaps I wouldn't need the crowbar after all.

'Take a good look at that engine, Mr Hunter,' I said eagerly, gesturing him to stick his face right up on into it. 'See how beautiful and shiny she is. And take a good whiff, too. Glorious, no?'

'Oh, aye. She's a beauty, aw right. A fuckin right shag and a half.'

Richard took a long, hard, up-close-and-personal sniff of the engine as I positioned myself right beside him. An inch away from where the latch held up the heavy and solid metal bonnet.

'Yes, she is.' I replied. And with my adrenaline at boiling point and without even hesitating a second, I placed one free hand on top of the raised bonnet, gripping it tightly. I swiped the latch with my other hand. In another split second, I used both hands to bring the heavy steel bonnet crashing down upon Richard's skull and upper back, as hard as I could. His entire upper body crumpled and collapsed instantly on top of the engine. He let out a strange, sickly gasp and a breathless yelp, which sounded more like a gag reflex. I wasn't done yet, though. Not by a long shot.

Another second passed and I raised the bonnet again, high above Richard. This time I slammed it down even harder upon his head and upper body. There was a sick crack. Possibly some ribs or his head splitting in two. Richard seemed barely conscious as he slid down to his knees and onto the concrete floor of the lay-by. His head still rested upon the lower half of the engine while the rest of his body slumped unnaturally against the rear end of the car.

I raised the bonnet one last time.

Only his head, neck, and gripped fingers lay within the bonnet's perimeter. I held the bonnet up high, one last time, with one hand, as high as it would go. With my other I grabbed Richard by the back of his mopped hair and pulled his head and neck out and away from the bonnet's reach, leaving only his fingers, still tightly gripping the framed edging of the hood. Again, and without hesitating, I slammed the bonnet down hard, as hard as I fucking could, right on top of his fingers. Only his thumbs were saved from the sheer force of the slam and the unhealthy cracks and pops that followed. The jolt of immense pain was enough to wrench Richard right out of his unconscious heap. He roared with the most horrific agonising screams, desperately trying to pull his fingers free, but it wasn't happening. As he continued to howl, wriggle, and struggle away, I took out the crowbar from the back of my trousers. I raised it high and out to the side. I swung it with a solid hard and ferocious stroke, straight into the line of his mouth and lower jaw. Facial bones shattered. Teeth and blood sprayed and splattered all over the closed shiny bonnet of the car while Richard slumped against it once more. His body and mind returning to another state of unconsciousness.

Not wishing to draw unwanted attention from passing cars, I quickly raised the bonnet, releasing Richard's shattered and crushed fingers. He fell to the floor, slumping in a heap. His fingers looked flat, crooked, bloodied, and unnatural. Bone even splintered through the skin of three of his fingers.

By the time I lifted him into the passenger seat and began tying him up, his fingers were bruising and swelling severely. A smug satisfaction overwhelmed me. Even if I were caught right this very second, before seeing through the final act of my plan, Richard certainly wouldn't be raising any more fingers towards women, children, or beast ever again.

Once I had him securely fastened against the seat, I drove back to the secluded coastal spot that had caught my eye. There was only a small fence separating the high road from the overgrown field which led up a shallow incline towards a clifftop with a fairly high drop in the distance. A drop which led directly down into a rough and rocky, high-tide, chilling North Sea.

I pulled over onto the side of the road, half on the grass, half on the concrete, and waited for an oncoming car to pass. As this was happening I realised that we weren't too far from the beach where Celine and I had driven yesterday. Where we playfully skinny dipped like a bunch of demented teenage bampots in the freezing cold waters.

The road became clear. The recent gallivanting thoughts about Celine and I evaporated to the back of my mind. Quickly I accelerated up and off the road, ramming through a small shoddy wooden fence that was guarding the field. I drove over the long unkempt grass and weeds towards the clifftop. I brought the car to a halt with only a hundred or so metres until the clifftop's edge.

Richard sat with his head slumped to one side on the seat beside me. He was still unconscious, yet making shallow and faint breaths. His blood had dried and crusted all over his mouth, chin, and tracksuit top. His fingers had swelled enormously, each one half the size of his own palm. He looked disgusting, yet eerily at peace.

I pulled out another cigarette and lit it. I began thinking about ways I could wake up this walking piece of dog shit. I noticed some anti-freeze and car oil were in the boot. I could throw it on him, make him smell it. Even better, shove it into his mouth and let him choke on it. I could even burn this cigarette onto his cheek; that might do the trick. For a second I felt a slight twang of remorse, regret, even sympathy about what I was doing and going to do to this sick fuck. Did this torture and abuse I was inflicting upon him make me just like him?

Perhaps!

Then I thought about some of the things he'd done to me as a defenceless child. Things I hadn't thought about in years. Things that felt like they'd happened to somebody else, and not me, which they probably had, too. How many other children had suffered and had their lives destroyed because of this sick bastard monster? How many lives was I saving now by going through with this deed today? How many innocent lives could I have saved if I'd only done it sooner?

I couldn't wait any longer. I had to wake up this prick. I couldn't sit there in view of the next passing cars, one of which would no doubt inform the cops about the presence of a nice, shiny silver Porsche Turbo perched on top of a cliff like it was a re-enactment of *Thelma and Louise*, thus putting an end to my act of vengeance.

I shook him. Nothing. I prodded and poked at his ribs. Still nothing. I squeezed one of his swollen, shattered, and broken fingers. He stirred. I wiggled and squeezed harder. He stirred even more, then moaned with a pained whimper. Slowly, the sick fuck was coming round. He shook his head. Still dazed. Still wildly confused.

'Wake up, you sick fuck!' I said, squeezing his cheeks and shaking his head back and forth. He dribbled blood mixed with saliva from his mouth. He tried to say something, then spat out a large gulp of more blood and saliva. It flowed down his chin and onto his tracksuit, mixing with the crusted blood already stained there.

'Ma heed! Ma fuckin heed!' he moaned. He tried to move his hands and fingers to his face, but the rope tied around his arms and upper body prevented him from doing so. 'Ma fuckin fing-urs in aw, ahhhhhhh.' He continued moaning in agony as he tried to wiggle his broken, purple, swollen fingers. 'Whit the fuck, man? Whit the fuck es goin oan here, man? Whit. The. Fuck!' He roared again, angry, hurt, confused. He struggled even more, jolting back and forth, but his struggles were useless.

I took another draw from my cigarette and watched.

'Whit the hell did ye dae tae me, man? Why the fuck am ah tied up like thus, ye cunt, ye?' And ma fing-urs. Ma fuckin fing-urs!' he screamed, then sobbed while glancing down at his unrecognisable purple and black, swollen, shattered hands. 'Ah cannie feel ur move ma fing-urrrrrrrrrrrrs! Arrrgghhhhh.'

I couldn't help but chuckle at the ridiculousness of it all. Especially this pathetic man reduced to crying like a big baby. Finally, I broke my silence. 'You really have no idea yet, do you, Richard? Not one fucking clue why you're in this little predicament, you sick, sick bastard, you.'

I took my burning cigarette and held it to within a few millimetres of Richard's face. His eyes widened with fear. His sobs and moans ceased for the time being. I had his attention now, the cunt. I raised the fag slightly towards his nearest eye. He pulled away, struggling hard. But he had nowhere to go.

'Well, let's see if I can jog your memory a wee bit then, shall I?'

Richard struggled immensely, yanking his head back and away from me like he was having an epileptic fit. It didn't matter, though. He was going nowhere. I stubbed out the burning cigarette on his cheek. Richard howled in pain before breaking into a fit of desperate sobs. He looked so utterly pathetic. Unrecognisable, in fact, as the big, powerful, hard man who used to stand over me as a boy. I shoved the remainder of my cigarette hard into his mouth. Was I actually enjoying this on some sick and twisted sadistic plain? Surely not. He quickly spat the cigarette out and onto the floor.

I took off my jacket and opened my white silk shirt, pulling the top end down beneath my left shoulder. A small cluster of cigarette burns, scars, and mementos from Richard's very own abuse upon my own body were revealed. Richard glanced at the scars for a beat, no more, no less, before turning away in utter shame.

'Looks like we have some of the same scars now, Ricky boy, eh?'

Richard sobbed again, clearly upset and breathing hard. He knew his end was nigh. 'Liam! Liam Walker,' Richard sobbed in between soft, muffled breaths.

'I was just an innocent and pure wee defenceless boy when she brought you into our lives, you sick fuck! You disgusting, pathetic excuse for a human being.'

My emotions were getting the better of me. I could feel the tears welling up in my eyes. The anger and rage building up inside, higher and stronger than I'd ever felt before.

'You took away my innocence, my childhood, my trust in people. My self-confidence. My self-belief.'

'Am sorry, Liam!' Richard sobbed. More tears and saliva dripped down his face. 'Am so, so sorry. Please...Am so, so sorry.'

I felt so angry. How dare this sick fuck ask—in fact, beg—for my forgiveness? How dare he. How fucking dare he. I wanted to pound and slam my fists into his face so hard, open him up. Break even more of his broken jaw, more of his face. For the moment, I refrained.

'How many others have there been, eh? HOW MANY OTHER CHILDREN AND THEIR LIVES HAVE YOU DESTROYED, YOU MONSTER? HOW MANY, EH?'

Richard closed his eyes and slumped his head to one side. His sobs were uncontrollable.

'Yeah, you keep those fucking eyes shut tight, you sick fuck. You don't even deserve to see what fate I have in store for you.' I poked my finger hard into his skull. 'Because inside there, pal. Behind those closed fucking eyes. Well, that's the only place left for you to hide now, you fuck. You sick fucking fuck.'

In an instant rage, I turned back to the steering wheel and started the engine. I slammed down upon the accelerator and sped right for the clifftop edge. With fifty metres to go, I hit ninety on the speedometer.

'I sure hope you enjoy hell.'

Richard screamed in terror as the cliff's edge approached us fast, faster than I'd expected. In another split second, I yanked open the driver's door and dived out of the car without time to spare. I hit the soft, long grass harshly and rolled over half a dozen times, never taking my eyes off the roaring Porsche as it took flight and nosedived over the cliff and into the cold, deep, rough, and rocky waters below. Quick as I could, I exploded back up onto my feet and rushed over to the clifftop edge. By the time I reached the edge and peered over the side, I could just barely make out the blurry back end of the silver Porsche underneath the murky grey waves below.

***

Ten minutes later I was walking back along the main coastal road, back towards Dunbar. It was the closest town from where I'd ended up, and from there I could get a train or taxi back to

Edinburgh. A black sugary coffee wouldn't go amiss, too. Another car passed by on the quiet road. I stuck out my thumb like it meant something and just like the last few cars that whizzed on by, this one didn't stop, either. I must have looked a right state to any passing drivers. Hell, even I wouldn't have picked me up. Mud and grass stains all over my fancy black-suited trousers. A blood-stained white silk shirt. Imagine if a police car passed by. I chuckled at the thought and shook my head. Maybe it would be better to keep off the main road for the time being. Walk through those fields on my left instead, or that light forest on the right. I was about to do exactly that when I heard the sounds of yet another approaching car from behind me. I turned around, feeling less than hopeful, yet still I raised my hand, sticking out my thumb with a default monotonous gesture.

Shite!

My heart sank to the bowels of my stomach. A bloody police car with a lone male driver was approaching and had already slowed down. Brilliant! How the hell was I going to explain this? Or my mucky and roughed-up appearance or why the hell I was out here in the middle of nowhere in the first place? As soon as he found out who I was, it would be game over. How many warrants would there be for my arrest by now?

The police car pulled over just a few yards ahead. He parked halfway on the grass and half on the road. The young, tall, clean-shaven and well-built policeman exited the car. He even leaned back inside to grab his hat, which had been lying on the passenger side of his vehicle…you know, just to make it official.

'Hello there,' said the policeman, walking round the back of his car towards me. 'You're a bit out in the middle of nowhere here, no? Where you heading?'

'London Town actually, mate,' I replied, putting on my best cockney accent. I was good at mimicking accents once upon a time. Back when I had parties, friends, and people to mimic.

'London! Jesus! You are a long way from home. What are you doing all the way up here?'

'Oh! Well, last night was my stag, do ya know, mate. And my friends thought they'd be a bunch of poncey comedians, yeah, and get me really drunk, ditching me up in ere in blaady Scotland.' I continued to slaver. It was the first thing that leaped into my head, to be fair.

'Nice pals.'

'Yeah, Ar used to think so too in all, mate.'

The policeman stared me up and down before pulling out a small notepad. 'How'd you get that blood on your shirt, sir?'

Shite. I glanced down at the blood stains. They weren't glaringly obvious, but they were there and showing.

'Ad a bleedin nose earlier, ya know.'

'What's your name, sir?'

'Michael! Michael McNabb...and you are?'

'McNabb! You don't sound very Scottish.' He grinned.

'Scottish parents mate, init. Born and raised daan saath though, ar'm afraid. Support Scotland for the rugby though for my blaady sins and England for the footy.'

'Do you have any ID on you, Mr McNabb?'

'If ar still had my bleedin ID and wallet do you think ard still be walking daan this bloody road right now, mate?' I chuckled.

The policeman hesitated. He gave me another suspicious once over, then gestured towards his car.

'Do you mind stepping into the back of the police car, sir, for one minute while I do a quick wee check, aye?'

Fuck. I think I'd been rumbled. I needed to do something and fast if I wanted to see Celine again...but what?

'Yeah, Ar do mind, mate. Where's YOUR bleedin ID? You could be anyone, mate. Maybe one of my friends hired you in all to dump me off somewhere else.'

'I can assure you, sir, I am the real deal.'

He pulled out his own ID. Shite, I was making this worse, much worse. I knew it was game over, but I wanted to buy myself a few more seconds to build up the courage to go through with what I was about to do next to that poor bloke.

'Yeah, nice badge that. Just lovely, mate. Ar have a fake student ID back home just like it in all.'

The policeman looked fed up. He took a deep, frustrated breath and a step back. He pulled out a small radio speaker strapped to his chest and spoke into it. 'Base from Sierra Echo twelve over.'

'Come in Sierra Echo twelve over' went the radio, with an attractive female voice on the receiving end.

'I need a background check on one Michael McNabb...' He turned his gaze back to me. 'What's your home address, sir?'

I hesitated. This had to be done. If I had any chance of being with Celine for whatever short time I had left, this had to be done right now.

The policeman continued to glance over. 'Your home address...sir...?'

Shite, shite, shite! This was so bad. This was so fucked up.

'Sir!' The policeman raised his voice impatiently, stepping towards me.

I closed my eyes, let out a deep sigh, and took a step towards him. At the same time, quick as a flash, I brought up my right knee, fast and hard, right between his legs, right into his crown jewels. The policeman keeled over immediately, clutching his balls for all they were worth. He looked speechless, breathless, and paralysed with pain all at once. I was about to punch him square in the jaw, too, sending him even more helplessly to the ground, but I pulled back at the last second. It wasn't needed. He'd almost staggered to the ground anyway. Instead I nudged him over onto the grass with ease. He fell to the floor like a sack of potatoes.

'I'm sorry, mate! Really, I am,' I said, my voice returning to its soft Scottish normality. I grabbed his handcuffs, unhooking them from his trousers. I forced him over onto his belly and wrapped his arms around his back. He groaned in pain, still too paralysed, helpless, and winded to struggle. I cuffed his wrists together and left him there on the side of the road. I was sure he'd be all right. Backup would come for him soon enough when he didn't answer his radio.

***

I jumped into the police car. A sexy yet firm and official female voice on the car radio called out for the real owner of the vehicle, but he was currently indisposed and wouldn't be replying any time soon. I switched off the radio. The keys were still in the ignition. I turned on the engine and accelerated away, not even looking back for a second. All I could think about was getting back to Celine and our new life together, packing up our shit and getting the hell out of this goddamn country once and for all. Just take off to France like Celine had suggested and make a go of life there on the continent. Of course, I felt bad for Mum, too. I thought about driving back down to the borders to see her again, if only for ten minutes, apologise for what a horrible bastard shite of a son I'd been all those years. How I'd never kept in touch with her. That I'd never looked after her and cared for her like any good son should have done for his only parent. I'd never even told her how much I loved her, not once.

I shook those thoughts from my head. Realistically, there was no time. I would phone her, either on the road south with Celine or whenever we reached wherever the hell we ended up. If I owed anything in this life to the woman who had given birth to me and done the best she could at raising me, I owed her that much...

***

I sped through another set of red lights, almost ready to pull over and chance my luck on foot when I spotted a speed camera dead ahead. No better parking place, I suppose, than on top of my second pet hate of all time—second, that is, to traffic wardens. So,

I headed straight for the contraption, ramming into its steel grey pole exterior and completely uprooting it from the ground, then slamming the main body of the camera box down hard onto the concrete road in front.

A couple of passing cars beeped their horns, cheered, and waved at me with sheer joy as they drove by. Some young ned teens across the road waiting at a bus stop started applauding and cheering me on, too. One even toasted an already half-drunk can of lager into the air like he was accepting me as one of their own. A smashed-up police car on this estate was worth more than any million-pound lottery win, that was for sure.

I exited the police car and waved back at the neds and all the passing drivers still beeping their horns. I smiled and took a bow before getting the hell out of there. I legged it over a nearby stone wall and made my way towards the southeasterly foot of Arthur's Seat.

***

I entered the front doors of the Balmoral Hotel. I walked through the main reception at a fast pace and headed straight for the lift to the top floor, where both my penthouse room and Celine lay in wait. Thank Christ I'd paid cash for our suite or else this little wild adventure of ours would surely be well and truly over by now.

When I entered the suite, I immediately called for Celine. We had to leave. We had to get the hell out of the country immediately. Too much had happened these past few days for any return to a normal life.

She didn't answer. I stepped inside the main bedroom and called for her again. Still nothing. I noticed that the bed had been made and there was no sign of Celine's handbag or clothes. I continued to call her name as I entered the bathroom.

Another empty room.

A sinking feeling engulfed me. She was gone for sure. I didn't know what the hell to think or do. My mind was in such twists and turns of turmoil. She'd abandoned me and done a runner. She'd finally woken up and seen sense or perhaps had even caught a glimpse of me on the news, already stealing Porsches and police cars, terrorising seemingly innocent civilians and traffic wardens on the streets of Edinburgh, and now a killer on the run from the police. Fuck this shite, she'd probably thought and gone back home. Right back to her old life.

I switched on the TV and scanned the news channels. There was nothing related to me and my recent criminal activity in the slightest. Even on the local newsreel or the red button news. I switched it off and stepped over to the window. The view was absolutely cracking of Edinburgh's city centre, stretching from southeast to southwest. All the way from the bowel rock tunnels of Waverly Station, Arthur's Seat and the vibrant North Bridge to the Prince's Street gardens, the steep mound and galleries. If you squeezed your face just enough right up against the window pane, you could almost see the entire width of the gothic castle perched high upon its proud volcanic peak. It calmed me immensely to look over and stare in awe at this beautiful wee city. It almost took my mind away from the task and troubles at hand...almost, but not quite.

I turned my attention back to the North Bridge. It looked so busy down there, vibrantly buzzing, in fact, with both traffic and pedestrians. Everyone and everything going back and forth, to and from somewhere. Home, work, the shops, wherever. Maybe Celine had just grown bored of sitting around in the hotel room all morning and afternoon by herself waiting for me to return. Maybe she'd decided to go off and do a little bit of shopping instead, keeping herself entertained and her mind away from our clouded and uncertain future.

Okay! I slapped my cheeks and shook my head, trying to clear my mind. So, she'd popped out for a bit, that's all. Either she'd gone shopping or went away home to get her things, her phone, her clothes, her belongings, whatever. I'd just wait here for a while longer before switching my panicked head back on again.

I turned and glanced over at that big, beautiful, comfy, and scrumptious-looking king-sized bed. Perhaps I'd lay down and have a quick power nap, recharge the old batteries before Celine came back and we finally left this place to make our way south and to France that very evening. Aye! A wee power nap sounded brilliant right about now. And the more I thought about it, the more exhausted I became.

I made my way onto the bed. I let myself fall onto the thick, soft duvet, which lovingly embraced me, moulding itself around my body like a new, warm, thick skin. God, it felt like pure heaven. My mind wandered to a vision of Celine coming through those beautiful hotel suite doors, back from her successful shopping spree down Princes Street. She'd see my sleeping body lying flat upon the bed and immediately drop all her shopping bags and dive right on top of me, waking me with playful glee. We'd kiss, we'd cuddle, we'd caress. We'd have one more wonderfully raunchy lovemaking session before beginning our next crazy, wild adventure together down on the continent.

Before even a whole minute had lapsed, I'd fallen into a deep, joyful, and wondrous sleep.

Chapter 15

I woke up. I felt more awake, recharged, and full of beans than I'd ever felt in my life. Jesus Christ, I'd needed that nap. Then I noticed the light outside and my heart sank. The sun was setting. It must've been around 7 or 8 pm. I'd slept for almost five hours. Still lying on the bed, I twisted my head back and forth, glancing all around. The room remained empty of a second body. Everything was so damn quiet. This wasn't good. This wasn't good at all. Where the hell was Celine? I had a bad feeling about this. I immediately jumped off the bed and flew out of the hotel room. There was only one place in my mind where I needed to go.

Outside the Balmoral and before making my way over the North Bridge, I jogged over towards the beginning of Waterloo Place, where I'd left Celine's car parked the night before. Oddly, it was still there. Why was it still there? I was sure Celine took the keys off me last night and put them into her purse. Surely she'd have remembered to take the car, or at least check up on it if she'd left the hotel earlier. Curious. I noticed, plastered across the windscreen in thick black and yellow stripes, my old familiar friend 'the parking ticket.' I'd forgotten to put more money in the metre this morning, but it was the least of my worries.

I jogged over the North Bridge, still busy with pedestrians, most of them standing about waiting at the various bus stops to go somewhere. I approached the Royal Mile Crossroads at the Old Bank Hotel and continued my jaunt down the high street, straight towards Celine's' apartment building on the Canongate, not far from the bottom. The sun had set behind me and darkness was quickly spreading its black wings over the city.

When I approached her apartment block, my heart swelled and relief swept over me. Her curtains were drawn but there was clearly a light shining inside her ground-floor flat. I grinned, shook my head, and imagined her still packing up her belongings for our great adventure. The outside door was locked, so I pressed the buzzer for her apartment. Within the space of a few seconds, she buzzed me in. It didn't even cross my mind at the time that she didn't ask who I was. When I approached the door, I could hear the bolt moving inside and the chain being unlatched. I was full of smiles and ready to hug her tightly. Perhaps even slip in for a quick wee coffee. Help with packing her things, then get the hell out of there.

My frown quickly turned upside down when Celine's front door was casually opened by a young, pretty Korean girl wearing a sexy nightdress. I was very confused.

'You are David, yes?' said the girl in broken English.

'No. I'm Liam. Is Celine...here?'

The girl hesitated for a brief second, then motioned to close the door over.

'I sorry. You must have wrong address. Good day.'

She closed the door, but I quickly slammed my foot in the gap. I pushed the door open with ease and barged my way inside. The young Korean girl cradled and shielded her body like I might strike her and backed away, looking scared. Another young Korean girl entered the hallway from the living room. She looked scarred by my presence, too. She clutched a mobile phone in her hand and immediately began dialling a number.

'Look, guys,' I protested, holding out my hands. 'I'm not here to cause any trouble, okay?'

The second girl continued dialling.

'Please. Put down the phone and just talk to me for a minute, then I'm gone, okay? Understand?'

The firmness in my tone must have gotten through to her because she stopped dialling and glanced at me instantly. The first Korean girl composed herself too and stood upright again.

'You no want to rob us, no? You no here to beat and rob us, no?' said the second girl, still panicking.

'No,' I grinned, shaking my head.

'Because we are Petrov girls. He our boss. He very violent man when it comes to his girls and money.'

That Petrov name popping up again. A red flag went up in the back of my mind.

'I just...I'm just looking for Celine, that's all. I haven't seen or heard from her since this morning. Do you know where she is?'

'We do not know any Celine,' the first girl replied while glancing back at the other.

'This is her flat, right? She was living here yesterday. You must at least have some rough idea about the girl who lives here. Or used to live here?'

The two girls paused and stared hard at each other. 'You perhaps mean...girl who worked here before us?' the second Korean girl replied.

'Yes. That's exactly who I mean. The girl who worked here yesterday, before you.'

'Well...this our place now...from this afternoon. They move her somewhere else.'

'When did this happen? Where did they move her?'

The two girls looked at each other again anxiously. 'We do not know,' replied the second girl. 'We never saw anyone here since we move. Only some of Petrov men and clients. Maybe Petrov took her back to sauna. Or maybe he move her to another apartment. He has many apartment here for girls.'

The second Korean girl went for her phone again. 'You want I call Petrov and find out? He answer your question. I have his number here. I call him, yes?'

'No! No...don't call Petrov. Just...just tell me which sauna I can find him at.'

'Usually...I think...Blair Street! But lately he been spending lot of time at our old sauna on Pilrig Street. Maybe try there first.'

I took a deep breath and gently nodded. 'Okay. I'll do that. Thank you so much, girls,' I replied with the utmost sincerity. I didn't want to leave them all anxious and scared and calling up every bloody pimp in Edinburgh telling them that some loony guy with a crazed look in his eyes had just forced his way into their new apartment asking about Celine. 'And I'm really sorry about barging in like this. Really sorry.'

Just then I heard a tap-tap-tapping at the half-opened front door. I turned and opened it fully. A nervous-looking gentleman in his fifties, wearing a business suit, stood there looking nervous.

'David, right?' I said with a wink.

'Yes, how did you...?'

I gently patted him on the shoulder and beckoned him inside at the exact moment I walked out. 'Your ladies await.'

***

I walked to the bottom of the mile, along Abbeyhill and up Easter Road towards Albert Street. I then cut over towards Leith Walk and eventually Pilrig Street on the opposite side. It was quite a walk, as the low and gothic streetlights and dark night above swarmed around me from all angles. It must've been at least 10 pm. I spent the next hour or so walking up and down Pilrig Street looking for any indication of the bloody well-hidden sauna. Even the slightest hinted sign would be welcome, yet I found nothing. Nothing! Not even a bit of graffiti. It was mostly just rows and rows of bed and breakfasts and guest houses spread all over. I decided to give up and either head back to chat more with the Korean girls or make my way down Leith Walk, heading back over to the Old Town and the Blair Street sauna, which was a lot more obvious to the eye and stuck out like a sore thumb. Then a really slim, pretty, yet pale brunette wearing a short, black, sexy skirt came seductively towards me from the Leith Walk end of Pilrig Street. She gave me an intense sexual stare before releasing a mischievous grin right at the point of passing me by. I froze, then turned around to watch her. She noticed my reaction and stopped in her tracks, then turned around to face me.

'You look for business, baby?' the sexy girl replied in broken English. Her accent sounded Russian or at least somewhere from Eastern Europe.

'No. Sorry,' I replied. ' I just thought...it doesn't matter.'

Another time, another place, a different frame of mind and I would have surely snapped up her offer, but not this time. Not today. Not now. My heart and soul belonged to one girl and one girl alone.

She shrugged, pouted her lips like she could suck a tennis ball through a hose pipe, and went on her way. I continued to watch her wiggle seductively down the footpath. Then it dawned on me that she might be heading for that sauna place around here somewhere, the one which was so well hidden. Surely it was no coincidence having a sauna or massage parlour somewhere on the same street that I found a working girl. I was about to shout her back, ask her if she knew where this sauna was located. Perhaps she even knew Celine or this Petrov character. But I decided against calling her back. Instead, I moved across to the other side of Pilrig Street and followed her.

After a short walk, she veered off to the right, down a dark and grotty cobbled lane before taking another sharp left down a dark and creepy alley. The alleyway led down the backside of some of the main houses situated on Pilrig Street. I poked my head around the corner of the new lane. It was dark, dirty, secluded. Some old garages gathered at the bottom end. The working girl veered left towards a steel gate at the back of one of the larger houses on her left. Before she'd even gotten close, two large, brutish-looking men came out from behind the steel gate, stopping her in her tracks.

'Ye shud uv been back fuckin ages ago, ye stupid wee Polish tart, ye,' shouted the smaller thug with the skinhead. He spoke with a thick Scottish accent.

'I from Ukraine, no Poland, sweetheart,' replied the girl, trying to sound smart when her best option was probably to say nothing at all. That point was further emphasised by the Scottish thug when he slapped her hard across the face. The girl squealed but stood her ground.

'Whae gees a shite, ye fuckin durty hoor, ye! Hoo much money did ye mak today anyhoo, huh?'

The girl ignored him and continued to hold her face. The thug grew impatient and slapped her again.

'HOO MUCH, HUH?'

She backed away. 'All right, okay. Stop hitting me. I have to make living from this face, you know. Fuck.' She pulled a wad of cash from her purse and showed it to the small Scottish thug. He grabbed the money from her hands before spitting in her face.

'Es that et? Were ye suckin cocks oot thir fur fuckin free the night hen, eh? Jesus Christ, woman.' He grabbed her by the back of the neck and forced her through the gate and down some steep basement steps. 'Geet the hell in thir, ye stupid wee Polish tart. Yul fuckin make yer money the night anyhoo, that's fur sure.'

The second, taller thug remained by the gate, as if standing guard.

Shite! I didn't know what to do after seeing that violent display. Call the cops? I almost chuckled. No, I needed to get inside. Needed to find out if Celine was in there and see if she was okay. There's no way she'd go willingly back to these brutes. She must be in there, being held against her will, or if not here, somewhere around town. No matter what, I had to do something. I had to at least try and find out.

I took a deep breath and stepped out into the lane. I walked casually towards the tall thug standing guard at the gate. He saw me coming towards him. I could see him tense up as he watched me approach, staggering a little for effect.

'You open the night pal, aye?' I said, putting on my best thick Scottish jakey accent.

The tall thug looked me up and down. Finally, he spoke with an Eastern European accent. 'And what exactly do you think we are open for, my friend?'

'Wet fanny man likes, eh? Bin a lang, hard day et wurk fur sum uv us ken. Noo av goat baw bags the size uv fuckin beach baws to drain.'

'Have you been here before, my friend? I have never seen you around.'

'Naw, never here pal, naw. But am pretty regular at that yin on Blair Street and the yin on Rose Street ken. Am actually a regular uv Celine's tae in aw likes. Ken that braw French lassie whae wurks on the mile in her ain flat? Ah actually went roond tae hers the night like ken, but they say she's moved ken. They suggested ah try here.'

The tall thug smiled. It looked like I was winning him over with my slavering shite Scottish patter. 'Oh yes, my friend. That French lass is a great girl. Some nice pair of titties on her too, no? So, you seen her a few times, huh?'

'Oh, aye. Braw lassie, that yin. Jist. The. Best. Ken.' I said this while kissing the tips of my fingers for effect.

'Bloody expensive though, ja. My God, she could break your bank account into tiny little pieces after just a few hours in her company.'

'Aye and break yur fuckin baws tae in aw like pal, ken. Ha.'

The tall thug roared with laughter at the joke. 'Ha, ha, my man. You a funny guy. Funny guy! You know, you actually in luck too, my friend, you know.'

'Oh aye! Hoo's that likes.'

'Celine is working here now. Just started this afternoon, actually.'

My heart nearly exploded from my chest there and then, but I had to keep my composure. Whatever I did, I couldn't give away my game even though it almost ripped my heart out. Especially if it was against her will, which it had to be. I couldn't think of any other explanation. Something had gone drastically wrong from when I'd left her in bed this morning to the time of my return earlier this afternoon.

'Aye. That right, aye. Nice yin! Hoo she wurking here though, likes? And no at the flat anymare?'

'I do not know, my friend. Some change of plan by management.' He grinned smugly and every fibre in my body wanted to cave in his goddamn skull before plucking out his stupid grinning teeth one by one with my bare hands. He must've been referring to this Petrov dude when he'd said management.

'And now she working the sauna again. She gonna be so much more cheaper, too my friend. So, you better get in there quick fast before you find a queue for her services all the way back to the castle.'

The tall thug laughed hard. I could do nothing else but laugh pretentiously along with him when in my mind, the thought of such a thing, other men having their way with my unwilling angel…it ate away at me. Ate away at my soul and much worse than the cancer ever could.

As his laughter died, I patted him on the arm and made my way past. For a second I thought he might stop me, but instead he only made a move for a packet of cigarettes in his jacket pocket.

'You have a good time in there tonight, my friend. Do not spend all of your hard-earned paycheck at once.'

'Oh, dinnae worry boot that, pal. Al be sure tae save a tenner fur ma wife and bairns sausage suppers the night.'

The tall Eastern European thug laughed again as I descended the steps. When I reached the bottom, I was confronted by a dully lighted steel door. I tried to push it open, but it wouldn't budge. I pulled it, but it still wouldn't move an inch.

'Just give it a knock, my friend. Maggie will open up for you,' shouted the tall thug down at me. I could hear him, but couldn't see him.

'Aye, cheers pal,' I shouted back.

I knocked hard upon the steel door. After a few moments, a small rectangular-shaped shutter in the middle of the door slid open. A pair of squint-narrow eyes stared back at me.

'Hey,' I said, sounding as friendly as I could.

The small shuttered peephole closed and I could hear the sound of locks turning from inside. The door was eventually opened by a stern middle-aged Chinese-looking woman.

'Hey! How ye daen, hen,' I said, again keeping with my thicker Scottish accent for appearance's sake. Although now that I was past the door security, I felt pretty damn sure no one gave a shit how I spoke anymore. I mean, in the past day I'd conversed with more people with accents from all corners of the world than I had in my entire life.

'Me Maggie. You looking for some hot action fun tonight big boy, ya,' said an overly enthusiastic Maggie. She beckoned me into the hallway as she closed the steel door firmly over behind me.

From a first impression, the underground basement sauna seemed fairly busy. I could already see two skimpily dressed women at the end of the long corridor dead ahead. One of the young women, wearing only underwear and stockings, led a young, shy-looking man out of a distant room before taking him into one of the five other sealed doorways along the corridor. Presumably all bedrooms. She closed the door firmly shut behind her.

A large, bald, thuggish-looking man in his mid-thirties stepped out from another room on the left. He made his way up and along the dimly lit corridor, heading towards a large oak door at the very back. He paid little to no attention to anything else, and when he reached the large oak door, he knocked and waited for a reply.

The room he'd just left, right beside me, still had its doorway half open. I glanced inside to see another two men. One was the small Scottish thug I'd previously seen outside hitting the Ukrainian prostitute. The other was yet another brutish, well-built man with scars a plenty carved all over his face. They had just started playing cards at a small round table at the back of the room. I noticed a handgun lying on the table beside the scarred thug. Maggie saw my distraction and interest in the room and quickly closed the door, blocking my view.

'No juicy pussy in there for you, cheeky Scottish boy. Now go to end of hallway, turn right, and enter pink room. Then choose girl. You give money. You go fuck, ya!'

I felt taken aback and a little shocked by her bold and forward words, but just nodded in agreement. 'Aye. Sure thing.'

Maggie ushered me farther up the corridor. I put one foot in front of the other and started moving. I tried to take my time, carefully weighing my options for when I finally found Celine, but my mind was coming up blank. At the end of the corridor someone must have shouted from behind the oak door for the large bald thug to enter because he made his way inside and quickly closed the door.

'You should try Lynn Mai! She very popular choice! She make you very happy. She very, very excitable. Very vocal! VERY horny. She what you Scots call...a bloody good ride, ya.'

Maggie laughed ridiculously at her own words. I could only force a smile at her comfortably forward ways. I kept walking the length of the long corridor. I had almost reached the oak door and the pink glowing open doorway beside it. I imagined that the sealed doors on either side of the corridor were all bedroom/playrooms for the punters to take the girls and have their wicked way with them. I'd been in one or two saunas in my long-forgotten past and knew enough to grasp the set up. Where Maggie was urging me must have been the waiting room or lounge area where the working girls put their assets on display for the paying punters to ponder over.

I cautiously approached the end of the corridor and the open doorway situated to the right of the large oak door. From within, a pink glow engulfed me. From what I could make out, the entire room was painted mostly in pink with slight areas of black here and there. Even the furniture, seats, tables, couches, and carpets were a mixture of pink and black.

When I entered the room, a drunk, arrogant, and neddish-looking prick of a man caught my attention almost immediately. He sleazed over three half-naked girls upon the farthest away of two large couches on my right. One girl looked Chinese and wore a skimpy white bra and short white mini skirt. Another was the Ukrainian girl whom I'd seen outside only five minutes earlier. With her jacket removed, she was wearing only her sexy short black skirt with stockings and suspenders underneath and a skimpy black top.

My heart sank and skipped a few beats, not for the first time today.

Celine was the third girl.

It took a few long, hard seconds to recognise her at first, but it was her for sure. She wore her hair in pigtails and wore a matching black PVC skirt and bra. My eyes widened and my heart sank even more when I saw her badly bruised face and black eyes.

Celine glanced up at me and froze. Time almost stopped for both of us. Everything felt so surreal. I felt faint and queasy. What the hell was happening? What the hell had I gotten myself into here? And how was I going to get out of this? How was I going to get us both out of this?

I was about to say something. I was about to call her name when Celine's eyes widened with fear and she gently shook her head like she was telling me not to recognise her. I glanced at the two girls sitting beside her, who both smiled up at me before returning their attention to the ned. My eyes moved around the rest of the room. Two large men at the back caught my eye. Another two thuggish brutes sitting at the far end of the room. One of them sleazed over a young black girl while the other, a well-suited man, flicked through a newspaper. I turned my attention back to Celine, the ned, and the other two girls.

I had to make a plan of action here.

The first thought that came to me was that I should pay Celine for her services. Take her to one of the bedrooms along the corridor and then pray to whatever powers there may be in the universe that we would find a window or some other easy escape route. I felt sure that if we could just speak and have a few moments to ourselves behind closed doors, we could come up with something. Yes. That's what I'd do. A ray of hope lit me up inside. Getting her out of here could end up being a lot easier than I had previously imagined.

My thoughts and plans were rudely interrupted when the arrogant dumb fuck ned began roughly rubbing his hand up and down the thigh of the Chinese girl beside Celine. He slid his hand all the way up to her crotch. He started laughing. The girl tried to playfully push him away, but I could tell she hated his touch.

'Cum oan hen, eh? Jist huvin a wee bit uv fun naw.'

He turned his attention away from the two girls on his right and focussed upon Celine, who hadn't taken her tearful eyes away from me the entire time. Spontaneously, he grabbed and squeezed her breasts, playfully rubbing them against her will.

The rage consumed me. Watching another man sleaze all over Celine right there in front of me. It just happened in a flash. I had absolutely no control over my reactions. I knew in that moment that all bets were off. Celine tried to push the arrogant fuckwit away, but he quickly came back for more. Pinching her nipples this time like she were some docile slave pet or piece of meat.

'Owe. That bloody hurt. Stop it,' Celine cried as the ned laughed in her face.

'Cum oan, hen! Av awready paid fur the baith uv ye,' he said, winking back at the Chinese girl. 'Can dae whitever ah like noo.'

The other two men sitting at the back of the room chuckled at the ned's aggressive antics without looking away from their own distractions. Celine glanced back at me. Tears filled her eyes even more, threatening to pour down her cheeks like mini waterfalls. She looked utterly helpless in the moment and it completely ate me up inside. Eating into the very core of my soul.

The ned grabbed Celine by her pigtails and roughly forced her face into his groin, all the while laughing giddily like a misbehaving schoolboy. In that moment, I wished I'd brought a goddamn machine gun with me. But all I had was my courage and rage, which had reached a new peak and eventual breaking point.

'Cum oan tae fuck lass. eh. Sucky, sucky. eh! Sucky, sucky.'

Celine pushed away. The ned continued to laugh giddily. The two thugs at the back laughed again, too.

'What are you like, Rab,' said the man reading the paper, grinning and shaking his head. He had an accent, but I couldn't place it, possibly Northern English. 'Take them to a private room already, for Christ's sake.'

'Yes, take them. Take them,' Maggie insisted, chuckling. Meanwhile Celine tried even harder to resist the ned's overly aggressive playfulness.

Christ, I knew the odds were stacked against me. Perhaps I should've kept my cool and mouth shut until I could come up with some new plan of action. A plan that would more than likely mean biding my time and waiting for this dirty piece of shite to have his wicked way with my girl, my angel, my Celine. My new reason for living.

It wasn't going to happen, though. I couldn't control it. It's not who I was anymore.

I can't remember the exact moment I snapped. I just know that I finally lost that composure and control. The rage consumed me entirely. I dived for the ned, adrenaline pumping through my veins like heroin. I grabbed the cunt by the roots of his thick, scruffy hair and yanked him violently onto his feet. The whole room was cast into a web of stunned silence, from the ned and thugs at the back to the working girls and Celine at the front. Finally, the ned roared with pain when he realised what was happening.

I heard Celine screaming. 'Liam, no! Please!'

But it felt distant. Like it was coming from another world. Without thinking about it, I slammed my fist right through the ned's face as hard as I could. I felt and heard the sickly crunch as I flattened and embedded his nose deep into his face. Blood, bone, and snot splattered from the new split in the bridge of his nose and his newly demolished nostrils. Engulfed with rage, I pulled back my arm, ready to smash him yet again when I should've been keeping an eye on the other two men at the back of the room. Before I could unleash my next punch, someone grabbed my arm from behind. Immediately I released my grip on the blood-soaked ned and turned swiftly to face the man who'd been recently sitting with the black girl on his lap. He still held my arm and took a swing at my head with his free fist. I instinctively ducked and with the man leaning in and off balance, I brought my knee up hard, slamming the bone cap of it into his groin. He hit the deck like a sack of spuds dropped from a great height. But no sooner had I brought my knee back down to balance myself when the second suited man, the one reading the newspaper, rugby tackled me out of nowhere, wrapping himself around my waist and sending us both crashing down and through a glass coffee table.

The suited man looked and felt fit and athletic and gained his composure in no time to scramble on top of me. I was soundly winded by the hard fall through the table and felt lost in my confused daze. The suited man was quicker to act. He began punching my ribs and face continuously. Over and over again. I felt like his temporary punch bag. I struggled to wriggle free and push him away. I heard Celine scream as I desperately tried to shield myself with my arms and elbows.

'Please stop! Don't hurt him. Please don't hurt him,' Celine screamed again.

I caught a glimpse of the solid oak door in corridor opening. Then the huge bald man emerged from within, followed by another suited man with bleached blonde hair and a narrow, beady face. They entered the pink room.

'What the fuck, guys?' shouted one of the two new men. I wasn't sure which as I desperately tried to wriggle free from the athletic man's frantic blows. Somehow, I managed to get a good hold of the prick on top of me and wrestle him onto his side. Now I had gained the advantage. I had the momentum to roll on top of him and rain my blows down upon him when...my head snapped to the side. A sharp agonising pain spread throughout my jaw, my skull, my neck, then my spine. I almost blacked out. Someone had booted me in the side of the head with a good, hard kick. My energy drained instantly. I glanced up for a second, on the verge of unconsciousness. I think it was the large bald man who'd booted me. He certainly seemed closer to me than anyone else.

The suited athletic man beneath me quickly took advantage of this distraction and punched me square on the other side of my jaw. I fell down. Deflated and defeated. Landing on my back beside him. I was done. I felt barely conscious. A loud ringing in my ear blocked most of the surrounding sound and movement. I could barely hear Celine screaming and sobbing wildly.

'What the fuck is going on out here?' I heard someone shout. I think it might have been the blonde man again.

'No! Liam, no,' Celine cried. I think she tried to rush over to see if I was okay, but the big bald thug who'd booted me in the head bundled her up with ease before throwing her back upon the couch.

'What the fuck is all this about, huh? Jesus Christ,' said the blonde, suited man again.

'It must be her fancy man come tae rescue her, boss,' said the large bald man. He had a Scottish accent too, but not so thick. I saw the scruffy bleeding ned standing over me. He held his bloodied nose and face, yet was clearly laughing hysterically. He kicked me with a sharp toe poke in the ribs, but I was too winded to even wince.

'Ya fuckn fanny, ye. Look at ye noo big man ye are eh?' roared the ned.

'What dae you want us to do wi him, boss?' asked the large bald thug.

'Pick him up and bring him into my office,' said the blonde man.

'Call him an ambulance, you shit heads. He's dying. He has a brain tumour. He's ill. He's very ill,' Celine yelled.

Both the blonde and the bald man chuckled at that. 'Looks like we saved him a slow and agonising death then, did we not?' replied the blonde man.

'Call him an ambulance, you sick bastards, please. Just, please, do something, I beg you, please...' continued Celine.

There was a groan beside me. Someone was trying to move. I think it was the first thug whom I'd kneed in the balls. The suited athletic man stood from his own kneeling position and began helping the man up, but it looked like it might take some time. Another two guys appeared from down the corridor. I think it must have been the first Scottish thug who'd slapped the Ukrainian girl outside and his scar-faced 'card-playing' mate.

'Everyhin awright, Petrov?' asked the skinhead Scottish thug.

'Everything is fine now. Just a slight altercation, my pal.' replied the blonde man, obviously Petrov. 'Now bring to me the antagonizer. This so-called brain-tumoured delinquent into my office immediately. And also bring in Celine. Chop, chop.'

I still felt dazed, confused, and weak as the large bald thug dragged me into the room behind the large oak door. Petrov's office. He plonked me upright upon a large black couch. I was still in a great deal of pain, especially all over my head, neck, and upper body. Thankfully, I could still move all my limbs, so I didn't think anything had been broken. Although if I lived to see another day I'd surely have a healthy swelling upon the left side of my face.

I felt myself becoming more conscious as the seconds rolled by, which could only be a bonus. The scar-faced man pushed Celine down beside me. He backed away towards the oak door along with the large bald thug, yet they never left. Everyone else, bar Petrov, must have remained inside the pink room. I think there was some music playing in the background. Guns and Roses. But somebody turned it down. Possibly Petrov.

Eventually Petrov walked calmly in front of both Celine and me in silence. He took a few steps back and leaned upon the front of his large oak desk in the middle of the room. The room was as high as it was wide. All the walls were painted black while the ceiling was painted white and glittered with spotlights. On the floor lay a black-and-white chequered carpet. I noticed the faint sign of an old window at the back of the room behind Petrov. It had been deliberately blackened out and almost blended into the black wall.

Petrov stared at us, not saying one single damn word. He just looked, watching and waiting. I stared right back at him. Celine appeared calmer while still regaining her breath. Her glance went back and forth between both me and Petrov. For a second she rested her hand upon my thigh. Oddly, I could see the gesture from the corner of my eyes yet I could not feel it. My veins were still pumped full of adrenalin and a throbbing pain that I quickly put down to my lack of sensations.

'Are you okay?' Celine asked softly.

I didn't answer. I didn't even look at her. Instead, I gently nodded while keeping my eyes firmly upon Petrov. If I had any way of killing him and his bastard arrogant henchmen in that moment, I wouldn't have hesitated to see it through. Even trading my own life for the deed. The pleasure and satisfaction would have heavily outweighed the cons.

At least I was feeling more conscious. My senses were coming back to me. I even began to feel and taste my own blood trickling down my throat. It must have been coming from either a gash on my face or a wound upon my nose. Perhaps both. I could feel it dripping down my cheeks and chin, too.

'So, this is the pathetic reason you came to see me today Celine, yes?' Petrov said, finally breaking his intimidating silence. His tone condescending. 'And why you informed me that you no longer wished to be represented under my management?'

He sounded like a literary agent.

'All for this pathetic-looking bag of shit and piss right here? This is where you found your redemption, your heart, your soul, your true meaning and purpose in life?' he continued with a dismissive chuckle. His two henchmen beside the door, both with their arms folded, sniggered at his words.

'I love him,' Celine replied proudly.

All three men burst out laughing.

'You love him!' Petrov replied, his eyes almost popping out from his head. 'Ahhhhh. But what does a whore know of love? Huh?'

Celine looked ready to say something else, but refrained at the last second.

'A whore knows only about greed and lust. Filth and manipulation. Ways of the flesh. Sins of the body. Pleasures of the damned, or in simpler terms—sucking and fucking. Spit or swallow.'

The two henchmen sniggered again, clearly enjoying Petrov's speech.

'A whore cannot fall in love no more than a bird can swim or a fish can fly.' When he said that, I almost chuckled as images of penguins and flying fish filled my head. Who the hell was this arsehole?

'Once a cocksucker, always a cocksucker, as my mother used to say. You will never escape that stigma.' He continued with his pathetic rant.

I raised my left hand to my face in a slow, calm motion before cleaning the sweat and blood from my eyes. Petrov paused to watch me do this. He looked somewhat fascinated by my calm and controlled movements. Then I returned my hand to my side.

'What is your name, my friend?' Petrov asked, staring right into me.

I remained silent.

Petrov grinned. The large bald thug took a threatening step towards me. He was going to strike me on the face.

'It's Liam...' Celine cried, leaning her body in front of mine to block the bald thug. 'His name is Liam.'

Petrov raised his hand and waved the thug back to the door. I gulped more blood down the back of my throat.

'Liam. Nice, simple name,' Petrov replied. 'I like it. Well, Liam. Can you believe that this stupid bitch right here actually had the audacity to walk into my sauna today? To walk right into my working men's establishment right here. Like she owned the fucking place. My fucking place, and tell me how it was going to be. My best fucking escort. My money cow. She had some crazy,

crazy idea in her head that she could just walk away from all this. From me. Our beautiful setup. No questions asked. No compensation on my behalf. No warning. Just...it's been a pleasure working for you, but now I have to leave.

'She even tried to tell me some bullshit story that her own mother is sick and that she must go back to France immediately to care for her. But Johnny here...' he winked at the big, bald bastard thug. 'He soon obtained the truth from her. A few little slaps to the face. A tickle of the ribs. A delicate punch or two for the stomach. A dunk of the head down a toilet. She soon sang the truth for me like a ned on ecstasy at an Igleston rave.'

I half turned to the large bald thug who had dared laid his hands upon Celine. He grinned, his eyes gleefully wide and boring into me. I glanced at Celine. The bruises on her face. The black eyes. She turned away shamefully. I remained calm on the outside, but inside I was beyond livid. If I had my way, I'd have that smug bald cunt's head on a stick if it were the last thing I ever did on this planet. I'd have them all, in fact. I turned casually back to Petrov when he began to jabber away again.

'So, of course, I became very anxious to meet this reason for her sudden eagerness to depart from my fruitful employment. To get away from this great rich and resourceful life that I have given her. I knew it would be only a matter of time before you turned up here to find her. Although I must admit, I did not expect you here so soon or to act in such an aggressive manner towards my staff and clients.' He tutted. 'Yes, that was most unexpected, Liam. I truly believed you might even come here to negotiate a compensation fee for her contract release instead.'

There was a long pause. I took this time to run over everything in my head. Everything Petrov had just said and implied. I felt sure they weren't going to kill me now and dump my body in the River Forth. I genuinely believed this guy wanted to make some kind of deal.

'How much do you want?' I asked.

'Ahh! It finally speaks.' Petrov grinned as his tone turned to one of condescension. 'Now I want you to say this one little thing for me before we continue our negotiations. If I...want Celine...then I am going. To have. To pay. For her.'

I felt confused. What the hell was this Mad Hatter talking about? He wanted me to repeat that statement out loud.

Petrov saw my hesitation and leaped on it, winking at the large bald man. 'Hit her,' he said, gesturing to Celine with a nod.

Within a second, the large bald man stepped towards Celine and viciously scelped her hard across the side of the face. It was a stinging blow that echoed throughout the room. Celine screeched in pain. I immediately jumped, making a dive for that large bald prick, but he punched me ferociously in the chest, winding me again and sending me hurling back down onto the couch. I could feel the bruise swelling already. That one was gonna hurt in the morning.

'Now say it. Or next time I make him slap her with his big, fat cock.'

'Okay, okay,' I coughed, protesting. 'If I want Celine...then I'm going to have to pay for her.' I took a deep breath. I had to regain my composure quickly.

'Good lad. But you are quite right, Liam. You will have to pay and it will not be cheap. She is...or she used to be...my very best whore. And I have a signed oral contract with all my best whores that when they eventually do wish to leave my company, they must give at least three months' notice. Or...they can happily buy themselves out of the contract.'

'You are a liar,' cried Celine, spitting. 'You never told me any such things.'

'Are you really going to sit there, my dear, in your predicament and call me a liar to my face?' Petrov grinned.

'You told me once that as long as I didn't just up and leave, but instead came to see you, face to face, any time I wished to leave, there would be no problem with my moving on.'

Out of nowhere, the large bald thug slapped Celine hard across the face again. He must have caught her with one of his rings because now a small gash on her face opened and blood trickled out.

'Enough,' I roared, turning and spitting at the large bald man, who just grinned sadistically back at me. 'Just...please. Enough already. Please stop hitting her. Please.'

Petrov raised his hand to the bald thug, who backed away.

'I'll do whatever you want, mate. Whatever it takes. I'll do it. Just please stop hitting her, please.'

'Do you know how much business and money I get from the Russians and Japanese every time they come over here to set up some business with Brad, huh? And all we have to do to keep them happy during their little stay is supply them with all the girls and drugs they ask for. And you very well know that Celine is who they ask for the most. Yes, my dear. Always you. The beautiful French Princess. So, you owe me now. At the very least you owe me the time to find a good and fine replacement.'

'I don't owe you a bloody goddamn thing,' Celine spat.

The bald thug moved to hit her again, but Petrov waved him

back. 'You will be working your notice here for the next three months, my sweet. I mean, I cannot very well send you anywhere decent now, can I? Especially with that bashful swollen face of yours. So, for the next three months you will live here. You will eat here. You will sleep here and you will work here. On your back or on your hands and knees. Twenty-four hours a day, seven days a week for the next three months or until your pretty little boyfriend here turns up with some cold, hard cash to purchase you.'

'You can't do this, Petrov. It's insane. It's illegal. It's not right.'

'Celine. My little princess. I answer to Brad and no one else, and as long as I keep answering to Brad, I can do whatever the hell I like in my working establishments. Now, you will stay here and fuck as many of those scabby, jakey, ned, drunk, lowlife, nasty, scum bastards who come through those doors every day. As many as it takes to pay me back for what you owe me.'

'How much do I need to get?' I interrupted, unable to listen to any more of this nonsense. If I had to, I'd rob a bank this very night to free Celine from this insane imprisonment...unless...another drastic option came to my mind. I shook it away for the time being.

'One hundred thousand sterling, my friend.'

I shook my head. Disgusted. Rob a bank it is, then. There was nothing left for it...unless...the erratic and insane thought came back to me again. It was a mad crazy risk that kept entering my head. A drastic, desperate last-ditch attempt to rescue Celine from this maddening situation that very night.

'But I am a fair man, Liam, and I will not have anyone say otherwise. Ninety or so days is more or less three months, I think. Which is around one grand a day or just slightly over. I was never any good at maths at school. So, every day that passes is a thousand pounds off the final bill. You cannot get any fairer than that, my friend, no?' Petrov grinned smugly again, then gestured to the large bald thug and his scarred mate.

'Now get him the fuck out of here and do not come back until you at least have some hard currency for me, yes? Or else come back in three months to this very day and pick up whatever is left of your whore girlfriend.' He grinned at Celine. 'Who is now going to be working on her back twenty-four seven to make up for her breach of contract.'

The two thugs made a grab for me. I didn't even try to fend them off. The ball was well and truly out of my court at that moment. They dragged me to my feet. Celine cried for them to stop, then put her hands to her face and sobbed when she realised there was nothing within her physical power she could do to stop them.

'Oh, and if you even think about going to the police for any help, my friend...' Petrov chuckled. 'Any help at all, you are in for one hell of a shock.'

If he knew only half my antics these past twenty-four hours, he'd realise that this plan of action would be the very least of his worries.

'But please, do try. I am sure they would be most happy to pass the case on to one of their most respected and senior detectives, whom you so kindly almost paralysed when kneeing the poor laddie in the balls just a moment ago. Now get him the fuck out of my sight.'

The two thugs lifted me by my armpits and dragged me through the large oak doorway.

'Send to me that Ukrainian bitch Lydia,' I heard Petrov shout through into the pink room as I was dragged farther along the corridor. I heard Celine cry my name again. I called out for her, too. I tried to say something else, like be strong! Or hold on. I'll be back! But the words wouldn't come out. My throat and chest still felt winded and swollen. I could hardly even shout, let alone breathe.

I noticed Maggie at the far end of the corridor, watching us coming towards her.

'Open the door, Mags!' said the large bald thug. Maggie did so immediately, unbolting the locks and holding the door wide open as the two thugs continued to carry me outside. They dragged me up the steps. The tall Eastern European guy standing guard at the top beside the gate turned curiously to watch.

'Hey! What happened to this guy?' he asked like he might actually give a damn.

'He attacked wee Charlie, Rab, and Don and now he owes the boss a shit load of money.'

'No shit. I thought he was a nice, funny guy. Just goes to show you, huh?'

The two thugs continued dragging me up and along the alleyway, then right down the next lane leading out onto Pilrig Street. They threw me into the cold, hard mud just shy of the pavement. The two men backed away, smug looks smeared all over their faces.

'See ye in three months then, Liam, eh?' said the large bald thug, still grinning from ear to ear. 'And dinnae worry yourself tae much aboot Celine noo, pal. We'll take good care uv that yin. Well, at least until you get yursel sorted oot ken.' He winked before turning away, returning to the darkness of the narrow lane.

I remained lying upon the hard, muddy ground for a good minute or two. I closed my eyes. I breathed slow, deep, and hard, trying to regain my composure. I actually enjoyed the feel of fresh air upon my face. The liberty of being outside, alone and unrestrained, was a relief. My thoughts soon became clear and calm. A new urge overcame me. I suddenly craved a cigarette; a taste of whisky, too, wouldn't go amiss.

I tried to stagger to my feet. Jesus Christ, I was in a lot of pain. Nothing felt broken, but the aches, pains, and swelling all over my upper body told me that I might be recovering from this beating for a few weeks to come. I tried to stand upright. The agony hurtling through my chest every time I breathed or took a step forward made me want to vomit and fall immediately back down to the ground, curl into a little foetus ball, and be completely still. I kept walking, though. I had to keep going. Celine's wellbeing was at stake.

By the time I staggered towards the end of Pilrig Street and onto Leith Walk to horrified gasps from a few pedestrians, I began feeling a bit more stable. I breathed a little easier. The pain throbbing throughout my head and upper body seemed to be subsiding. My body was adapting. It felt worse if I stopped, that was for sure, but if I kept moving, I could handle the physical hurt.

I paused on the street corner. I didn't know what to do. I debated whether I should get a taxi or a bus back to my home. What I really wanted to do was get a hold of a couple of guns. My mind flashed and I remembered the gun on the table inside that room in the sauna where the two thugs had been playing cards. I shook the thought from my head. I glanced down the street. I clocked a small closed supermarket, then a newsagent's next door. The newsagent's was still open, so I headed straight for it.

Inside, the store appeared quiet. A friendly, middle-aged Asian man greeted me from behind the counter. His expression turned to one of sheer horror when my bruised, beaten, and bloodied body entered his well-lit store.

'Jesus Bloody Christ, my friend!' said the Asian shopkeeper with an Indian accent. 'Were you just in a bloody car crash or something? You need a bloody hospital, man?'

I approached the counter. 'Later,' I said, coughing. 'First I need you to phone the police and a couple of ambulances. Tell them to get their arses to that sess pit sauna at the back of Pilrig Street. Can you do that?'

The Asian shopkeeper nodded while staring at me blankly.

'Tell them there's been a couple of murders or something, you know?'

The Asian man nodded once more. To his left I noticed a small TV screen which caught my eye. It looked to be the latest Scottish news…and my face was plastered all over the screen. Ha! Finally, some coverage I thought. They had taken their bloody time.

The screen cut away to an interview with that Harry salesman bloke from the Porsche garage who, I'd abandoned on the bypass that morning. The screen then cut to more images of me. I gestured to the TV.

'In fact, pal, tell them you saw this guy go into the sauna. That should get their attention and bring them here pretty pronto.'

The Asian shopkeeper remained speechless as he glanced at the screen, then back at me, then back at the screen again and finally back at me. Meanwhile, I spotted a half bottle of Jack Daniels Honey sitting behind the counter. I gestured towards it.

'I'll take that half bottle of honey jack in all, mate.' I reached into my pocket for my wallet.

'I'm sorry, pal, but it's past ten o'clock. You can't buy booze after ten.'

I slammed down a hundred-pound note. His eyes nearly popped out of his skull.

'Give a condemned and dying man a wee bit of joy in life, huh, mate? Just don't put it through the till and keep the change, yeah?'

The shopkeeper turned in silence and took the bottle from the shelf.

'Oh, and some Marlboros and a lighter, too. Cheers.'

'Lights or regular?' asked the shopkeeper, still looking and sounding quite dazed.

'Regular.' I grinned. 'You only live once, right?' I opened my wallet and laid down a couple more hundred-pound notes.

'I do not think I have much change of anymore hundreds, my friend. Do you have anything smaller?'

'No mate, don't worry, it's all for you. I'm not gonna need it where I'm going. I just need you to do what I asked. Oh, and one more small wee favour.'

The shopkeeper gave me a look of great doubt.

'If you're a small store, right, you must get your fair share of dickheads coming in here now and again, no?'

'Oh, most certainly we do, sir.'

'So, you must have a little special something behind the counter there for those certain wee dickheads...am I right?'

The shop keeper hesitated. He glanced at me, then at the money, then at me again, then back at the TV. He was about to say something...he hesitated...he glanced at me again, then down at the money. He reached underneath his counter.

Chapter 16

I stood outside the shop and lit a cigarette. I took a long, hard puff, then opened my newly purchased bottle of whisky. I took a big, gulping swig of that, too. With the warm buzz of the nicotine and alcohol combined, I felt a little better physically and a lot clearer about what I had to do.

I left the cigarette in my mouth and used my free hand to grab hold of a hard steel baseball bat which I'd just purchased from the Asian shopkeeper for a couple hundred quid and which was now tucked firmly underneath my armpit. With another long swig from my whisky, I made my way back onto Pilrig Street towards the dark, narrow lane and the sauna. Where the lane turned left towards the gated basement, still guarded by the tall Eastern European thug, I came to a halt. I gulped down another huge portion of whisky and gasped, almost in agony, as it stung the back of my throat. I quietly threw the empty bottle onto a small patch of grass. I took one last, long, hard, deep draw from my cigarette before throwing it, too, upon the dark ground beneath my feet.

All I held was my new steel baseball bat. I gripped her hard and tight with both hands. She felt good. She felt powerful. I felt like I could do some damage with this force of nature. That I could at least make an uphill effort to change the odds. Put down some kind of marker before I got my arse handed back to me again, most likely, this time, from a plate I would not be getting up from again.

I took a hard swing into the dark, thin air.

I felt ready.

I glanced back around the corner and saw the tall Eastern European thug standing outside the gate, smoking another cigarette. He stood sideways on from my approach, so he would easily see me coming if I stormed right on in. How to play this? I thought hard, but couldn't think. If I charged in full steam ahead, he'd have ample time to defend himself. He could shout down to the sauna for help. He could even have a gun or a knife tucked away in his pants, somewhere. I wondered how he'd react if I just staggered on up to him again, pretending I'd come back to plead my case to Petrov or to see Celine one last time. Surely, he'd let me get close enough to smack him in the face or the knees with the bat? The bat though, shite. What to do with that? Perhaps tuck it down the back of my trousers to hold it in place. One thing was sure, I couldn't just stand there and debate it all night. Surely someone would come out of the sauna eventually. Or even worse, walk in from the street lane behind me and discover my sinister presence. The sauna was an all-night business, after all.

I raised the bat. I was about to place it behind my back when the tall thug received a message on his cell phone, which he quickly pulled from his pocket. He took a quick glance all around. He looked satisfied that he was alone and leaned against the side of the steel gate with his back positioned towards me again. He began typing away on his mobile.

That was it. This was my chance. I didn't hesitate another second. I had to do it now.

I moved forward, doing my best to keep myself tucked away against the side of the dirt track and fences belonging to the other houses and buildings. The tall thug continued to type away on his phone, utterly engrossed. I stepped on a few pebbles and crunching twigs. The sound felt excruciating to my senses. Surely the thug had heard, yet still he typed away.

I moved closer. I pulled out the bat from behind my back. I was only a few feet away. I could see the back of his short-cropped, brown-haired head. A large vein bulged from his lower neck along with a bulge of bone upon the back of his skull. I gripped the bat with both hands and gently swung it out to the side. This was happening. This was going to happen right now. In a split second, I had to decide. Smack him on the side of the head. Smack him in the knees.

I grimaced and went for the side of his head. I swung ferociously and made impact with the right back side of his skull. I saw the bone crush like putty. Like the skin was just so soft there that it imploded. He immediately looked paralysed. His phone dropped from his hands and onto the concrete path. He crumpled to his knees. I was about to strike the fucker again, just in case he was still good in the head, so to speak, but he fell forward. Flat on his face and into the dirt and patchy grass. He looked either very unconscious or as though I'd killed him outright. Whatever was to become of him, it seemed too late for regrets and remorse, and far too late to stop and turn back from this path I'd chosen.

I turned him onto his back. He was a heavy fucker. I had to use both hands to move him while still holding my bat. I checked for a pulse. He didn't seem to have one. In fact, he didn't seem to be breathing at all and I couldn't see any blood. I left him where he lay and proceeded with caution down the steep, winding steps towards the basement sauna. The large steel door was closed over again. I prayed to the god of cancer that in the thugs' haste in dragging me outside, they hadn't bothered to lock the main door upon their return. If they had, then shite, I'd have to knock once more. Play dumb or some shite. Or hide that body and wait for a punter to show up. I didn't know for sure. Perhaps I'd even find another way inside. There must be a small bathroom window or something.

I took a deep breath. As quietly as possible, I tried to pull the door gently open. To my sheer delight, the door moved. It was unlocked. I felt a wave of relief flush over my entire soul. I peered through the crack in the opened doorway. I couldn't see anyone or any movement inside. Only the dim light of the hallway and the continuing corridor ahead. I opened the door just a little further. I could see into the opposite doorway on the left where the scarred thug and the Scottish thug had been playing cards the last time I found myself in this doorway. I think they were back inside the room again. I could definitely see another two figures in there, but their backs were turned. One stood upright looking at something on the table while the other leaned over the table.

I slipped quietly through the gap in the front door and gently closed it. I stepped lightly towards the opened doorway where the two thugs were still standing. Still leaning over the table with their backs towards me. I stepped through the doorway. I could see that they were browsing through a suitcase full of money and a brown leather bag full of white- and brown-powdered packets. Drugs, I assumed, and not various brands of supermarket sugar and rice. The handgun lay tucked in between the two bags.

'Do we really have to count this fucking money again?' said the scarred-faced man.

'Fucking aye. He's no happy wi the last count likes,' the small Scottish thug replied.

I snuck even closer behind the two men, almost on my tiptoes. I raised the bat up and over my shoulder. I decided to swing for the scarred thug first. He looked bigger and meaner. When he bent his head slightly just as I was about to swing, I decided to swing for his knees instead. I smashed hard into the side of his left knee cap. The crack sounded sickening and even excruciatingly painful to watch. He fell to the floor immediately, clutching his knee with sheer agony while howling like a drowning wolf.

The Scottish thug turned instantly, first glancing in shock at his fallen mate, then gazing right at me. By that time my bat had already been swung with a vicious uppercut blow to his lower chin and jaw, both of which cracked, splitting wide open. Blood, teeth, and bone, along with bits off tongue he'd bitten clean off with the sheer force of the blow, splattered everywhere. He fell backwards against the table, then slid onto the floor to join his mate. Dead or unconscious, I couldn't tell. His jaw and chin were moving in an unnatural position, that's for sure. They would probably take years of surgery to correct…if he were lucky enough to get those years.

The scarred thug continued to howl in pain while clutching his broken knee for dear life until I brought down my bloodied bat upon the exposed side of his face and jaw. It took two quick swings to shut him up for good.

Inside I felt dead. Like a robot. Swinging the bat into the first man's skull outside had shocked me with the ease of it. Especially the sickening impact and the shattering of his skull. But now I felt immune to it all. I felt completely emotionless and devoid of any sympathy for those three men. All of whom I'd floored in the space of two minutes. I had no idea whether they'd recover from the horrific injuries I'd inflicted upon them. And the truth was, I didn't care. My only thoughts were of Celine and getting her the fuck away from here and this life, as fast as possible. If I survived intact, that would be a bonus. If I could take out as many of these smug, arrogant cunts with me in the process, including Petrov, then big Christmas bonus.

I reached for the handgun on the table. At that very moment, the large bald thug—the one who'd slapped Celine in Petrov's office, the one who'd grinned and winked at me while I sat there helpless, the one who helped drag me out of the sauna, dumping me in the mud outside—suddenly barged into the room like a raging bull.

'What the fuck is goin...' he roared. He hesitated when he saw me standing over his fallen comrades. I turned to face him when I should've gone for the gun. He charged at me immediately. Full steam ahead. I swung the bat into his arm and shoulder hard, but he still tackled me into the table. We crashed through it, sending everything flying all over the place. The drugs, the money, the gun, paper, a stapler, pens, cards, coffee cups, everything. The bat flew from my hands as I landed.

We wrestled back and forth for a few seconds, rolling around over the spilled table contents. The large bald thug wrapped his hands around my throat and put his life's worth into strangling the soul out of me. I managed to slip my knee between his legs and used it to knee him repeatedly. Over and over again in the balls until he released his hold. Then I head-butted him in the face over and over again. The burning rage inside had consumed me. I thought of nothing else but ending this smug bastard's life. Both my mind and body were in places of such anger, aggression, and violence. Something I'd never experienced before. I felt like I was fighting for my life, and I was.

I finally ceased head-butting the large bald man. Blood sprayed from the bridge of his nose like a burst water main. He instinctively placed one hand upon his groin and another over his face.

I didn't stop there.

Immediately I made a grab for something, anything, within my reach. I felt cold, hard metal on my fingers. I thought it might be the gun. When I snapped it up, I had to do a double take. It was the stapler. Shite. The large bald thug had recovered enough to make another grab for me with a slow yet dazed movement, so I opened the stapler and slammed it hard against his cheeks. I went crazy. I stapled his entire face and head over and over again. He screamed, he cried, he howled. Then he fell still where he lay. I continued to staple his face until no more staples were left, then I began bashing in his face with the stapler. Blood oozed everywhere, splashing all over the two of us. I could feel it dripping down my face and neck. His blood and mine. After a dozen or so more blows, he wasn't moving or reacting. I stopped hitting. Like the other three, he was either unconscious or not of this world anymore.

I rolled off him. I got onto my knees. I saw the handgun lying on top of some scattered cards. I leaned over and picked it up, then stood to my feet. I glanced down and saw my bat. I picked it up, too. I scanned my eyes over the carnage. Three bodies bloodied and unconscious lay all around me. I turned my attention back to the door and made my way towards it. Handgun in one hand. Baseball bat in the other. I re-entered the main corridor without looking back. I couldn't even say what the hell was running through my mind as I walked up that corridor. How many more of Petrov's men were left? Would someone jump out from one of the bedrooms along the corridor and shoot me? Stab me?

I thought about Petrov.

Up ahead, his large oak door was sealed tightly shut. I could hear loud thumping rock music coming from within. Guns N Roses again.

As I reached the end of the corridor, I could see that the door leading into the pink waiting room had been closed over too. Guessing that Celine would most likely be in there, I put my hand upon the handle and casually entered.

As I made my way inside, it seemed obvious that the occupants weren't that bothered or aroused by my entrance. I took a quick glance to my left as I opened the door. I could see the suited athletic thug I'd wrestled earlier and the newspaper-reading thug—the police detective, I think—whom I'd kneed in the groin. Both sitting back in their chairs again, distracted by each other's concerns for their injuries.

On my right the ned whom I'd punched in the face and whose nose I'd broken was sitting back upon one of the three couches, holding a bloodied cloth to his face. At the same time, he was being attended to by two of the working girls, the Chinese woman and the black woman.

Celine looked a sad, pitiful sight. She sat all on her own upon the next couch, sobbing into her hands, which covered most of her face. She, along with the others, still hadn't glanced over to see who had entered the room. Too distracted by the aftermath of the previous scuffle.

It was the skinny, scruffy ned who turned to stare up at me first. A look of pure and utter shock, horror, and disbelief engulfed him. As soon as he lowered his bloodied towel in protest and made the move to stand, I stepped forward and swung the solid steel bat right at his head. He half yelped while trying to claw and block the vicious blow with his hands and wrists, but he was far too slow and weak. The swing cracked him hard in his already-broken nose. More blood splashed out, this time splattering all over the girls sitting beside him. They screamed in horror when a few of the ned's teeth ended up in the Asian girl's bra.

Now I had everyone's attention.

The two thugs at the back of the room were already upon their feet. Ready to attack once more. Meanwhile, the ned crumpled back down onto the couch. Almost unconscious. I cracked him on the side of the head again with the bat for good measure. Surely to fuck, he'd never get up from that strike.

Celine took her hands away from her red and tearful face. She glanced at me with a mixture of raw emotion flooding throughout her face. Joy, shock, confused terror, then dumb awe.

The other two girls seemed like they were about to scream again, but nothing came out of their mouths. They just stared at me in a bewildered silence. Eyes wide and mouths open. Probably scared stiff that if they screamed again, they would be next.

My eyes locked with a speechless Celine for a brief, flickering heartbeat. Then I tore myself away from her gaze and stepped towards the two remaining thugs. They both looked shocked and enraged. Shocked that I was there. Enraged that they had to fight for their lives. They stepped towards me, ready to pounce. Two against one. They must have felt confident, like the odds were soundly in their favour.

I took a step towards them and raised the handgun I'd tucked into my pocket. Both men froze immediately. I could almost see the confidence deflate from their bodies like a burst rugby ball.

Both men raised their hands like it mattered a damn. I aimed for the well-suited athletic man's head first. The one who'd rugby-tackled me to the ground and pounded me with a sly punch the last time I'd set foot in the place.

'Please, man...'

I shot him twice in the head. He fell lifeless to the floor in a crumpled heap. I turned to the remaining thug. He backed up against the wall. Fear filled his tearful eyes. Wet patches began staining his trousers. Piss flowed down his legs and trickled onto the carpet, dampening the pink material.

'Please, man,' he pleaded. 'I'm with the police. I'm undercover...don't do anything stupid...I've got a family. A WIFE...'

I shot him once. Then shot him over and over again. One bullet after the next. Unloading the bullets until the gun finally fell empty. Even then I kept shooting. Click, click, clicking away on the trigger. My mind caught in a robotic trance.

The gasps and terrified moans of the girls behind me gradually brought me out of my cold and emotionless robotic state. For the first time, the realisation hit me like a tank that I might have just killed as many as seven people here. Two or three for sure. I didn't even want to think about the consequences or the future. A vision entered my thoughts. Celine and I driving an open-topped convertible through the hot Mediterranean roads of South France. Laughing, smiling, singing. Our hair blowing in the warm, fresh wind. I dismissed the thoughts as soon as they entered my head. All I wanted to focus on in this instance was the present. No more, no less.

I turned around to face the front of the room. The two working girls, the black girl and the Chinese girl, remained where they were on the couch, huddled against one another and staring at me in frozen terror. The black girl looked to be almost hyperventilating. The bloody-faced ned still lay unconscious, sprawled out on the other side of the couch.

Celine was on her feet. Her hands clutched tightly against her face, desperately trying to hold back her sobs and tears. Frozen in so many mixed emotions, but mostly fear and shock over what I'd just done. Then joy and elation at seeing me again. Whatever happened from here on in, nothing would even be the same again. We would either make a run for it and start a new life together or I'd be going to prison. No doubt about that.

I lowered my gun and stepped towards Celine. The faint sound of rock music and the pounding of a booming bass faintly filled my ears. It was still coming from the room, Petrov's office, next door.

As I approached my darling, fragile, angel Celine, her emotions overcame her and she burst into a fit of sobs and collapsed into my arms. I still held the steel bat in my other hand as I hugged into her with all the love in the world. She, in turn, hugged even harder into me. She sobbed her heart and soul into my upper chest. The other girls watched.

'Liam...Liam...' Celine continued to sob. Like she couldn't even believe I was there or real or what the hell had actually happened. 'I can't believe you came back for me. That you're all right...that you did...all of this.'

'Hey!' I replied, comforting her and holding her and hugging her just as tightly as I could. 'It's okay. Everything's gonna be okay. I'm getting you out of here right now, Celine. You're safe. You don't have to do anything you don't want to do any more. You're free to live your life for as long as you have left to live.'

'I love you so much. I really, really love you, Liam. I'm sorry for all of this...thinking I could just come back here and talk my way through it somehow...I'm so bloody stupid.' Celine's sobs turned into a nervous laughter.

'None of that matters anymore, baby. I love you too. I love you sooo much.' I chuckled and smiled back.

The loud music coming from Petrov's office distracted and shifted my thought process. Where the hell was that prick? Was he still in his office? Had he left? Had he heard the commotion? The gunshots? The shouts? Was he hiding in there, waiting for me to come in and get him? Or was he just sitting in there now, listening to his music and thus never hearing a single damn thing that had happened out here?

'Where is Petrov?'

Celine took a few beats to compose herself and stepped back.

'I don't know, I don't...maybe in his office still. They took Lydia into him about ten minutes ago. I don't know if they're still in there or if he left already...I don't know.'

I turned away from Celine and glanced towards the large, thick oak wood door leading into Petrov's office. He must still be inside. And if the working girl was in there with him, I'd take a fair bet that something sexual or drug-related would be going on.

'He takes girls in there to fuck them, yeah?' I said bluntly, yet with a non-judgemental tone. I knew that most of these girls had no choice in who they spread their legs for in this place, whether it was willingly or not. Celine included. I didn't really want to think about it, as it just enraged me and clouded my judgement further.

'Yes,' Celine replied softly, looking ashamed as she lowered her head and eyes.

I took another step away from her and headed towards the

doorway leading back into the main corridor.

Celine reached for my arm, trying to pull me back. 'Please, Liam,' Celine pleaded. 'Just leave it. Let's just get the hell out of here right now. Please, let's just go.'

I ignored her and shook away her hold. I stepped into the corridor. One of the bedroom doors opened and a half-naked working girl along with her half-naked punter stepped out curiously, obviously disturbed and concerned by all the commotion.

'What's going...' said the working girl. But when they saw me looking like some extra from The Walking Dead and holding my baseball bat covered in blood, they looked like they wanted to do a runner.

'Get the fuck out of here,' I roared, waving my bat. They quickly turned and scampered down the corridor towards the exit as fast as their bare legs could carry them.

I turned back to the oak door leading to Petrov's office. I glanced at the handle. I could see the door gently vibrating with the loud bass thuds from the sound system inside. I tried desperately to listen. All I could hear from within was the music. Guns N Roses, 'Sweet Child o' Mine'.

I dropped the empty handgun and raised my bat, gripping it tighter. I placed my free hand upon the door handle.

Celine approached the doorway to the pink room and stopped, concerned. 'Please...don't.'

I glanced at her for an overly long moment. I turned back to the door. I put some force into pushing down the handle and carefully opened it. The incredible loudness of the music coming from within took me by surprise. It must have been some kind of soundproof room or door or something because the increase in noise levels was immense. I knew then it would have been too loud in here for the room's occupants to hear anything that had happened in the rest of the sauna. Still, when I fully entered Petrov's office and caught his line of sight, he would see me. He would see who was entering his domain without permission. I prayed he wouldn't have a gun pointed right at my face or perhaps be lying in wait behind the door with his own baseball bat.

I nudged the door open farther. Gently I poked my head around the wooden frame, preparing to whip myself back and away from any blow to the face or shot to the head. Finally, I caught a peek inside. The music still pounded so loud, I could barely hear myself think through my throbbing eardrums.

I heard something.

Very faint moans, grunts, and groans, really faint. When I

carefully looked, I could see the back of Petrov, his suit jacket still on. His trousers and pants were around his ankles. The backs of a woman's silky-smooth legs were visible, spread slightly in front of his. It was the Ukrainian girl, Lydia. He had her bent over his large oak desk and was taking her hard and rough from behind. His bare bum cheeks clenched back and forth and were almost comical to watch.

With a new surge of confidence that this siege was almost over, I stepped forward in silence amongst the noisy vibrations of the sound system. I positioned myself close behind Petrov as he pounded away at Lydia with his hips. Over and over again against his desk. The girl looked neither into the act nor against it. Just a plain old numb, get-it-over-with neutral.

I gripped my bat tighter and raised it above my shoulder. In all fairness, I could've hit the cunt anywhere to my liking, choosing my sweet spot with the utmost of ease. The back of his knees. His upper or lower spine. His arms. His shoulders. His skull! But I wanted the fucker to see me. I wanted the satisfaction of looking this bastard stone cold in the face and having him die with the knowledge that it was I who had ended him.

I almost smiled when I glanced down again at his pumping, back-and-forth, bare buttocks. There was only one place I wanted to drive that baseball bat.

I swung, really fucking hard.

The steel bat smacked him right against his bare, pale buttocks. He buckled, then howled above the music, which I didn't think would've been possible. I think Lydia assumed he'd just come big time because she half-turned in the moment with a look of relief. Like the dirty deed was finally over.

Petrov backed up in a great wave of pain before almost keeling over. It seemed like it was far too painful for him to bend down and sit, yet even more painful to remain standing. His reaction looked as comical as his fornication techniques. I think I might have broken his tailbone.

Lydia instantly stood to her feet when she saw me. She turned fully around and covered her breasts. Like I said, she didn't seem too upset that Petrov had been screwing her over his desk, but neither did she seem to be enjoying the act. If she worked here for her keep, I guessed she'd grown immune and accustomed to these raping sessions by now. And let's not kid ourselves. That's exactly what they were.

Petrov made some fleeting glances in my direction, his face filled with shock, fear, and surprise…but most of all, immense and total pain. Of course, his physical actions were much more concerned with grabbing a hold of his butt cheeks and trying to soothe the pain. What he needed was a good old-fashioned ice bath.

I swung again for the sheer hell of it. I hadn't ever thought for one second that I'd enjoy acting out such violence, yet I could no longer deny that I secretly and sadistically did. Perhaps that sick sense of enjoyment could be achieved only by acting it out upon a certain type of person. If that were the case, I had found my type.

This time I went for his legs and cracked the side of his knee with another vicious and violent blow, one that sent him thumping to the floor. He squirmed and wriggled around in more agonising, hysterical pain. Like he couldn't even decide which part of his body to cradle and comfort first.

I gestured for Lydia to leave. Right away she nodded and scurried away towards the door. I walked casually over to the large digital sound system packed into the nearby wall and began smashing away at the speakers and main stereo. Memories flooded my mind from days earlier, when I'd done the exact same thing to the electrical contents of my neighbour's bedroom. It seemed like a year ago...so much had happened since then. Finally, the music stopped and all I could hear were the agonising groans and sniffling howls from Petrov filling the room.

I stepped back around the table to stand and face him. When he saw me coming, he quickly huddled up to the back of his desk. Desperately trying to regain his abandoned composure, yet still whimpering like a badly wounded animal. I raised the baseball bat ever so slightly, which sent him into a fit of protesting hysterics. He raised his hands, making a begging gesture. Inside, I let the rage build up again. Gearing myself up to unleash hell and a series of pounding, devastating blows upon him.

'Now wait one minute! Just wait...one fucking MINUTE...' he spat and yelled. Trying to get out his defending argument. Yet it was like his mind was working far too quickly for his mouth to catch up. My own breaths were deep and hard. I felt myself exploding inside the more I gazed upon him. This pathetic man who had dared give me an ultimatum. Who had dared believe that he had the power to take my Celine away from me. To spew his threatening and patronising words of shite at us while I sat there defenceless upon his couch. And he hiding behind the protection of his so-called men. To dare believe that he had some kind of psychological power over us just because of the people around him and the untouchable arsehole he believed himself to be. At the tail end of it, he was just another narcissistic, delusional, wannabe gangster given a wee bit of power that had instantly gone to his head. A victim of his own overactive self-awareness. A self-awareness that had led him to believe he was, without a doubt, a somebody. A somebody better than others. A somebody better than all the other nobodies like me. Invulnerable and untouchable with massive delusions of grandeur.

Well, he had no one around to protect him or his ego anymore. Now his true pathetic, snivelling, whimpering, naked self was exposed raw for my world to see.

I raged at him like a wild, savage dog. Snarling and roaring before the attack. I raised the bat high, high above my head as he begged, pleaded, and shrieked for his life.

'WAIT...WAIT...'

I brought down the bat hard and fast upon him. Raining down blow after blow upon his unprotected body. The first hit was the knees of his cradled legs. The second ferocious smack and crack was upon his protecting and defensive hands and arms. After five continuous blows, I could both feel and hear his bones shatter. Then his arms and legs fell limp. Stripped of all movement and exposing the rest of his vulnerable body. I continued to pound him with the bat. Over and over again. His chest, his neck, his face, his skull. I smacked and smashed him over and over until his face shattered. Opening like the Red Sea, his bloodied, unrecognisable head caved inwards while blood, snot, pus, and grey brain matter splattered out from within his skeletal shell. After twenty blows to his head, I stopped counting.

When there was no more head and face left to pound, I finally stopped. In all truth, I could barely raise my arms or the bat any longer. I felt drained, knackered. Sweat poured down my face like mini Highland waterfalls trickling down a mountainside from all angles. I had nothing left to give. I'd never felt my heart beat so fast and I'd never heard myself breathe so hard. In that moment, I wanted to lie down. Drop to the floor and fall into a long, dark, deep sleep forever.

Then I realised that my job was far from done here. I had to find the energy somewhere to get Celine the hell out of here. Maybe even the two of us if the universe was still shining its favour upon us and somehow begin our journey to France, towards our new life. If that was still possible. I had no idea what lay ahead for me around the next corner. Even as far as the next corridor, I didn't have a clue.

The sickly smell of death filled my lungs. It felt disgusting. The smell of faeces, too. The poor guy must have literally shat himself. A wave of queasiness engulfed me. When I glanced back down at Petrov, I could no longer recognise this bloody pulp mesh of a man in front of me. I winced, then bent over. I couldn't stop myself from vomiting all over the bloodstained floor.

I composed myself and staggered backwards. I turned and headed back through the large oak doorway. Out in the corridor Celine stood, still sobbing while hugging herself so tightly I believed she might pop. Lydia stood beside her, rubbing Celine's shoulders. Comforting her. Without words, I approached Celine and kissed her forehead. I glanced at Lydia and she nodded softly yet approvingly.

'Thank you.' she said.

I took a quick glimpse into the pink waiting room. The other two working girls were huddled together on the couch, still in shock. The ned remained lying, spread out beside them in the exact same position I'd left him, still unconscious or dead. Hopefully dead.

I took Celine by the hand and led her down the corridor. We had to leave this place. We had to get the hell out of there right now. Right this very second. Surely the Asian shopkeeper had done what I'd asked of him and called the police. If they're weren't pulling up outside at this very second, they were sure as hell close by.

Halfway along the corridor, I heard the faint sound of a toilet flushing. All three of us paused in our tracks and gazed at one another. Before any one of us spoke, the end doorway along the bottom of the corridor opened and Maggie, the Chinese hostess, stepped obliviously out. When she finally turned to see us, her eyes widened, almost popping out from her head. A rage overcame her and she looked as if she might explode. She began yelling and screaming while edging towards us, pointing and shouting louder.

'GUYS! GUYS! RABBIE. JOHNNY! HE BACK. HE BACK. GUYS.'

All three of us remained still as Maggie stepped closer, still roaring for someone, anyone, to come to her aid. She seemed so convinced that someone would come a' running soon. But there was no one left. And three out of four of us knew it.

As Maggie stepped nearer, only a few feet away, I was about to grab her by the throat and lock her in a room or cupboard somewhere. But from the corner of my eye I could see Lydia tensing up. Her face twisted to one of great anger and bitterness. Before I could make my move, Lydia unleashed a surprisingly ferocious kick right between Maggie's legs. It caught her by surprise. When Maggie instinctively bowed down, wincing and trying to protect her groin, Lydia punched her square in the jaw with a vicious crack. Maggie fell to the ground in a winded and dazed heap. Lydia took one more sly hit and unleashed a hard kick to Maggie's' gut.

'Why don't you suck and fuck that, huh?' Lydia raged.

I didn't say a word. I just thanked my lucky stars that Lydia wasn't with Petrov. I glanced and smiled at Celine, who was still shaking. I then led her down the corridor with Lydia at our backs.

When we reached the end of the corridor, I really believed we were going to do this. Make a lucky escape. I couldn't hear a single damn siren outside or even the slightest bit of commotion. I thought we were going do it. I really believed we were going to make it out of there. Celine and me.

As we made our way past the side door where I'd laid out three of Petrov's thugs, I allowed myself a brief glimpse, a quick little flash into my and Celine's future...

As I closed my eyes for just one overly long second, I could see us driving that damn fine-looking convertible on a tantalisingly hot and gorgeous summer day. Not even the faintest hint of white clouds could be seen anywhere in the ocean of rich blue sky above our heads. We had the roof down. We were laughing. We were horsing and fooling around like two reunited childhood sweethearts without a care in the world. As the lusciously warm wind rippled through our hair, we sang along loud, proud and with an infectious heart, to any goddamn tune that dared play out at us from the car radio. My God, we were so happy and in love.

As we continued to drive, I could see the beginning of some mountains emerging on the distant left- and side, while a delicious carpet of rich blue sea stretched out into the smooth horizon on our right. For one heartfelt moment, I could both smell and taste that raw and exciting salty sea air in my nostrils and the back of my throat, while also feeling those radiant rays of sunshine smothering my tanned skin with their delicious, tender, affectionate kisses of warmth.

When I blinked again we were naked on a magnificent golden, secluded, sandy beach, our stripped clothes strewn here, there, and everywhere. We were playing around like big kids again, spinning and jumping on the sand, then onto each other before wrestling ourselves down onto the silky, smooth sand beneath our bare feet. Soon we were running and chasing one another into the cool, calm sea before diving freely into the deliciously inviting and invigorating waves of the crystal-clear water.

We swam, we played, we talked, we laughed, we whispered sweet nothings, we kissed and hugged with great tenderness, then made love with an even greater fiery and furious passion before continuing our romp on the shallow, sandy shores of the stunning beach. The ocean waves lapped against and massaged our entangled, naked skin, enticing us to come back in for more.

We looked so happy. We looked so in love.

Real or imagined, it was the most perfect moment I'd felt in my life. I'd never experienced such pure and utter joy before, so much good, raw, and positive emotion, until those short-lived but heavenly gifted last moments with her. I wished it could have lasted forever. I wished beyond all shadow of doubt, hope, and fear that it could have been real. That it should have been real...was it real? Was it really real?

If I just kept my eyes closed tightly shut, surely the moment would never end. It would last, always and forever, in my mind, just so long as I didn't...open...my...eyes.

When I opened my eyes again and saw the big, sharp knife coming straight for my gut, it was too late. By the time I blinked, the cold steel blade was already inside me. I felt the tip slamming against the front of my spine. Everything went numb. I had let my guard down. I had let my emotions take over my thoughts at my most vulnerable moment. I knew it was over. Even when the big, long, ridged knife ripped out from my stomach and inserted itself inside me for a second time, this time deep inside my chest and right next to my heart, cracking my rib cage in two...I knew my time was finally up. My fine ship that had dangerously set sail a few days prior, without any lifeboats or life jackets, had almost made its way into the next harbour...almost. But upon trying to take the shortcut through the reefs, she was sinking now without a trace. Right in the middle of the cold, lonely ocean on her very first voyage. There would be no coming back from this.

I think I heard Celine scream hysterically as the first stabbing blow entered my gut. Someone had been hiding and waiting for us behind the doorway of the first room. That was the only explanation I could conceive of as plausible. Everything had happened so fast. As the blurred figure of a man stabbed me again, this time more devastatingly harder in the chest, I heard him roar. 'Die, you fucker. Die!'

My vision became distorted. I couldn't see anything for a few long moments. I felt half sure it was the large bald thug who'd stabbed me. Who'd ended my innings here in this life. The one who'd wrestled me through the large table in the side room and whom I'd eventually gotten the better of as I stapled his face repeatedly before bashing him unconscious with the stapler itself.

Right now, all I wished for more than anything in the world was to fall down and sleep. I felt weak. I felt sick. I felt like my energy and life force were draining from my body at a rapid rate.

I felt like I was dying, and fast.

As I fell to my knees, I could still hear screaming, then lots of commotion. The thug was about to violently strike me for a third time with his knife. The blow coming straight for my face. It would've ended me there and then rather than giving me some precious last few moments with my angel, my love, my Celine.

Someone leapt past me.

I think it was Celine. I think she had bravely dived for the thug and dug both sets of her long, sharp nails right into the big man's skin above his already bloodied, stapled eyes. Then, with a violent downward motion, she almost ripped his face clean off as she clawed downwards, shredding most of his skin all the way down to his jaw.

I was resting on my knees. Not wishing to fall flat on my face just yet. I still believed I could help Celine overcome the attacker. But in all honesty, I was utterly done for. I had nothing left to give. Even balancing myself upon my knee caps was more effort than I could afford to give.

The big bald man dropped his knife as he screeched and covered his face with his palms. I felt a slight wave of relief. Celine began throwing frantic slaps and scratches all over his upper body until finally I think he just kicked her brutally hard in the legs, knocking her to the ground behind me.

Someone else scrambled over the top of me next. I saw a short skirt. Then those sexy, smooth legs. Ha. Even now. During my last few dying breaths, I still felt urges. It was Lydia. She had dived desperately for the dropped knife. The big bald man had noticed, too. He tried to crouch, moving his hands away from his blood-soaked face, looking more like a blind man as he desperately waved his arms back and forth, searching for his knife.

I couldn't hold myself upward anymore. As I fell backwards, I could see Lydia grabbing the knife. I could hear more screams, grunts, and groans. Celine was back on her feet again, too. Lydia moved to slash at the large bald man. He blocked her instinctively, but when Celine stamped on his foot, it distracted him. He let his guard down. Lydia didn't hesitate. I'd hate to think what would have become of Celine if it hadn't been for her. Lydia dived for the big man, stabbing him over and over again. Without any remorse, guilt, or hesitation. She stabbed him in the side of his throat, the front of his throat, deep in his shoulders, hard in his collarbone, his chest, his arms. The big bald man fell to the ground faster than I had. He landed flat on his face with a squelchy thud. Yet Lydia, like a demon possessed by the devil, continued to stab him over and over, at least another half dozen or so times all over his back. Finally, out of breath and her energy draining, she stabbed him one more time. This time she left the knife fully embedded in the middle of his spine. Unlike me, there was no life left in him.

I finally fell all the way back and hit the floor. Celine turned and immediately crouched at my side. By the look on her face and in her eyes, I could see it was bad. There must have been blood everywhere. I couldn't see it, but I could feel it. Feel its warmth and thickness oozing out of me. I could taste it, too. It was filling the back of my throat and my mouth, thick and fast.

Celine couldn't fight back her tears. They flowed down her cheeks, covering her face just like the blood flowing from me. I tried to speak but nothing came. I coughed and spat up more blood. Celine lifted my head and shoulders, resting them upon her knee in a position where I could see her face. She started stroking my cheeks and chin, wiping away the blood. She ran her fingers through my hair like she'd done during my very first night at her place.

I managed a quick glance at Lydia. She sat upon the floor, resting against the wall next to the dead, bloodied body of the large bald thug. She looked emotionless, her demeanour filled with little empathy. I glanced back at Celine. I tried to speak again. I coughed and spluttered, then finally spoke. I desperately wanted to tell her how sorry I was for getting her into such a mess. I wanted to tell her how much I loved her. I wanted to tell her...so much...everything!

'I'm sorry,' I finally whispered.

Celine looked flabbergasted that I was apologising. 'What are you sorry for? You have nothing to be sorry about, baby.'

'I'm sorry for the last few days. For coming into your life like this. For hurting you. For causing you this pain.'

'Are you kidding me, Liam? You are my hero and I fucking love you. I love you so much. These last few days with you have been the best of my life. The utter, most unbelievable best...'

'So, you finally...trust me now?' I said, almost smiling. I could feel my heartbeat getting slower and slower. My life was ending, one slow heartbeat at a time. How many beats were left...

'Of course I trust you, you idiot...completely. You have my heart.'

I always imagined I'd die alone someday, whether as an old man living out his last days in a nursing home or in some rundown council flat in the middle of a shitey jakey scheme. Hopefully just falling asleep in front of the telly and never waking up. It had always terrified me. But here, now, knowing the end was so close, so damn close... lying in Celine's arms as she held me, stroked me, comforted me, loved me. I didn't fear death anymore. I didn't feel like I was dying alone.

'I can feel your warmth and it feels good. It feels really, really good.' I think I said it aloud or in a whisper. I was fading back and forth from unconsciousness. When I opened my eyes, I saw Celine. So beautiful, smiling, concerned. When I faded into the darkness, I could see us so clearly and radiantly driving along that coastal road once more. Just the two of us. Happy, joyful, laughing, in love. A future that would never be, yet a future I was now living and falling into.

When I closed my eyes for the very last time, Celine was beside me in that car. She touched my face. She kissed my cheek. She whispered something in my ear as the warm, luscious wind whipped over us. She whispered something I couldn't quite make out. I'm sure she said it in French and I smiled, listening attentively.

'Trois allumettes une à une allumees dans la nuit. La première pour voir ton visage tout entier. La seconde pour voir tes yeux. La dernière pour voir ta bouche, et l'obscurité toute entiere pour me rappeler tout cela, en te serrant dans mes bras.'

I remembered. It was the poem she'd told me in French a few days ago. The one she teasingly refused to translate. Not until she trusted me, she'd said. She held my head even tighter in her arms. She kissed me on the cheek again. Smiled that angelic, radiant smile of hers. Then softly whispered what she'd just said into my ear, but this time in English. I felt some of her tears splashing down upon my face as she spoke.

'One by one, three matches are lit in the night, my love. The first to see your face. The second to see your eyes. The last to see your lips. So when it's dark all around, I can remember it all...while holding you in my arms.'

The End

Thank you for reading my book 'Lust for Life.'

If you enjoyed this novel and would like to help, then you could think about leaving a review on Amazon, Goodreads or anywhere else that readers visit. The most important part of how well a book sells is how many positive reviews it has, so if you leave me one, then you are directly helping me to continue on this journey as a fulltime writer.

A huge big thank you in advance to anyone who does.
It means a lot.

Cheers and many thanks for your time and interest in my self published work.

Printed in Great Britain
by Amazon